The Perfect Sheriff

Karen Tucci

True Heart Romance

Contents

Character List		1
Karen's Other Books:		5
1.	Chapter 1	7
2.	Chapter 2	16
3.	Chapter 3	25
4.	Chapter 4	30
5.	Chapter 5	37
6.	Chapter 6	41
7.	Chapter 7	47
8.	Chapter 8	49
9.	Chapter 9	60
10.	Chapter 10	69
11.	Chapter 11	77
12.	Chapter 12	85
13.	Chapter 13	96

14. Chapter 14	105
15. Chapter 15	111
16. Chapter 16	120
17. Chapter 17	127
18. Chapter 18	131
19. Chapter 19	137
20. Chapter 20	144
21. Chapter 21	152
22. Chapter 22	157
23. Chapter 23	162
24. Chapter 24	173
25. Chapter 25	180
26. Chapter 26	188
27. Chapter 27	198
28. Chapter 28	207
29. Chapter 29	217
30. Chapter 30	229
31. Chapter 31	235
32. Chapter 32	241
33. Chapter 33	250
34. Chapter 34	258
35. Chapter 35	262
36. Chapter 36	267

37. Chapter 37   279

38. Chapter 38   284

39. Chapter 39   291

40. Epilogue   300

How About a Review?   307

41. When the Dust Settles: A Sweet Romance with a Navy SEAL   308

About the Author   317

Character List

In any series, it can be difficult to remember the characters. Below, I've listed them and a short description to help you. Happy Reading!

Gerard McDugal - Haven Ridge's sheriff. Determined, flirty, and insecure about his past.

Willow Payne - the pastor's daughter. She's beautiful, sassy, and hiding an important secret.

Zeke Roberts - Haven Ridge's newest teen. At 16, he aspires to write for The New York Times.

Jack and Marilyn Lawrence - Amelia's parents, who've since passed on; her mother of cancer, and her dad in a tractor accident on the ranch.

Amelia Lawrence - the owner of Big L' Ranch. Overcomes her past insecurities and loves her new life married to ranch foreman **Quinton**

Richards. Together, they raise **Emmanuel**, his autistic son from his first marriage. Find their story in Book 1: The Perfect Kiss.

Raddix Lawrence - Amelia's grumpy cousin and cattleman on Big L' Ranch.

Married to psychologist **Lily Peters**, who arrived in Haven Ridge from CA when she was being stalked. Find their story in Book 2: The Perfect Cowboy.

Damon Richards - known as the horse whisperer, has three kids: **Dean**, **Dominic**, and **Darlene**. He's married to Harlyn, who arrived in Haven Ridge when her abusive family was tracking her. Find their marriage of convenience story in Book 3: The Perfect Match.

Sean Lawrence - Raddix's recluse dad and cattleman. He befriends **Violet Skillings**, the flower shop owner to help with his grief. Find their story in Book 4: The Perfect Christmas (novella).

Tanner Brooks - a former hot shot bronc rider, turned employee at Big L' Ranch. He is flirty, adventurous, and determined. Find Tanner and **Dr. Jenelle Merriman's** story in Book 6: The Perfect Doctor.

Val Taylor - co-owns Haven Ridge's only salon and Haven Horizons with Willow. The story for this caring, over sensitive, people-seeker and **Axl Hughes** will be Book 7: The Perfect Partner.

Selena Whittaker - Haven Ridge's resident bully. Find Selena and **Blake Johnson's** story in Book 8: The Perfect Contract.

Jeff and Katy Hughes - This married couple is who many of the young couples look to for advice. He is the butcher at BIg L' Ranch and she runs the store at the ranch. Their son Axel moved away in book 1, but he will return in Book 7.

Cash and Caroline Nelson - This married couple works seamlessly together as full-time chefs at Big L' Ranch since Amelia was a young girl.

Reneé and Rocco Hamilton - she homeschools the kids on the ranch. She recently expanded to include the neighboring children. He is the full-time veterinarian for Big L' Ranch. They have three kids: **Addison** 16, **Ivy** 14, **Sam** 12.

Cora and Pastor Myles Payne - Willow's well-respected parents.

Harper Richardson - midwife for Haven Horizons and cosmetologist. She's married to **Ryan Richardson** who owns the third largest ranch in Haven Ridge: Richardson's farm.

Hazel and Frank Evans - this married couple owns the town's only diner. She is one-third of The Troublesome Trio, working to match up all the single people in Haven Ridge.

Doris Barnes - is another member of The Troublesome Trio. Her trademark saying is, "Pish posh," ignoring anyone who goes against her plan to unite Haven Ridge's singles. Think Golden Girls -- fashionable like Blanche; hair like Rose.

Myrtle Hill - is the third, most dangerous of The Troublesome Trio. She wears outlandish clothing and spends every waking hour planning and scheming. She doesn't back down to anyone, even villains she needs to whack with her purse!

Annika Mallory - she joined Haven Ridge as a waitress at the diner. Her son, **Jackson,** attends Reneé's homeschool group. She is a single mom with a plethora of troubles; one of them being **Rudy Watson**. Find their story in my G & G Security Series: Book 3: Keep my SEAL.

Karen's Other Books:

Stand Alone Books:

When the Dust Settles: A Sweet Romance with a Navy SEAL

G & G Security Series (Coming 2025)

(The characters from When the Dust Settles cross-over in this series)

Operation: Heal my SEAL Book 1

Operation: Find my SEAL Book 2

Operation: Keep my SEAL Book 3

Operation: Train my SEAL Book 4

Second Chance Series:

Starting Over

Moving On

Big L' Ranch Series

The Perfect Kiss: Book 1

The Perfect: Cowboy Book 2

The Perfect Match Book 3

The Perfect Christmas (Holiday Novella)

The Perfect Sheriff Book 5

Best Friends Series

Let Me Carry You

Let Me Marry You

YA Cumberland Christian Prep School Series

The Big Score (Coming 2025)

Chapter 1

It was mid winter, the make-it-through-the-cold-season... Have you ever considered the notion that you are just a meticulously groomed cattle? Gerard had... The auctioneers, three troublesome, but loving septuagenarians, had been calling his number... Initially subtle — a low thrumming, like a distant drumbeat of doom, rumbling in his chest, growing steadily stronger until he could hear the barter holler vibrating through his very bones. The time to protest was now ... Sweat, thick as air, ran down Gerard's back as he inhaled. Letting that breath out slowly, he locked eyes on his target and stepped into the diner...

Cupids, paper hearts — acting as place mats on each table — dangling sparkly loops hanging from the ceiling, and puffy red, white, and pink hearts perched on the wall hooks assault him. He wouldn't mind this holiday so much if it wasn't a flashing neon sign slapping him in the face, reminding him that he was alone. No, that he was pushing forty <u>and</u> alone.

Gerard cleared his throat as he approached the back of the diner. Myrtle, Hazel, and Doris huddled over papers scattered on the table, too preoccupied to even notice him. No doubt orchestrating their next scheme, hence his unease.

Be sure to leave me out of your shenanigans.

"Morning, ladies."

"Sheriff." Doris looked up from the scribbles she wrote on one sheet.

"You know, Eisenhower used less paper planning D-Day. Please tell me that whatever you are conjuring up won't land you in my jail cell."

He startled, his eyes widening. Possibly because of Myrtle's hooting laughter or her hot pink leggings and black shirt with neon green flames that burned his retina. Either way, the place reeked of gossip and mischievousness, telling him to leave immediately before he gave them any fuel for their fragile hope that he would fall madly in love and keep their matchmaking record secure.

Myrtle was still laughing. She even threw in a few knee slaps, most likely to prevent him from asking more questions. No such luck. He had more patience for the ladies than anyone else in town even after what they did to him after the festival a few months back.

"Seriously, what plan are you hatching up?" When the women, perfectly coined The Troublesome Trio, hadn't responded, Gerard continued. "I'd prefer not to be involved in your plans. I think two hours in a shed with the pastor's daughter was enough meddling for a lifetime."

Who trapped people against their will anyway? Apparently, these ladies. Other couples in Haven Ridge had shared their stories of matchmaking and were happily connected with their soul mate. But not him. He was fine as the single sheriff. The last thing he wanted was another relationship to blow up in his face.

Full disclosure, he hadn't complained about being trapped in the shed either. If he was being honest, during that time with Willow, he saw her inner strength and alluring charm shine through. Her hazel eyes, filled with desperation, had finally softened and begged him to rescue her, and he had, in a way. He was the one to call his deputy and tell him to rush to the church and free them before his phone died.

He swallowed a lump in his throat when he recalled how her silky blonde hair cascaded down his arm when she leapt onto his lap at the sight of a scurrying mouse. Willow refused to leave his lap until the door opened. He felt a profound gratitude for the small creature.

For those two hours, her coldness toward him had almost vanished. He couldn't remember the last time a simple touch breathed life into him, an foreign awareness he rather enjoyed.

Yet, lingering issues remained.

Willow was the pastor's daughter, and he was intimidating, especially to a man with Gerard's past, but he wasn't ready to let everyone know about that. Furthermore, he continued to question his and Willow's age differ-ence, past kissing debacle, and her seven year absence. Though all of these were reasonable concerns, it didn't explain why Willow gave him attitude.

He shouldn't have been surprised though. No woman had ever considered him good enough to stick around, including his mom. Who could blame them? His less-than-honorable past caused him to keep his distance. Willow deserved a good man.

What was he? He'd say a five out of ten, if anyone asked for his opinion, but that was not good enough. Not for Willow.

"We apologized for that," Hazel interrupted his thoughts before he trudged any further down the pity path he'd traveled many times before.

"The wind blew the door shut," Myrtle's tone, less than convincing.

"Okaaay," he said, disbelieving.

If he was to believe any one of the three women, it would be Hazel Evans. She was more of a mother to him when he first arrived than his own had ever been. Despite being full of energy, she was more calm and quiet than the other two. That is probably due to owning the diner with her husband. She'd never scare customers away, on purpose.

Doris Barnes, the second most dangerous with information, sat directly across from Hazel. Doris's eyes were as mischievous as her smile. However, if you got her mad, watch out! Gerard recalled the perfectly primped woman in front of him standing on a chair telling an unwanted visitor how things were going to go.

Then, there was Myrtle Hill. She was the ringleader when it came to schemes. She never hid her stunts. He knew from experience. A vivid memory of this woman blasted through his mind. She'd hit that same unwanted visitor with her purse before one of the cowboys could stop her.

"It really was a misunderstanding, Sheriff," Hazel cooed.

Okay. Now his trust in Hazel had diminished a fraction.

"Yet, one of you put a bar between the handles, trapping us in there for hours until Jimmy rescued us."

"Sorry, Sheriff, but our crew is here," Myrtle pointed toward the door as they gathered their papers and shuffled off.

Of all the... Gerard silently exclaimed. He never got straight answers from these women. No one did.

A bell rang at the open window between the diner and the kitchen. Frank, Hazel's husband, spotted Gerard. "Morning, Sheriff. I think you're next."

Gerard looked between Frank and the trio. His face must have reflected pure fright, causing the owner to laugh. Before he escaped into the thralls of his kitchen he said, "Don't fight it. You'll lose."

Would it be so bad to lose? Willow was so easy to talk to when she wasn't sassing him. That sneaky thought gave him a sudden urge to spill his guts. Would she care to listen? Even thinking about growing closer to her seemed ludicrous. He needed to get his mind focused back on the action happening in his town.

He smiled at the entourage of community members pouring. Best town ever, no doubt about that. Being the sheriff here was an honor. These people were his family. A pang of despair shot through Gerard's chest when he watched a few of the married couples doting on each other. Would he ever find a beautiful woman to be with? *Lord, please. You gave Adam one, saying that man needed a companion. I'd appreciate one that won't tempt me to commit condemning sins, though, thanks.*

"Hello, everyone! Rohan is here!" The owner of the dance hall entered like he was announcing himself as the next contestant on a gameshow.

Gerard made a face. Oh, brother. This could get interesting.

"Who's ready to plan the Valentine's Day dance?" he asked in his boisterous voice, often used when acting as the DJ during events.

Not him. Gerard pulled out his phone, checking the time, wondering how he'd get out of the diner without insulting anyone.

Ah ha. An idea came to him. "Where's Randall this morning? Doesn't he usually join the group?" Gerard asked.

"Not always. Sometimes he can't find anyone to man the store," Violet, the flowershop owner shared.

"I hear congratulations are in order," Gerard heard Cora say to Violet.

"Thank you," Violet gushed, holding up her left hand, eyes sparkling. "Sean gave it to me on Christmas. We won't walk down the aisle anytime soon, but he said he wanted everyone to know that I was his."

Cora's lips curved up in a smile. "That's wonderful. Baby steps are better than nothing." Her eyes darted to Gerard.

Good grief. A bead of cold sweat popped out on his forehead, slick and cold against his skin. *Was Willow's mom implying that I should make a plea for her daughter? Does she know something I don't?*

With a nervous gulp, Gerard clutched his coffee mug as if it were a lifeline, his eyes darting around the room, desperately trying to avoid Cora's piercing stare. Uneasiness gnawed at him. Could Willow's parents ever embrace him if they knew about his past?

"Sheriff, are you going to join us?" Cora's pleasant voice silenced the room as she gestured to the chair next to hers.

Gerard, avoider of dating and socializing, let the question linger in the air, causing him to tense as all eyes fixed on him.

Despite being over a foot shorter and at least a hundred pounds lighter, Willow's mom had an intimidating power over him, just like her husband. They were good people and he was a former criminal. What more did he have to say?

Carrying that weight around all these years was taxing. More than that, he'd worked hard to hide the growing feelings blossoming in his chest for Willow.

Besides the Troublesome Trio and Lily, who caught Gerard ogling Willow at the summer festival, nobody knew he was interested in the pastor's daughter. Heck, he only admitted it to himself a week ago. Thinking about Willow's sweet mother potentially turning rabid if she found out a former criminal wanted more than friendship with her daughter made him cringe.

If he was lucky, maybe Willow would join them today? Whenever she didn't have a client, Willow was an active participant in town activities. Maybe he should wait a little longer to see if she arrived?

"Willow usually sits here, but she's running errands and can't join us today."

That answered that.

He shook his head. "I wish I could, but I'm going on patrol. Randall's store is my first stop." He should be here. After losing his wife a couple of years ago, he'd drowned himself in work. Getting together with the other business owners in town was his only social interaction, besides his customers.

One could accuse him of drowning himself in work, too, but he had no choice, right? He had a whole town to protect.

Meanwhile, he found himself enjoying bantering with the fiery hairdresser and had made a New Year's resolution to stop isolating himself, at least when it came to her. How pathetic was he? Very. She would stomp all over his heart and he'd be picking up the pieces before Valentine's Day. Yet, he couldn't stop himself from gravitating toward her.

James and his dad, Harvey from the hardware store, which also served as the feed store for the ranchers, entered last and found a place at the table. Studying the menu, Harvey said, "We have to scarf down our food and run. We don't feel comfortable leaving the store unattended for too long."

"No offense, Sheriff," James quickly filled in for his dad.

He knew they were referring to the string of unsolved break-ins, the ones that had his entire town on edge. A wave of guilt washed over Gerard, heavy and suffocating, each pang a painful reminder of the criminal still running free.

Between him and his deputy, they were patrolling their entire shift, leaving the station void of any authority. Only the town's dispatcher could be found at the station. Gerard made sure the doors were locked, but that wouldn't stop a determined criminal.

This wasn't the way he'd wanted to start his morning. First Cora, then Harvey. Gerard felt the urge to remove his hat and wipe the sweat from his brow, but that seemed too revealing, given that it was the first week of January and only twenty-two degrees out.

"Hopefully, sometime soon, you can—"

A loud screech blared through his police radio, cutting Violet's words short.

"Dispatch to Sheriff."

He pressed the button on the side of the device, resting on his shoulder. "Go ahead, dispatch."

"Robbery in progress at Randall Brown's store. The offender has fled on foot. Age approximately sixteen, a yellow hoodie, jeans—two sizes too big—and bright white sneakers. He is said to be armed and potentially dangerous."

Gerard set down his mug and was at the door as a chorus of *"be safe; get 'em, Sheriff; put on your vest; let us know,"* reached his ears. He lifted a hand to acknowledge their well-wishes, pushed open the door, and let dispatch know he was en route.

Chapter 2

Heavy footfalls echoed in the now silent store. Willow remained facedown on the tiled flooring. A frantic rhythm vibrated through her chest, her heart thumping like a trapped bird, praying the steps veered in another direction, away from her. No such luck. She knew they were coming for her. *Dear God, please don't let him hurt anyone.*

The air grew heavy, alerting her of more potential danger. She felt the presence of a large figure looming over her. Releasing the clench in her jaw, quads, and glutes, she slowly let out the breath she was holding. Then it started. Oh, no. She knew it was coming. Willow's ragged, shallow breaths mirrored her frantic crawl into this space moments ago.

Rats! She'd done it again — chosen to run and hide. Why'd she keep doing that? That ended now.

Without moving, her eyes scanned the vicinity. Weapon. She needed something to attack the robber with, but what?

Her eyes landed on a mop. That will have to do. Like the ninja, she really wasn't, Willow did a push up off the floor, landed in a squat, while simultaneously grabbing the mop handle. With a flick of her wrist, she jabbed it in the intruder's chest.

"Ow!"

Well, that was not what, rather, *who,* she'd expected.

"Willow, it's me."

The familiarity of that voice, his chiseled jaw, and the twitch of his lip, no doubt, trying to thwart a grin, should have eased the prickling sensation at the base of her neck. Instead, it peaked to an all-time high, probably trying to outdo her racing heart. If anyone asked, it was a direct result of being involved in a robbery and nothing to do with her teenage crush standing in front of her, a billboard of masculinity.

"Give me that before you hurt yourself," Gerard stole the makeshift weapon from her hands.

Goodness gracious! Her fingers tingled when they connected with his large, manly hand. *Don't fall to pieces. He didn't like you before and he doesn't like you now.*

"Right. Only *you* and the bad guys can have weapons, while the rest of us are left defenseless."

Gerard's hand cupped her elbow as he eased her toward the door. "You're far from defenseless, Princess," he laughed out a breath. "Just start talking and criminals will run."

She pulled her elbow free. A distinct coldness replaced the once warm spot where Gerard's hand cocooned around her. She made it to the door, avoiding items from the shelves scattered and strewed all around, while Gerard stepped on a pink cut out hearts furnishing the floor. It pleased Willow to see that Randall continued decorating the store like his wife had.

"Come to think of it. We didn't have these break-ins until you came back from wherever you've been the last seven years. Did you bring them with you?"

How dare he? Everyone knew she was in California with her aunt, they just didn't know why. For many months, she'd been splitting her time between California and Haven Ridge now that she had her salon here. Wait! Did he just accuse her of bringing riff-raft into the town?

She'd grown up a lot in the last seven years, too fast if she was the judge. But that was what happened when life gave you road blocks. You either sat idle and waited for the cones, or boulder in her case, to move, or you veered to the left, right, or reverse and made a fresh path.

Willow wouldn't change her outcome if someone paid her. She would, however, change the path she took. Oh, well, no time to dwell on that now.

"Am I free to go *Mr. I'm the letter of the law in this town, yet, I don't actually protect it.*"

"Hey," he growled. "I'm always on call, and so is Jimmy. We do what we can."

Her smirk resembled his from moments ago. "Yet, here we are. Nice work *patrolling*, officer." She snarled, shooting him a venomous glare.

"It's Sheriff," he yelled at her back seconds before the door slammed shut. She huffed at the irony of another slamming door and her connection with the *sheriff*. At least this time, she hadn't embarrassed herself by kissing him.

She'd spent her teen years watching Gerard, her heart twisting with every new woman on his arm, each one a painful reminder of what she couldn't have. Why couldn't she? Yeah, she'd made mistakes, but who hadn't? Her parents, Gerard, and probably a slew of others in this town. The thought of her old ways and her parents' disapproval felt like a heavy American Quarter horse, suffocating her with its weight.

Embarrassed to admit, over the last seven months, she'd noticed that Gerard had dated no women at all. That seemed odd considering how women from neighboring towns came to every event in Haven Ridge and smothered the man.

"Wait." Gerard's returned-to-calm voice stopped her, but she didn't turn around. Could this be the breakthrough she'd wanted for years?

"You need to give your statement before you leave. I'll be out after I talk to Randall."

Nope, I guess not. "Whatever you say, *Sheriff.*" She inhaled more powerfully than she intended and let her breath release through her nose, similar to a raging bull one might see in a cartoon. Like the bull, she too was misunderstood. She wasn't mad, just frustrated, and she didn't know how to fix it.

A short while later, Gerard sauntered over and was by her side as he held the car door open for her. A subtle touch of his chest against her shoulder sent a spark racing down her arm.

Traitor! Her heart thumped against her chest, acknowledging the accusation.

How long should she resist the pull she felt towards this man? Anticipation pulsed through her veins, each beat of her heart a countdown to her surrender.

What was she thinking? Since she'd returned to Haven Ridge, they rarely spoke without insults. But after the Troublesome Trio imprisoned them in the shed, her mind fixated on the man's caring disposition and, of course, his firm muscles. He'd never believe her if she told him she wasn't afraid of mice. That would be her little secret.

The slams toward one another hadn't stopped since. In fact, his charming wit flustered her more than she was willing to admit.

As natural as getting dressed in the morning, Gerard placed his hand on her low back, guiding her to take a seat.

She flinched. A nervous energy ripped through her body and short-circuited a wire to the part of her brain that reminded her she had already humiliated herself with the sheriff her senior year and had no business crushing on him now.

"You okay? Did you get hurt during the robbery?"

Just peachy. "I'm fine."

Willow attributed her racing pulse to the robbery and coached herself: *his tender touches don't feel good. They come from a civil servant helping a victim in a crime scene.*

"Is that a real *fine* or a woman's *fine?*" Gerard asked, releasing his hand from her back. The heat from his hand disappeared, leaving behind a chilly absence, and she shivered. "Do you need a blanket?"

Willow imagined his words were part of a script memorized from the academy, but his soft tone, caring brown eyes, and alluring cologne left her stomach fluttering.

A woman's fine? Willow bit the inside of her cheek. *No laughing. He's not funny.* Her mind ordered. "I'm all set with the blanket, thank you, and it's real."

"Is Mr. Brown okay?" Willow asked, looking up at Gerard.

"Physically, yes. Can you tell me what happened?" Gerard had his notebook out, pen in the ready position, but he didn't move. His eyes bored into hers, channeling his inner Superman, probably hoping to see into the depths of her soul. Good luck.

"Same," she hesitated. "I don't understand why or how a teenager gets a gun. Why does he need to steal in the first place?"

"Something has gone drastically wrong in his life, I would assume," Gerard replied like he understood the kid on a personal level.

As she told him what she witnessed, a pain shredded through her chest like the shards of the glass counter the boy created when he slammed the gun into it. She could have ended up like him if she didn't have her aunt. Her parents were great, but she'd kept them in the dark, unable to live with the disappointment she knew she'd bring them if they knew her seven-year-old secret.

"I wish my center was open. We could help him."

"How's that going?"

"Every day, things are coming together. The ladies and I haven't decided on the official name, but we've been praying—it will come."

Mr. Brown appeared, and Gerard stepped aside. Closer to Willow, her stomach thundered like horse hooves pounding a dirt trail. *Darn him!*

"Are you okay, sweet child? I'm so sorry. Things could have gone very differently. I'm just glad you're okay."

The adrenaline that pumped through her veins moments ago slowed to a trickling, but steady faucet drip. Embarrassment now replaced that rush. *Sweet child? Really? Is that how Gerard looked at me, too?* She'd turned twenty-five a few months ago. Even if Randall considered her a child based on age compared to his, her experiences were far from child-like.

She placed her hands on his to relieve his shaking. "Like my dad says, if God wanted it to be different, it would have been. You have nothing to be sorry for, Mr. Brown."

"Rest assured, Randall, her dad would kill me if anything happened to her." Gerard stated, seemingly out of nowhere. She wanted to know where that came from, but she let it go for now.

Instead, she smiled at the ludicrous idea of a pastor committing murder. *Why did he care what my dad thought?*

"Well, If I'm done here, I'll be leaving," announced Willow, standing quickly.

Gerard stepped in front of her, blocking her way. "We're not done here." His commanding police voice was down right dreamy and irritating at the same time.

"Yes, sir," she sassed, saluting him with two fingers.

"I'll leave you two at it. Thanks for taking care of things, Sheriff," Randall said as he escaped back inside.

Maybe crime scenes were second nature to Gerard, but this was Willow's first robbery, and she didn't appreciate his rough tone, so she gave a bit of her own sass.

"Could you hurry? I have better places to be."

"I'll do my best, Princess," he returned fire.

Willow plopped back on the seat and dropped her chin into her hands. "Ugh." Willow caught a glimmer in the man's eyes and it lit her belly on fire.

"Hey Sheriff," Gerard's deputy, Jimmy, drew Willow's attention. She watched as he whispered something into the sheriff's ear.

"Wait here. I'll be right back," Gerard spat.

Geez. "That man is infuriating. Is he always so bossy?"

"Well, he *is* the boss," Jimmy replied with a shrug.

He had a point.

"Go easy on him. He's a good man."

"Perhaps you and I define 'good' differently." She gave him a wan smile.

Jimmy chortled. "He's different on a scene. Focused. Determined. The fact that you were involved makes it even more important to him."

Her eyes widened. Before she could ask him to clarify, Gerard was back and assigned Jimmy another task.

Her stomach hollowed out when Gerard leaned against the open door with his ankle crossed over his foot and his arms folded over his brawny chest. He asked, "Are you ready to give the rest of your statement, Princess?"

Jimmy grinned as he walked away, making Willow question what he knew even more.

"Yes, provided it gets me far from here."

"You wound me." He mocked hurt, placing his hand on his chest.

She retorted, "Thank you for the invitation." Willow winked at him subconsciously.

Chapter 3

Willows's fruity perfume, a mix of berries and citrus, still clung outside the store, teasing Gerard's senses. She was trouble with a bold capital T, or more accurately, *he* was in trouble being around her.

"Sheriff," a young officer from a neighboring town approached. "Did you see this?"

Eyeing the rectangular gold nameplate on the officer's chest, Gerard greeted Officer Darcy with a nod as the man handed him bagged evidence. "A matchbook from The Red Mill. What do you make of that, Sheriff?"

"That's over fifty miles away." Gerard shook his head as he stated the obvious with a confused voice. *What would cause a teenager to travel such a long distance?*

Fear pricked at Gerard's spine as his mind drifted back to his past. A chilly familiarity, mirroring what he endured alone on the streets, with nothing and no one but himself to rely on until coming to Haven Ridge. *I have to find that kid!*

"Check that for prints," Gerard said, his tone demanding.

After nodding and casually saying, "Sure thing," the officer turned around and walked away, his boots echoing on the pavement.

Gerard's fingers squeezed the side button on his radio until his knuckles turned white. "Sheriff to dispatch."

"Go ahead, Sheriff."

"Issue a state-wide BOLO. This kid could be anywhere by now."

With such a small team, Gerard and Jimmy would double as detectives, investigating the teen's motive, but first, they required clues; something to lead them to his whereabouts.

Gerard hoped the prints would reveal the boy's identity, while at the same time prayed they didn't, because that would mean he'd been in trouble before.

"You got it, Sheriff."

With things running smoothly, Gerard's focus shifted back to Willow once again. Her return to Haven Ridge seven months ago hauled him into a state of sleep deprivation and the exhaustion weighed his muscles down. He sighed, leaning against the front fender of his SUV.

He dragged his palm down his face. Night after night, he counted the spots on his ceiling, unable to sleep, wondering why she'd left before she graduated, and recalling the last memory he had of her. The night he celebrated his victorious win in his first race for sheriff, Willow stayed to help him clean up. She was a fresh eighteen-year-old while he was two years shy of thirty. Unfazed by their age difference, she kissed him. But when he pushed her away in shock, she ran with haste out the door. He cringed at the memory. Talk about a colossal mistake. The next time he saw her was seven months ago when she returned to Haven Ridge all grown up.

Now she had his full attention. Her wavy blonde hair, always just so, and her nails were equally beautiful, not surprising, given her profession. She'd matured into a striking woman with never-ending curves. Though her outward appearance kicked him in the gut regularly, her fiery spirit challenged him, and most days, that was fine. But her open animosity, post robbery, was frustrating.

Sadly, she wasn't his only challenge. Gerard only had one year left in his term. Unopposed in his last run for sheriff, he could face heavy opposition this time if he didn't stop the crime spree from disrupting his town.

Maybe Willow would help him campaign again and they could get a second chance at that kiss?

A shred of guilt zipped through Gerard. He didn't need this distraction right now. A serial criminal in town demanded all his attention. But try telling his mind to avoid Willow; not going to happen.

As daylight dwindled, so did Gerard's mood. He'd spent the last seven months pampering Willow with flirty, playful banter, thinking it would win her over. Nope. Even an afternoon locked in a shed with her had yielded nothing, much to The Troublesome Trio's chagrin.

Jimmy teased Gerard about having feelings for her, or as he put it, a crush. Did anyone else notice? If Jimmy planted that idea in her head, Gerard would fire him. Not really, but the woman's repulsion toward him and potential backlash from dating the pastor's daughter deterred him from acting on his interest.

Besides, Willow traveled every weekend. Where to? He didn't know, but his ideal woman was a homebody — a wife who found joy in the simple pleasures Haven Ridge offered.

The weight of his age and unfulfilled dream of having a family, left a gaping void in the center of his chest, reminding him of his loneliness, making it difficult to take a deep breath. Those burdens seemed to seep into his limbs, zapping the energy and motivation from his body. He couldn't afford this diversion. Not now. The town expected him to find the teenager who held Randall at gunpoint.

A flash of anger surged through him, revitalizing his energy as he recalled the fear etched on Willow's face. Her trembling body spoke volumes as she relived the traumatic situation. The urge to wrap her in his arms and comfort her still pulsed through him. He could check on her after leaving here. It would be his civil duty, right?

He rubbed his palm up and down his jaw, letting the stubble stab into his palm. She would never allow him to ease her pain. Although, he didn't want the robbery to overshadow any type of relationship they could have. The Florence Nightingale Effect and Stockholm Syndrome were real. He'd already wasted a year of his life with a woman he thought might have been the one, save she wasn't in love with him after the effect wore off. That loss, coupled with his mother's disappearing act, Gerard had sworn off dating. So, what about Willow caused such an intense reaction he couldn't ignore?

Chapter 4

"Sheriff!" Gerard let out a heavy breath before ripping his eyes from his computer screen, thankful for the interruption.

Reviewing the reports of vandalism, shoplifting, and other petty crimes from the last month was hurting his brain. The robbery felt like more than a few hours ago.

The cheerful ping of his email notification made his breath catch. He'd been waiting for this. The report would tell him who had been creating havoc in his town.

Like a bully in school, the fingerprint report laughed at Gerard. A knot in his stomach threatened to constrict his intestines with the force of a vise, knowing this left his town vulnerable to another attack.

He even imagined a child sticking his tongue out, sneering, "Nananana-booboo, you can't catch me."

Gerard forced the laptop lid shut harder than he intended.

"Sheriff. Is everything okay?"

Shoot. He'd forgotten someone entered. "Hello, Myrtle. Everything's fine. What can I do for you?"

"It's not just me. Come on, girls."

Gerard chuckled at the expression as the septuagenarians shuffled into the station. Gerard respected these women, but he wasn't in the mood for whatever they were orchestrating.

"We just came to check on you. Getting a call like that can be straining. Do you have anyone you can talk to?"

No, but I'd like to talk to Willow.

"I'm good, ladies, but thank you for your concern."

Myrtle wasn't going to let this go. He could tell she was more assertive than usual this evening. "What about Willow? Were you able to debrief with her?"

He rubbed his palm down his face and sighed. Before he could say anything, Doris piped up. "We think you need to go on a date, Sheriff. We've lined up some women who we think would make a good match for you. While we narrow it down, tell me: a woman with a child, is it a deal breaker?"

What?! These ladies were pulling him from his work and he needed to figure out a nice way of getting them to leave.

Then God sent an angel through the station's door. *Thank you!*

"Ah, ladies look, Randall is here. How are you doing?"

Gerard flipped over the list of properties in town he needed to search — ones where a criminal might be hiding. The last thing he needed or wanted was the rumor mill to stir up in town. Would he find anything? Probably not, but he had to start somewhere.

The man smiled despite being robbed earlier. "I'm getting by. I came by to ask a favor."

As long as he could avoid answering the women who'd taken up residency in the chairs in front of his desk, Gerard would offer his assistance. "What is it?"

"Violet wants to set up a place here with food for all of the volunteers still helping to fix up the store, so I can open back up. Is that okay?"

The townsfolk were forever taking care of him and the others. Though he and Jimmy were the only paid employees, the volunteer EMT and firemen worked just as hard when the alarms blared.

"That's generous. Set up in the front room there. Thank you."

For the next twenty minutes, a string of townsfolk ushered in main and side dishes, drinks, and desserts into the station. As for The Troublesome Trio, they still hadn't left. *Ugh!*

"I'll let everyone know we're taking a break to eat," Violet said as she set the last dish on the table and waved to her friends before exiting.

Now, to deal with the women who act like meddling, but doting grandmas. His head whipped up seconds later when the door opened again. "Did you forget—"

His tongue lodged in his throat when his eyes caught a glimpse of her blonde hair pulled up in some fancy thing that only she could do, with loose strands curled, forming her face. He didn't miss six mischievous eyes bouncing back and forth between his shell-shocked expression and the woman who caused his temporary laryngitis.

Speak, you idiot. Why won't my vocal cords work? His mouth had gone dry, and his tongue felt ten sizes too big, as if he was having an anaphylactic reaction to seeing Willow.

"Hi, Sheriff," her voice permeated the room. He nodded his head, still staring at her like she was an optical illusion and her face would eventually morph into something else.

"Where can I put this?" She lifted the casserole dish in her hands.

Gerard stood with such force that his chair slammed into the wall behind him, startling both of them and making him even more jittery as he tried to walk toward her, reaching for the dish.

Their fingers brushed against each other, sending little jolts of electricity up his forearm as he rushed into the room with the warm dish and set it on the table. Turning, he found Willow in the doorway.

Say something. Tell her you like her hair, her perfectly painted purple finger-nails, ask her how she's holding up. Something.

"It's really cold out there, isn't it?" He winced the moment the words left his mouth, and he heard, "Geez, Louise," behind him.

Between that and the little quirk at the corner of Willow's lips, it broad-casted loud and clear that everyone thought Gerard was a fool. He didn't blame them. When she blasted him with snarky comments, Ger-ard handled himself well, but when she was sweet, like now, he became tongue-tied.

"There isn't much we can do right now, ladies. Let's go," Hazel ordered gently.

Myrtle shuffled close to the couple. "We'll be in touch, Sheriff. Willow, it's always a pleasure. Take it easy on this one; he clearly struggles around you." She winked at them as they departed. At least they were gone; fewer people to witness him making a fool of himself.

However, this wasn't new for him. A couple months ago, he made a twit of himself at the dance hall the night he got called in when goons from Harlyn's past attacked Damon. When he wasn't stuttering over his words, he'd accidentally knocked over her glass of water. It pooled on her plate and drenched her jeans. Gerard vowed to never approach Willow again. Humiliation had its limits, especially for a man.

Today was the first day since then that he'd interacted with her. *Really, God? Was a robbery necessary?*

He did fine with her at the scene, but that was his element. He needed to channel his inner flirt.

Before she answered his question, he rattled off another one he already knew the answer to, but, oh well. "How is the renovation going?"

Willow, Val, her friend and co-owner of the salon, and Val's sister, Harper, were renovating a house to help youth who were homeless or needed a warm, safe place to stay. Generous, right?

Her face lit up like a flash of sunlight when she described how close they were to finishing the process. "Soon, we can start welcoming teens through the doors. Val has already talked with a few pregnant girls who fear homelessness. She wants them to have priority."

"That is very honorable. Is that why Harper became a midwife?" One benefit of being the sheriff in a small town meant always being in the loop.

Willow's contagious smile still hadn't left her face. "Yeah. She's eager to deliver babies."

"What will you do if boys need a place to stay?" A wave of regret smashed into him when her smile vanished, replaced by a tight-lipped frown.

She shrugged. "Unfortunately, that's more of a challenge. We purchased the land next to the main house, but the abandoned house on the property needs a lot of work. The contractor said it will take him 'many man hours' to refurbish the heap."

He knew that place well. In fact, it was the first place on his list to hunt for Haven Ridge's newest criminal. Willow's assessment of that house was correct — the cracked foundation, windows, and siding were enough for every potential buyer to pass on that house over the years.

"But that's only part of the problem." She let out a big huff. "How are three women going to bring any peace, comfort, or security to teenage boys?"

He couldn't help but grin. Willow crossed her arms over her chest and gave him a '*What are you laughing at?*' kind of glare.

Gerard put his arms up in a surrender position. Things were going well; he didn't want her snarky side to come out. "I'm familiar with those three women, and I can predict exactly how your presence will affect the boys — likely causing unwanted distractions."

A sly smirk slowly formed on her face. "I'm glad you agree. I was hoping you'd be willing to work with us. You could help manage the boys, like a big brother-type program. With you being a sheriff, I can imagine that might help convince them to stay on the right side of the law."

"Perhaps," Gerard mumbled noncommittally, remembering the similar program he went through in middle school. The lessons vanished the moment he stepped into high school, like water through a sieve. Maybe he could do a better job of getting through to the boys than his mentor had. *No!* Blaming his mentor was unfair.

Not to mention, the idea of working this close with Willow would have its benefits. They might have some late nights and be forced to grab dinner together. She might get stressed or overwhelmed and need a shoulder to lean on, which Gerard would gladly offer.

"Perhaps nothing," she scoffed, placing her hands on her hips. "You're the sheriff in this town, and it's your responsibility to keep it safe. Giving teens a warm, safe home is a great place to start."

Her sass ignited a blaze within.

Chapter 5

Zeke

H e hit the jackpot with this abandoned house. Zeke cringed, realizing how sad that sounded. Oh, well. At least he briefly escaped the cold. He tossed his tattered backpack on the chilly, unforgiving cement while he located a bucket. Flipping that container over, Zeke settled down. Unzipping his bag, he retrieved beef jerky and two bags of chips. Not the food of champions, but he wasn't at all close to one, anyway.

He plucked out his notebook, stolen of course, and a pen, also lifted, to record today's dealings, with the goal of moving on soon. He couldn't risk staying in one place too long and getting caught. Too bad. Something about this place made him feel oddly enough like home, when home was safe.

Right now, he'd come to terms with this book being his only friend, so he wrote the heading Convenience Store: Haven Ridge, MT at the top of the next blank page.

Today, I almost got caught. The police sirens still wailing in the distance. I made another bad choice today, but don't judge, you probably would have, too. It's difficult when you only have two choices: steal food to survive or wither away a slow and awful death.

Ah, death sounds so wonderful right now. Well, maybe not wonderful, but definitely a relief. Death isn't a problem for me. It's the constant suffering. Haven't I endured enough? I'd like a break.

For the past two years, I'd made many choices, and it's time I share them with you since you are my only friend.

School or no school? Before everything happened, I loved school. I'd just started high school, and the freshman class voted me class president. I was the editor and lead reporter for my school newspaper, then I dropped out — one of the toughest decisions I've made, yet unavoidable. Guess I'll never work for the New York Times now.

Steal or beg? I tried the latter first and that led me to the dumpster behind McDonald's most nights, as I never imagined myself stealing something that wasn't someone else's trash. Once the police kicked me out of every fast food parking lot in my hometown, I'd stowed away in the back of a pick truck with Colorado license plates. Future lesson: never leave my vehicle unattended at the gas pump.

Zeke stopped writing when a scraping sound along the ground outside caught his attention. He stood on the bucket and slowly peeked his head out the small rectangular window, covered with a film of dirt at least a decade old. The crack down the middle forced his eyes to take an extra second to focus. Hearing nothing, he returned to his journal.

Unwilling to believe I'd be in danger, I'd curled into a ball on the chilly metal truck bed, excited for new scenery. Maybe people outside of California would be more generous. Little did I know that my chauffeur was heading to Montana instead. Not that it really mattered. Colorado would probably have been just as cold as here — my fingers are ice cubes.

These choices and more have led me here — tucked under the basement stairs of an abandoned house, eating stolen chips and beef jerky. I didn't mean to pull out my gun on that old man. He made me nervous, trying to get me to take more food. He was just stalling so the cops could catch me.

I've never taken my gun out like that before. My father gave it to me in case I needed it. I never should have taken it. Ending up like him is not an option. I never expected to use it, or wave it around like they do in the movies.

If he wouldn't have acted like he cared about me, I wouldn't have pulled it out. I hate it when adults lie. No one cares about me. If they did, I wouldn't be here, would I?

Where am I? Many states from home with worn and tattered clothing, treadless shoes, making me slip in dirt or on grass and now snow, and a thinning sweatshirt that's riding half way up my forearms covering my Sunday shirt. Sadly, it exposes cuts on my hand from slamming that glass counter.

Another noise diverted Zeke's attention. This time it was more like *clonk, clonk, clonk* — similar to small pebbles hitting against the window. He paused long enough that the sound disappeared and he continued writing.

You might think I'm donning a button-up, collared shirt. I'm not. I call my hole-y shirt my Sunday shirt. Get it? Holy? Sunday? Yeah, I guess it's not that funny, but my mom and I always laughed.

She was so funny. Too bad she left me. Not on purpose, so don't you dare think badly of her. God took her from me. Jerk!

I would still be in school if He hadn't taken her from me. I'd be visiting colleges and getting ready to graduate next year. Right now, the best I could do is get a GED. Well, not right now. Instead, I have to curb the monster in my gut, gnawing at my stomach lining.

"Wee-oo, wee-oo." Police sirens are echoing throughout my ears, warning me that my time is limited. Oh well. If my mom was right about God, things will be better on the other side. If that's the case, why doesn't God love me enough to let me see the streets of gold, or grass prairies with children running around carefree? That's how I've imagined Heaven, anyway.

A slamming door jump scares me. Heavy footsteps match the rhythm and beat of my anxious heart. The last chip in the bag is calling my name. The slightest movement and I'll have silver bracelets and probably dislocated shoulders. No doubt a result of my own stupidity.

Zeke froze, worried even the scratching of the pen would give him away. His breath hitched, and he refused to exhale when the doorknob jiggled. He morphed into a popsicle, hoping the sudden urge to pee went away before he needed to shift into his next choice — flight.

God, if you're out there, now would be a good time to show yourself. His silent prayer, a heartfelt final thought before a large officer kicked in the door and held a gun at him.

Chapter 6

"Can you believe he said that?" Willow spouted the next day while cutting Amelia's hair at the salon. "Perhaps? Really? Perhaps he'd like to continue being sheriff."

Amelia smiled at her, giving her a look she didn't have time to discern. "It took him a while to become that relaxed. It's better, trust me. That's how he and Raddix met and became buddies."

Amelia owned the ranch, and her cousin Raddix worked there. Everyone else at the ranch had worked there so long, Willow had forgotten the rest weren't a biological family.

As a child, Willow visited with her dad, especially when Amelia's mom was sick. Though put out, Raddix always 'kept her company' until her dad finished.

Since returning to Haven Ridge, Willow still felt like an outsider with the crew from Big L' Ranch, despite being an adult now. They were the older, popular kids, and she was nobody.

Not true! Willow didn't believe that anymore. God loved her, so she was somebody. She also had one very special person she visited every weekend who loved her.

It made sense to her now how she'd let herself fall into trouble seven years ago. At the first sign of interest, someone had completely captivated her.

"I know nothing about his high school years." Willow sprayed Amelia's hair with water and ran the comb through it before cutting an inch off the bottom. "He's the sheriff. Why wouldn't he jump at the chance to mentor boys so they don't get into trouble?"

"Maybe it has more to do with you than helping the boys." Amelia's words stabbed Willow like a dagger straight through the heart. That might be a little dramatic, but Willow's long-standing crush on Gerard hit her with the force of a blizzard wind, leaving her heart aching with a sharp, icy pain.

"Oh." *I didn't realize he disliked me that much.*

"You're not surprised, are you? I've never seen two people go at it like you guys." Amelia winked.

She had a point. Willow's shoulders sagged as she let out an audible sigh.

"Enough of that talk," Willow declared, imagining her eyes sparkled with determination as she set her sights on a New Year's resolution: return to Haven Ridge full-time for her center, and forget about Gerard.

That should be simple if she leaned on the everlasting arms of her Savior. Easier, at least, than the enigma she'd kept for seven years. The weight of her secret felt like lead in her stomach, so her final resolution was to tell her parents everything.

Clearing her mind, Willow asked, "Are you and Quinton going to the Valentine's Day dance?"

"Yes, of course."

"It was nice of Rohan to offer the dance hall," Willow said, snipping at Amelia's ends.

Amelia nodded, and Willow steadied her moving head with a smile and a wink. "Christmas was major, so I couldn't have hosted another event so soon."

Willow recalled that dance. Gerard spent most of the night stealing glances at her, making her self-conscious. Unable to hold his gaze, she always looked away. Then, a terse exchange had passed between them at the food table.

"Hi, Willow. Would you like some punch?" Gerard held out the drink to her.

She cackled. "Yeah, right! As if I'd accept an open drink from you." She wasn't sure where that comment had come from. Gerard had never put her in harm's way, so she blamed it on the hurt she still harbored.

"Willow, are you listening to me?" Amelia dragged her from her musing.

No. She smiled, unable to admit her mind drifted.

Amelia sat a little taller as Willow finished up the cut. *Thank God for muscle memory.*

"I said, Emmanuel is trying to convince us to let him take Darlene as his date."

Willow laughed, blowing out a hard breath simultaneously. "The way Damon wrapped his daughter under his arm like a football when he thought Emmanuel was going to kiss her under the mistletoe, I don't think it matters if you give him permission or not."

"Excellent point." Amelia raised a finger like she was going to use that information to her advantage.

"Emmanuel is adorable."

Amelia frowned. "Oh, don't say that too loudly. He's getting old now — his words, not mine — and he can't be called cute names like that anymore." Amelia laughed, but her pang of sadness echoed through the salon.

"They grow up fast, don't they?" Willow's heart swelled and her voice caught. Amelia's wide, curious eyes examined Willow, but she moved on before Amelia could question her further.

"What do you think of your cut and style?" Willow asked Amelia, holding a mirror behind her head for a better view.

"I love it. Thank you so much."

Willow unbuttoned the cape draped over Amelia. "My pleasure. Thank you for the business."

Moments later, Amelia reached the door. Turning back, she disclosed, "The ladies are having a get together on Friday. You're more than welcomed to join us at the ranch if you'd like. We meet at six thirty. Harlyn is leading the Bible study and then we talk and have fun for a couple of hours."

Aww. Willow swallowed twice, trying to dislodge the lump of emotion restricting her esophagus. "That sounds great. I'll check my schedule and text you. Thank you for inviting me, Amelia!"

"Of course. I hope you can make it."

When Amelia left, Willow pulled up her schedule on her phone. Although she had a color and cut at four on Friday, she should have plenty of time to reach the ranch in time.

In the meantime, Willow would pray for guidance and wisdom. The ladies at the ranch had had their share of secrets from their pasts. Maybe they could help Willow if she'd let them.

The year-round jingle bells on the doorknob alerted Willow of a customer. When she looked up, she saw a boy with scraggly hair — hair was always the first thing she noticed — worn clothing and a filthy backpack. But his bright white sneakers glimmered.

"Can I help you?"

He stepped in and shut the door, leaving the frigid air outside, but a chill ran down her spine and it had nothing to do with the temperature.

The teen in the doorway clutched his backpack strap, slung over his shoulder, and gave Willow a sheepish expression. She suspected that was due to being a young man in a girly salon.

"I sure hope so."

Chapter 7

Zeke

As he settled down in the basement of a different abandoned building, he second guessed getting a haircut. He hadn't realized how much extra warmth it added until it was no longer there. He chuckled at the similar, yet awful metaphor he called his life.

Trying not to think about the cold whipping through the cracks in the windows, he pulled out his journal.

Willow is the nicest person I've met in a long time. She reminds me of Mom — wouldn't take no for an answer. Fed me a couple of sandwiches and made me a few PBJ for the road. She washed and cut my hair; haven't had that done in years. Yes, I looked like a shaggy dog, or a rag-a-muffin. That was what my mom liked to call me when I let my hair get too long.

She didn't talk to me like I was some dumb kid, nor did she try to make me talk. I don't know how I would have explained running from that cop without telling her everything I've done. But she talked enough for the both of us. Apparently, she's opening a home for teens soon. If I can survive in this cold a little longer, I will go there.

"My mom was a hairdresser," I told her. I expected her to say something like, 'sorry for your loss,' or give me a pity look that's even worse than the words. Instead, she said, "No wonder why you have such great hair." No one had complimented him since his mom, well, you know.

That made me want to tell her about my mom, but in the end, I wasn't ready to talk. If she'd asked about my dad, I would have happily shredded him to pieces. Dirtbag!

The very idea of his father ignited a furious blaze of anger within Zeke's heart. That thing not only mistreated his mom by making her work to support him, but he further insulted her by drinking and cheating on her, causing her to be the town's laughingstock.

Zeke didn't believe his mom killed herself. She never would have left him alone. His father was responsible for her death. He may not have pulled the trigger, but he knew people who would.

As Zeke drifted off to sleep, he wondered if he hadn't left when he did, would his father have killed him, too?

Chapter 8

A sharp, pungent odor slapped Gerard in the face when he entered the salon. Eyeing Harlyn in the stylist chair with tinfoil pieces draped in her hair and clear plastic gloves covering Willow's petite fingers told him he should have picked a different time to check-in.

He knew she'd be working alone today since he already visited with Val and Harper at the center. He chuckled inwardly, recollecting Willow's reaction when he said he might help her with the potential teenage boys arriving at her establishment.

Wow! She was full of sass today. That glare could have sliced through him. Well, it wasn't actually a glare, more of an initial pleasant look, expecting to greet a potential customer, turned cold as she ripped her eyes away from him.

Each day that passed, he noticed her reluctance to look him in the eye for longer than a couple of seconds. What did that mean? He knows what he'd like it to mean.

"Well, hello, Sheriff. How are you today?" Harlyn's cheery voice echoed through the salon.

He moved further in before answering. "Another day; another dollar," he responded with one of the many clichés people use when they know others are looking for a quick response and not the truth.

"Puh." Gerard knew her venom was about to spew. Warning! Do. Not. Engage.

As if he could stop himself. Gerard moved even closer. "Something wrong, Willow?"

"Oh, no. But now I know why we have the problems we do in Haven Ridge."

"Pray tell." He knew he was in for a tongue lashing, but he couldn't stop himself from encouraging her.

"When the Sheriff refers to his job as just another dollar, towns slide downhill."

"Is that supposed to hurt?" He rested his hands on his hips, catching her subtle raised brow and pursed lips.

He'll take that as a yes. Okay. If she only realized that it did hurt, would she care?

"You wounded me," he masked the pain by placing his hand over his heart.

Willow shook her head. Smarter than him for not engaging in enemy fire. She peeled open one end of a tinfoil piece, then pressed it back in place. She repeated that with a couple more.

Pulling other tinfoil pieces out of Harlyn's hair a few minutes later, she kept her eyes trained on the back of her client's head. "What can I help you with, Gerard?"

"I wanted to discuss your plans for boys at the center." When she didn't respond, he continued. "I could get us some lunch at the diner and bring it back," he offered.

"I'm not hungry." Her stomach growled like a lioness going after the kill.

He raised his brows in question, even though she refused to give him the slightest bit of attention. "Wanna try again?"

"She'd love that," Harlyn piped up. "We should be done in about twenty minutes or so. You head to the diner and I'll make sure I'm gone by the time you get back." The woman's eyes beamed brighter than a flare in the sky. He'd noticed that same look in Myrtle's eye all the time.

Since Willow didn't object, he nodded and hurried off.

Before the door shut, he heard Harlyn squeal. "I told you. I can't wait to tell the girls. Friday night, we'll have something to talk about."

Good grief. It appeared that he was right. Harlyn seemed to be making a great protégé. Hazel, Myrtle, and Doris would be proud.

True to her word, Harlyn was gone when Gerard returned. Willow had One Direction blaring through her speakers. One might assume she had it so loud, trying to feign not being able to hear him when he returned. He wouldn't let that happen.

Gerard knew Willow's deep love for at least two of the members of the band when she was a teen. She clearly hadn't moved on from her boy band days. He watched her sway her hips for a few more beats. Maybe he should have looked away, but this was reality, not some movie where the main character acted vastly. No single man would miss this.

God had been good to him, giving him great vision and he couldn't be happier for it at this moment. *Whoa!* She can have her boy bands if she continued to dance like that.

After setting the food down, Gerard snuck up behind her and spoke into her ear. "I can't believe you still like these guys?"

Willow jumped, bumping his chest with her back, sending a zing right through him. He steadied her with his hands on her now still hips, fire searing his palms. "You good?"

He shook his hands free when she turned and nodded. This close, he saw golden flecks scattered through her hazel eyes, which were more blue today.

"What's with this?" Gerard pointed in the air, referring to the music.

A slight pink hue formed on her cheeks. Adorable.

"No judging. Their music stands the test of time. What can I say?" Besides, when my fiancé died, I about died with him.

His eyes bugged out of his head. "Your what?"

Her giggle relaxed his features. "I always said I'd marry Liam one day. I wouldn't of had to change my name either. It's even spelled the same."

Phew!

"Should we chat? I have a client in an hour."

"Yeah." Gerard grabbed the food and followed Willow to a small room in the back of the salon. I feel like the Mayor of Munchkin City in this quaint little room, he thinks as he ducked to clear the door frame. When he sat down, he then felt like Buddy the Elf in elf school.

"Is anything standard size in this room?"

Her chortle hit him in the chest. "It is. You're freakishly big. Don't pick on my breakroom." She tossed her hair over her shoulder and he had to force himself not to close his eyes and take in her faint strawberry smell.

Freakishly big, huh? She'll pay for that one. "Okay, shrimp," he quipped.

Oh, her sass was intriguing! With every witticism, flip of her hair, or quick look, Gerard teased her more.

"So you want to help with the teens?"

Thank you for getting back on track, he thought.

Gerard handed her a chicken roll up and fries. "Thank you," she said and offered him a grateful smile.

"Yes, I do. I'm sorry I was hesitant before. My reasons are valid."

He reached for her hand. She hesitated. "For grace." The pink hue from before burned a little brighter this time, and he closed his eyes to center himself before he said or did something stupid.

When she said, "Amen" with him, she also pulled her hand free. Instantly, he missed her warmth.

"And they were?" Willow asked, prior to taking a bite of the wrap. Before he could reply, a soft moan escaped her lips as she tasted the food. "I'm sorry. This is so good. I haven't eaten lunch or dinner at Hazel and Frank's place since I was eighteen."

"Don't be. I'm glad you like it." Gerard realized at that moment he meant what he said. Joy bubbled in his chest, knowing he'd brought Willow a little pleasure.

The collar on his polyester shirt uniform suddenly felt like it'd shrunk like Saran wrap, snuffing out all his air. This woman was lethal to be around.

"I'm sorry. Are you going to make this easy, or will getting your reasons be like searching for the Holy Grail?" She returned the conversation back to him.

Decision time. If he told her, he risked others finding out if she spread the information around. On the other hand, he would learn if she was, for lack of a better term, a gossip. He wanted to tell her, to share his life story with her. What did that mean?

"If I tell you, I'd appreciate it not leaving this room, though not much else can fit in here."

"Hardy, Har, Har. I won't say a word to anyone. Unless you're about to tell me you're a danger to yourself or someone else, legit criminals, not included."

"I was a homeless criminal when I came to Haven Ridge," he blurted, not wanting to avoid the truth any longer.

Willow froze mid bite. Staring at him for at least three seconds before looking away. A record. "You were in high school, right?" she asked, putting her wrap back in the takeout container.

Most people's first question, "What did you do?" made him feel like pond scum. But not Willow. She was concerned about how old he was during that season in his life. His chest bloomed with appreciation and attraction for this woman that corded around his gut like a rope, with someone cinching it until he couldn't breathe. Would she ever ask for details? He was compelled to tell her, but not if she didn't want to know. He couldn't imagine darkening her world.

"I won't ask you what you did because, frankly, it doesn't matter. All I see is Sheriff Gerard McDugal."

Dang, this woman was reading his mind. When kind words, intended for him, came from Willow's mouth, it felt like springtime in Haven Ridge when the snow melted and God breathed life back into everything.

"Thank you."

"You didn't let me finish."

Here we go.

"This may just be me talking, so don't expect some loud speaker from God to fill this room right now, but have you considered thinking like a teenage criminal again so you can catch the one disrupting our town?"

Nope. He hadn't. He looked at his untouched burger, a tsunami of confused feelings crashing down inside of him. He didn't have a desire to eat. "That's a valid point. Thank you."

"You're welcome. I realized I never thanked you for being there for me after the robbery at Randall's store. And while those words alone are not nearly enough, I hope you know I appreciated you being there that day."

His heart ached — always a rescuer, never a keeper — not long-term, anyway. "Thank you for saying so. You weren't very happy with me that day. Is there anything I can do to make you feel better?"

"Sheriff McDugal, you scoundrel. What would your mother say?"

He couldn't see himself, but based on the heat he felt, he imagined his face had turned a few shades of red and a wave of nerves flowed through his stomach.

"I'm sorry. I never should have said anything. In all the years I've known you, you've never mentioned your family, so I should have known better. I'm sorry."

She'd noticed he hadn't talked about his family. This woman was surprising him even more. What had he missed out on all these years without her?

A smirk formed on his lips, letting his playful side return. "I was going to suggest I buy you an ice cream. What did you have in mind?" He cocked an eyebrow and leaned his upper body closer to her.

He watched a red streak creep up her neck and into her cheeks. Her eyes dropped to his lips and his pulse kicked up. For the briefest of seconds, he thought about the many hurts she could erase with a simple kiss.

That thrilling thought erupted into a pillow of smoke when Willow wrapped up the remains of her food. "I'm full. Thank you so much for lunch." She stood with so much force the chair nearly tipped over, but Gerard caught it with his hand.

Now standing next to her, he pointed out, "You didn't even touch your fries."

"Well, you can have them with your untouched burger." She always had to have the last word.

When she threw her wrappers away, Gerard packaged his lunch back up; he'd eat on the road. Willow's suggestion to think like a teenage criminal gave him an idea.

One advantage of the small room and his 'freakishly big body' was when Willow tried to walk around him. There wasn't anywhere for her to go. The temperature rocketed at least fifteen degrees with Willow that close to him.

If he would have said the first thing that came to his mind, it would have been, can I kiss you?

But instead, he stated, "We didn't discuss how I can help with your center, but I'd like to, so let me know what I can do."

Time seemed to trail off as he gazed into eyes for a split second before her gaze veered off. It was as if she were looking for an escape route. Gerard blocked her way by placing his arm on the closest wall. Her sudden gasp, then quick intake of breath, the only noise in the room, rippled through his chest.

He would never keep her anywhere she didn't want to be, but he needed to know if she felt the chemistry, too.

Her eyes continued to evade him like usual. Not. Right. Now. Gently placing his finger under her chin, tilting it until their eyes met. "You have the most beautiful eyes." She tried to dip her chin, but he refused. "Why won't you look at me?"

She shrugged. Oh, no. She wasn't getting away with that. "Come on, you know. Tell me."

Her neck pulsed faster than his heart beat following his morning run. Feeling brave, he brushed a strand of her hair behind her ear, granting him a window into her high cheekbones and flawless complexion.

Her silence urged him to make his next move, hoping she didn't slug him, but gave her the courage to talk to him. Leaning closer, he brushed his lips gently across her forehead and then her temple.

"Gerard," her breathy voice saying his name ignited an ember in his chest.

He whispered in return. "I'm safe. You can tell me."

Pulling back, Gerard studied her eyes. What was she hiding? She was hiding something. What was it?

A thick-phlegm-coated throat cleared at the doorway, slicing through the sizzling air, prying Gerard away from Willow. For a woman set on matching couples throughout Haven Ridge, she certainly had horrible timing, and he bet Myrtle would kick herself for interrupting this. Good.

The interlude, a stark reminder that he had a town to keep safe.

"My lumbago is acting up today, so I was hoping you could take me a little early," Myrtle chimed, way too happy for someone with an aching back.

Willow ducked under his arm. "Sure. We were just about finished here, anyway."

Ouch. Willow, darling, I'm just getting started.

Chapter 9

Willow barely made it through Myrtle's interrogation. She had no answers for the woman — heck, if she knew what'd gotten into the sheriff. Hopefully, a good night's sleep would provide her with answers.

Unfortunately, luck was not on her side. That night, a restless sleep had her waking up every hour and at five on the dot, she got a call from Bill, her contractor.

"What do you mean, you need another five days? Willow rubbed her temples, taking a deep breath. Very. Slowly. I'm supposed to move in tomorrow. What happened?"

Waking up the next morning to the contractor's delay left Willow with an excruciating headache.

She was supposed to move out of her parent's house and into the two-bed-room apartment attached to the new shelter she would soon open with her friends. The contractor finished the addition yesterday, but a problem persisted.

"I can't have you move in without the smoke detectors installed. Harvey spoke with the manufacturer, guaranteeing they would arrive at the feed store in five days."

Willow didn't blame him. He even promised to install them the moment they arrived. "I understand. Thanks, Bill." She tapped her phone, ending the call.

Unable to fall back asleep, Willow threw back the covers, hoping her day would get better. *It couldn't get much worse, could it?*

Thirty minutes later, she arrived at the salon. An icy dread seeped into her bones as she saw her salon door ajar. "This is so much worse."

Pushing it open the rest of the way, Willow thought, *the criminal strikes again.* "Why can't Gerard catch this crook?" She asked aloud when she entered her business and flicked on the light with more force than necessary.

"I'm trying."

"Ahhh!" Willow jumped in the air at least a foot. Her fist clenched, ready to ward off the intruder.

"Do you need your mop?" Gerard asked with a grin, rubbing his chest. She would have smiled at the memory of poking him with the handle, but the jump scare had distracted her.

"What are you doing here?"

"Trying to catch the crook, as you so eloquently called him."

She scoffed, relaxing her arms. "Clearly, you're too late, unless you've tried your hand at redecorating, and if that's the case, you need to stick to your day job."

"Ouch." He mocked offense. "Maybe it's time to hire more police to patrol." His gruff tone didn't affect her.

Willow picked up the rolling carts the thief knocked down and put the drawers in place before she collected the combs and clips and tossed them into a jar of sterilizing solution.

"Please leave things alone, so I can get prints," Gerard requested. His commanding police voice caused her stomach to do little flips.

I knew I should have eaten. The day had gotten worse, and now she had a stomachache. Hunger had never affected her like that before. Odd.

"I have clients coming in. Don't stop me from doing my job just because you can't do yours." She stood erect, dropping a cape from her hand.

His downcast eyes spoke volumes, causing guilt to crawl up and tighten its grip on her throat.

"I'm sorry. I didn't mean that."

Gerard barked, "Yes, you did. I get it. The town wants answers for this." His hands motioned around the room.

He walked closer. "Do you think I enjoy watching my friends, who should just be called family, suffer? Randall lost his wife. He doesn't need to deal with some punk holding a gun at him. Harvey and his son can't afford another attack."

The grit in his voice made her jerk back.

"I'm sorry—"

"No, you're not," Willow gave him the same answer he'd supplied her with a few moments earlier.

He shook his head, probably annoyed that Willow threw his own words back at him.

A pang of sadness swirled in Willow when Gerard didn't mention the most recent break-in — her place — when he listed his friends close enough to be family. Clearly, their encounter in the breakroom didn't affect him as it did her.

"Do I have to stop, or can I pick up my space? Doris is coming in thirty minutes and I don't want her to fall."

"It's fine. We already ran the prints; got them back an hour ago."

His admission riled her up even more. "When did this happen?"

"My guess, real early this morning. I found your door open at two this morning. Jimmy and I didn't want to wake you, so we took care of it. Sadly, the prints don't match the ones we found at Randall's."

"So, there are multiple people tearing up our town?"

Gerard smiled. "You're making it sound more dire than it is, but in short, yes."

"Wait," she exclaimed, as if just realizing something he'd said. "You already have your evidence? So you just gave me a hard time for your enjoyment?"

"You have a pretty high esteem of yourself, huh, Princess?"

Gerard pressed his hands inside his vest, letting his arms dangle, reminding Willow of chicken arms. Darn him! Fowl arms or not, he looked like he'd just walked out of one of those police charity calendars.

"How do you figure?" She crossed her arms over her chest, annoyed at his comment.

Gerard moved closer. "You must think you're pretty special if I'd do something just to irritate you." His breath, warm on Willow's cheeks, sent a trail of fire all the way to her toes.

Willow opened her mouth to retort, but her voice rendered mute. Instead, just to show him he couldn't fluster her and get away with it, she walked over to her purse, slid out a piece of gum, and handed it to him. "Here, try this. You've obviously been working so hard today you couldn't keep up with your personal hygiene."

She expected him to be upset. Instead, he smiled as he accepted the stick. He unwrapped the gum and bent it in half with his front teeth before he started chewing.

Her mouth dried up faster than the Sahara in the middle of summer.

"Thank you. That is much better. Interested in trying some?" he asked with a smirk before he held the minty treat between his teeth for her to see.

"You're incorrigible."

Gerard smirked. "I think you mean incredible."

"In your dreams, officer."

Before she could move, he was in her space. "You are there every night."

Her breath hitched. His liquid chocolaty eyes drank her in.

Time seemed to melt away until a sudden gasp, followed by a sharp intake of breath, ripped through the silence.

"Oh, my, what happened, Dearie?"

She welcomed the interruption; one she never expected Doris to cause. Any longer, and her lips would have been fused to his. A sweet and exciting fantasy that could never happen. Ever!

Taking a step back, Willow almost landed on her rear when she stumbled on the drawer the thief had ransacked, looking for who knows what.

Thankful for Gerard's quick reflexes, Willow smiled and whispered, "Thank you," when he caught her elbow and pulled her to his chest.

"Ahem." Doris cleared her throat, slicing through the electricity in the air, a stark reminder they weren't alone.

Doris's singsong voice rang through Willow's ears. "I'm happy to come back later if I'm interrupting anything."

"We're good," Willow answered at the same time Gerard replied, "Oh, thank you."

Willow narrowed her eyes at the man in front of her. Whatever game he was playing, she didn't appreciate the mixed messages.

"Oh, the girls are going to love this," Doris chirped.

"Look what you did," Willow growled, low enough for his ears only.

Gerard chuckled, then cleared a path to escort Doris to the chair.

"Thank you. If I was only thirty years younger, I'd be all over you like white on rice."

Oh, brother. Doris was full of it today. Willow's eyes widened, and she turned her head to suppress the laugh bubbling inside of her.

"Are you okay over there?" Doris asked Willow, who continued clearing the floor of debris.

The words, "I'm good," hung in the air, masking Willow's unreasonable envy of a woman in her seventies.

She retrieved clean tools from a station the thief ignored, and halted, shocked by the grandma's unexpected move.

Doris tapped Gerard's biceps. "Will these guys be back to walk me to my car?"

Looking at Willow, he asked, "How long will you need with Doris? Not that she isn't beautiful enough right now."

"Aw, you sly dog, you," Doris playfully slapped his arm as Willow rolled her eyes.

"Oh, please. No wonder you're single with lines like that."

"Jealous?" His eyes gleamed with amusement, letting her know he was teasing.

Yes! "Hardly."

"Are we doing anything different today, Doris?"

"That depends if Mr. Muscles can come back."

"I don't think he needs you to stroke his ego any more, or his head won't fit in the room."

"Pish, posh. You need to tell your man how great he is."

"First of all, he's not my man, nor is he all that great."

"Why else would he be here if he's not your man, Dearie?"

"Yes, Willow, who's man am I?" Gerard's eyes shined at her as he grinned, waiting for her to answer.

The thought of wiping that smug smirk off his face, a smirk that seemed to radiate pure arrogance, flashed through Willow's mind.

She shook her head free of that fleeting thought. "Doris, if you're doing the usual," Willow began, ignoring the sheriff's question, "I'll need about thirty minutes."

"Does that work for you, Sheriff?" Doris's cheery voice made Willow want to roll her eyes, but she refrained.

He rested a comforting hand on Doris's shoulder, keeping his eyes trained on Willow. "It does. I'll see you ladies in a little while." He smiled and tipped his hat at Willow before trotting out the door.

"Woo-ee! That man sets my panty hose on fire." Doris fanned her face as Willow burst out laughing.

Doris's lips drew a straight line, and she fell silent. But that was short-lived.

"You're going to lose that man."

"Excuse me? He's not my man to lose," Willow replied.

"And whose fault is that?"

Chapter 10

True to his word, Gerard returned. Willow greeted him with the near freezing attitude he'd become accustomed to, but Doris, the sweet woman, was all smiles.

After helping Doris to her car, she buckled up and said, "Don't let that one get away."

Gerard choked on his laugh. "I don't think I have much to say in the matter. That woman hates me."

"Pish posh. Someone once said that love and hate are of the same energy." Doris narrowed her eyes at Gerard. "We see it. You and Willow will be together one way or another."

Gerard's stomach dropped. "That sounds like a threat, Doris. You can get in a lot of trouble for threatening an officer of the law, ya know?"

"We girls don't threaten, we're all action. Speaking of the girls, I'm off."

Doris drove away as Gerard muttered, "Yes, you are."

He didn't want any trouble. If those ladies locked him and Willow in a shed again, first off, they'd freeze given it's January in Montana, but with the teenage boy and another unknown criminal still on the loose, the townsfolk would not be pleased if he wasn't available to catch them.

Gerard almost felt bad when the boy ran from him the other day. The gun definitely escalated the situation, but he didn't know what he was walking into.

Willow's singing when the salon was empty seemed to be a regular activity. He froze, gawking at her as she swung her hips and turned her head.

"Anything I can help with?"

Willow jumped at his question. "I thought you left." Her tone was terse, but he hoped it was a reflection of being scared.

"You could start by not jumping me."

Gerard almost apologized, but she'd probably have a curt reply for him and not accept it, anyway. She had to feel the same energy he did when they were alone. How could he help her let go of whatever was bothering her?

"Then you could catch the person destroying everyone's businesses. After that, you can figure out what I'm supposed to do with any teens that arrive at the center."

"Believe it or not, but I've noticed the energy you, Val, and Harper have put into the shelter."

"Thanks. Sadly, it won't be much of a refuge for the next week." Willow grabbed the broom and swept up the remaining debris on the floor. "Bill can't get us occupancy until he installs the smoke detectors."

"That's awful. When are Val and Harper getting back from their trip?" he asked, handing Willow the dustpan.

She smiled as a thank you. It was small, but he'd take it.

"You mean sister's retreat," Willow clarified.

Gerard held his hands up in surrender. "Excuse me. When do they return from their sister's retreat?"

"Don't shoot the messenger, I was just trying to save you from getting your head bitten off by one of them if you didn't use the correct term."

That might be the first nice thing Willow had done for him since she'd returned home. The meager gesture gave him hope he could repair their strained interactions and build a relationship.

"Monday, Val has an eight o'clock cut and color, so she'll be home before then."

His first instinct was to take the full dustpan for her. Instead, he remained still and Willow brushed against his shoulder. Was it intentional? A spark ignited in his solar plexus. It'd been a long time since his gut had reacted to a woman like this, but with Willow, he was in a constant state of good discomfort.

Their gazes locked when she faced him. The air crackled with an energy so intense, so potent, that it felt as if it might actually ignite between them. *What is happening?*

At the most inconvenient or perfect time, depending on how one looked at the situation, Willow's phone rang, and she pulled her attention away again.

She tugged her phone out of the front pocket of her hoodie. Without saying a word to Gerard, she answered.

"Hey, Mom. What's up?"

Willow yanked the phone away from her ear like it was on fire. Gerard could hear Cora across the salon.

"Are you okay? What are you still doing in that place if someone broke in?"

Willow rolled her eyes, knowing her mom had checked her location before calling.

He knew that she'd given her parents location access as a safety precaution since she spent so much time in California. A smiled formed on his lips, realizing they'd taking liberties to find her in Haven Ridge as well. Gerard could only wonder what it was like to have parents like hers. Willow didn't know how lucky she was.

"Mom. I'm fine. We've cleaned up the mess—"

Cora interrupted her. "We? Who's we?"

"Gerard."

He sensed her trepidation. Was he right that Cora had ill feelings toward him? Willow turned the volume down on her phone, or so he guessed when he couldn't hear Cora any longer.

"Alright, Mom. I'll talk to you later tonight." Willow disconnected and stuffed her phone in her pocket.

Gerard broke the silence first. "I take it your mom likes me even less now."

Willow whipped around, stumbling as our feet connected. He cupped her elbow, preventing her from tumbling to the floor. Heat seared through his chest the moment her palms latched onto him.

The air, heavy with so much expectancy, ratcheted Gerard's nerves up many notches. If he were a volcano, he would have exploded. His breathing picked up as his fingers grazed her arms and her visible shiver urged him to pull her even closer.

"S-she likes you," Willow sputtered out.

His gaze dropped to her lips, wondering what it would feel like to kiss the woman who seemed to dislike him. He let his eyes roam over her high cheekbones and back to her hazel eyes.

"I can't believe you just lied to me. We can't be friends anymore." He was taken aback by the look of confusion on her face. Was she questioning his statement or the wink that followed?

Willow stepped back, crossing her arms over her chest. "I do not lie," her tone, indignant.

"Settle down, Princess. I was just kidding."

"Right." Willow scuffed her feet as she moved toward her station. "You have it all wrong. My mom told me to invite you for dinner at my parents' house as a way to thank you for helping me today."

"Oh." He hadn't expected that.

Gerard didn't know what to say. This was uncharted territory. The woman in front of him had kissed him years ago and then disappeared. At the time, she was too young for him to consider, wasn't she? Now, their age difference didn't matter, but she was feisty as ever and a captivating temptation he didn't need.

"Don't worry, I'll tell her that you're too busy trying to capture the person or people who did this to take a break, and I'll get you out of this."

He inched his way toward her, wondering if she'd get upset again.

"Want to know what I think?" he asked, mere inches from her. He clenched his fist, controlling the desire to reach out and wrap her up from behind.

"Hmm."

"I think you do want me to come for dinner," he teased, cupping her shoulders and gently tugging her toward him until Willow's back was flush with his chest. Enclosing her with his forearm around her shoulders, he felt her heart thump like a drum in her chest. Her hair smelled of exotic fruit, sending his nervous system into mayhem. He leaned even closer and whispered in her ear. "Tell me I'm wrong."

"Y-you're wrong." Her tone, unsure and unconvincing.

If she'd only turn her head and look him in the eye, he could lean down ever so slightly and their lips could meet again properly, not like the little peck seven years ago.

Only their heads turned as they stared at each other in the mirror. In her eyes, he saw the same intense desire that consumed him.

"Whatever you say." He grinned. "Has anyone ever told you that you are incapable of lying?" his smirk, bigger than ever. This woman brought out the flirt in him, something he'd avoided for a long time.

"Ahem." A deep throat clearing at the door jumped Gerard, and he created a foot's distance between him and Willow. When he realized it was Pastor Myles, Willow's dad, he took another big step away from her.

"I hope I'm not interrupting anything."

"N-no, Daddy, of course not. Gerard was just making sure I was okay with things."

"Mmmhmm."

She technically wasn't lying, but the look on her dad's face left Gerard feeling unsettled.

Giving all his attention to Willow, the pastor got to the point of his visit. "Your mother told me to check on you since the break-in bandit has struck again."

Ouch. I'm doing the best I can. Jimmy, too. People are expecting a lot from two law enforcement.

Haven Ridge might be small in population, but the area is vast. Amelia's ranch comprised over a hundred thousand acres, and that was before she inherited Mr. Banks two hundred fifteen acres. She could hire her own security, void of any connection to the town, but no one recognized that. That doesn't include the Whittaker's sizable ranch, nor Harper's husband's. Richardson's farm, which is about ten miles past Big L' Ranch, has at least fifty-five thousand acres.

"Gerard, are you okay with that?"

"I'm sorry, am I good with what?" Gerard felt like an ant, waiting for a giant foot to stomp him to bits when he locked eyes with Pastor Myles.

"Cora and I would like you to come to dinner Friday to thank you properly for helping Willow."

Dinner at the Payne's house. You don't want your past to get out, yet you're considering dinner at the pastor's house? The one everyone refers to as a saint? The voice of reason, or maybe it was the voice of fear, reigned in his head. Don't do it.

"Sure, I'll make that work. Thank you."

Willow smiled. "I hope you all enjoy dinner because I won't be there."

Gerard's stomach dropped. What the heck?

Chapter 11

Willow blew out an exaggerated huff. "What am I doing? I don't have to do this. Doris created the problem; she should fix it." Her steering wheel was getting a tongue lashing like never before, poor thing.

Despite her irritation toward Doris for somehow swiping the sheriff's keys, and claiming she needed to bring them to him, Willow checked her hair in the rearview mirror. She dabbed the corner of her lips where a bit of lip gloss bubbled up. Pressing her lips together and releasing them with a *pop,* she was ready. Willow suspected this was another ploy to get Gerard and her together. How could Gerard have left if he didn't have his keys? She supposed he could have had another set, but this smelt like a setup, right down to the grandmas' floral perfume.

When she opened the station's door, that smug smirk filled Gerard's super handsome face, making her heart skip.

"I just saw you. Lemme guess, you couldn't get enough of me. Well, here I am." He opened his arms wide as if looking for a hug.

Awareness tingled throughout her body. Her long ago crush on Gerard McDugal had flooded back in waves of angst and desire. Those arms and that chest. They looked perfect, waiting for her to enter. With the way he looked at her recently, she wouldn't have been able to resist his kisses if they hadn't been interrupted. She glanced at his lips. They looked like perfect kissing lips. She ripped her attention away from his tempting lips, but her mind was still focused on him.

Could she return to Haven Ridge and build a family life? Her responsibilities were far greater than worrying about a man who rejected her once. The stakes were much higher now. Failure was not an option. Every cliché imaginable fit.

"Oh, my goooodness. You can read me like a book," Willow deadpanned. Her dad always corrected her when her sarcasm flowed freely. Thankfully, he wasn't there.

"Yeah, I think my book is overdue. Time to return it."

Though he laughed like he was joking, tears formed a concrete wall behind her eyes, reminding her of his rejection so many years ago. Does he even remember it happening?

"You're mean."

He froze, his gaze piercing her heart, making it too strong to hold. Her eyes gravitated to the floor, searching for anything to focus on and keep the tears behind her eyes from falling.

"Hardly," he said, low and husky, stepping toward her, the tips of their shoes colliding. Even still, he didn't take his eyes off her. She didn't need to look at Gerard to see he was staring at her. She felt his laser focus.

"Teaser?" Many men thought they were teasing a woman, but the delivery stung, probably because men never took the time to ask questions before opening their mouths.

"That's better, but only with you." He winked at her. Maybe he had a nervous condition because this wasn't the first time he'd winked at her. She told herself that he's just a great flirt and trying to get under her skin.

Willow's stomach lurched. As he leaned closer, the air shimmered with the unspoken desire, a palpable heat building between them. Their breath mingled, and his hands bonded to her jaw. At this point, her face must be scarlet red. She was on fire! She sucked in a breath. The air in the station, smothering her.

By the grace of God, she remembered why she was there. Releasing her breath, she blurted, "Here are your keys!" Willow dangled them in the minute space between their bodies.

The slow grin peaking his lips told her he knew the impact he had on her emotions and he was going to use that to his advantage.

"There you go, girl. Breathe." He brushed a strand of hair out of her face.

Those simple words had no business sounding as sexy as they did. She knew it had everything to do with Gerard's thick, gravelly voice and his intense mahogany eyes screaming, "Willow, I see you!"

Good golly, is it hot in here?!

"I only tease the ones I love." Now, inches from her, he cupped the keys and shoved them in his pocket.

What?! Has he lost his ever-loving mind? Her brain short-circuited, yet she was fully aware of Gerard closing the gap again. There was no way he loved her.

Then Jimmy swung open the door. "So boss—"

Gerard hung his head, but didn't seem in a rush to move away. Another interruption, and Willow thanked the good Lord above.

Reading the room that lacked a significant amount of oxygen for two people, Jimmy apologized. "Sorry, Man. I caught him just like you said, Gerard."

He entered the rest of the way with the kid she met a few days ago at her salon, where she gave him a haircut, food, and a thick sweatshirt from her trunk. She was happy to see he was still wearing it.

"Hey, Zeke, right?" she asked, creating a canyon of space between her and Gerard.

He nodded. "You remembered my name." His statement split Willow's heart in half. Obviously, someone had forgotten about this teen.

"Of course."

"You know him?" Jimmy and Gerard asked in unison.

"Yeah, she's my long-lost mother. Why don't you let me go now?" Zeke said dryly.

An ache in Willow's chest burned, threatening to engulf her into flames. Where was this boy's mother? His father?

"Why is he here?" Willow asked.

"This is the one causing chaos in our town. Breaking into the hardware store, Randall's and your salon."

"I didn't break into her salon," Zeke's fiery outburst told Wilow the boy hadn't touched her place.

"So you admit to the others?" Jimmy retorted.

"I would do nothing to harm Willow or her property. She fed me, clothed me, and gave me a haircut. I'm not a monster."

Aw. Willow's heart ached for the teen in front of her. "Enough. Put him in the cell, Jimmy."

"What about my backpack?"

"It's in my SUV. I'll get it to you, Sheriff, when he's secured," Jimmy answered the boy, but spoke directly to the sheriff.

"I'll head out so you can take care of this," Willow inched toward the door.

"Not so fast. You're going to tell me everything you know about this kid."

"What do you make of this?" Gerard asked Jimmy, pointing to Zeke's backpack he tossed on the table near the cell and a notebook slid out.

The words MY ACTIVITY in all caps donned the front cover. "I have reasonable suspicion that this notebook holds information about the crimes in town."

"I did arrest him with a brick in hand, ready to toss it through Randall's window like a baseball. He's not talking, though."

He flipped open the notebook. Staring back at him were the words: Convenience Store: Haven Ridge, MT. "Bingo! This kid is going down." Finally, the townsfolk wouldn't regret voting for Gerard and it might help him get reelected.

Flipping through the notebook, Gerard came across an entry that sparked his interest.

Before he started reading, he sent Jimmy home to get some rest. "Nice work today."

Seeing Willow's name in this kid's notebook made his stomach churn. Based on the boy's entry, Gerard believed he wasn't a monster. Clearly, the boy needed a Mama. The warmth and care Willow used to comfort Zeke mirrored the compassion she'd shown him when he told her that he was once a criminal. When he'd told her that he used her strategy of thinking like a teenaged ruffian, she ducked her head, but Gerard didn't miss the shy smile adorning her face. They made a great team. Now, all he had to do was convince her of that.

Another entry captured his attention, causing alarm to race through his mind.

As I slipped into the dark, frigid night, I felt like someone was following me. Maybe I should have accepted the ride and hotel from Willow? No, it was only my imagination. The bare tree branches weren't gnarled fingers trying to trap me in its clutches. Nor was the shadowy figure adorned in the snow a hatch for a portal that would transport me to a nefarious leader waiting to mold me into his protégé.

The smell of decaying animals mixed with damp earthy matter and a hint of pine from evergreen trees was not a sign that one day someone would travel the same path I did and smell my decaying body.

I never minded death before, but with nice people like Willow, why would I want to die?

I wish I had accepted the boots from Willow, but I refused to be her charity case. She had her own troubles; I wouldn't lay mine on her, too. Instead, I took off my sneakers and drenched socks. Hopefully they'd dry before morning, and I would have frostbite on my feet.

The air through the woods I traversed was filled with a sinister energy, whispering 'turn back'. With danger lurking around me, maybe he should heed that advice and leave MT. I dread the idea of leaving, especially since Willow said I should come visit her again, but I'm not sure I have many other choices.

He'd been there, so he understood Zeke's vulnerability. Gerard needed to help him before Zeke got out of control or ran off. But first, he needed answers. He stood in front of the cell door, staring at the teen's back.

"Zeke, is it? How old are you?"

Silence.

"Is Zeke your name or just what you told my friend?"

The boy scoffed. That's progress.

"Something funny?"

Zeke shook his head.

"What are you doing in Haven Ridge, Kid?"

"I'm not a kid," he barked.

Thank you, Lord. Our experiences help us in the future. Gerard knew calling him a kid would get to him.

"Then talk to me, or that's what I'll call you. Unless, of course, you prefer Prisoner 25." Where'd the number come from? Gerard didn't have a clue, but it sounded cool.

Silence again.

"I already have all the evidence I need to convict you of at least two crimes in town."

"No, you don't."

Hallelujah, the boy can talk. "You wrote about holding up the convenience store and stealing the notebook and pen."

"And what makes you think those are two different situations?"

Gut feeling. He had a point, though. It wasn't often he dealt with smart criminals. Gerard preferred the stupid ones. This case might not be over yet.

"Spill it — all the details. Start with telling me where your gun is." Gerard said in his commanding sheriff's voice.

Chapter 12

The days blurred together, leaving Willow exhausted mid week. Women occupied every chair at the salon, feeling the need for that mid-winter color and cut, but Willow's mind focused elsewhere.

"We're heading to check on Haven Horizons," Val and Harper announced after cashing out their customers.

Yes, they'd finally chosen a name, and she loved it. It was crazy to think that they were expecting their first teen to arrive tomorrow. The smoke detectors arrived early, and true to his word, Bill had already installed them.

Ten minutes later, Willow asked, "What do you think?" shaking her fingers through Reneé's color and cut. She was married to Rocco, Big L' Ranch's veterinarian, and she homeschooled the kids on the ranch.

"Would you ever consider expanding your services to other students in the community?" Willow asked with caution.

A peal of laughter, unexpected and joyful, bubbled out of her. "Oh, that's already happened. Sean and Violet offered my services to Annika's son, Jackson, so yeah, I already do. Why do you have more you want to add to the mix?"

Willow felt a little guilty for asking now. She didn't know that the newest waitress at the diner had her son benefiting from Reneé's teaching expertise.

Between all the kids at the ranch and Annika's son, Willow was more determined to tell everyone the truth and start building her family here in Haven Ridge. Would residents accept her? How about her dad? She'd left initially so he could save face. She couldn't imagine being the pastor of a small town and *my daughter being pregnant out of wedlock and at seventeen. Nope. He will be so disappointed.* She didn't know if she wanted to put Tate or herself through that. Hence, why she'd stayed away all these years.

"Well, I was wondering if you could educate the teens that came through Haven Horizons, *and my little guy, if I ever get the nerve to tell people the truth.*" The well-formed statement was more of a question, and Reneé knew as much.

Her brows shot up. "That'd be a lot, but I suppose it wouldn't be too hard if they study at the same level as one of the other students."

Reneé seemed to be thinking this through. "Yeah, I could make it work. I imagine Addison would help." She was Reneé and Rocco's oldest. "As a new driver, she begs me to drive all the time. I could have her bring assignments back and forth if necessary."

"I imagine the mom in you is so scared to watch her drive away." Willow was glad to have at least eight years before Tate started driving.

Reneé choked out a breath. "I don't wish this feeling on anyone."

"I'm surprised Rocco will let her go anywhere after homecoming."

Willow had the pleasure of making Addison look like a princess that day. When her date brought her home an hour late, Rocco screamed at the two of them. Or that was the story she'd been told.

"Me, too."

Willow wanted to ask if she would extend the invitation to Zeke, but she didn't know how long the boy would be in jail. She also wondered if people would welcome him in town if he was responsible for the break-ins.

The jingle bells on the knob sang as the door flew open. Willow glanced at Gerard, but looked away just as quick.

A feeling akin to giddiness peaked within her. "How do you like it, Reneé?" Willow fluffed the woman's hair.

"Love it, like always." Reneé handed Willow a hundred-dollar bill.

She shook her head. "This is too much."

"It's not nearly enough. Besides, I imagine it's seldom the two of you are alone." She thumbed over her shoulder at Gerard, looking as determined and attractive as ever. "I don't want you to waste time giving me change."

The woman grabbed her coat and with a passive, "Later, Sheriff," she was out the door.

His unpleasant stare, oozing with disapproval, made her stomach churn. Instinctively, she wanted to run, but he was blocking the exit, so instead, she attended to her mess.

Ha! Willow didn't miss the irony of that entire thought. She had to stop running from people's disapproval of her. It was her life; she had to answer to the Lord. She'd already repented for her sins, so he already forgave her. What man thought shouldn't matter.

"Why didn't you tell me about Zeke?" His tone, gruff.

"Excuse me. When did you become my keeper or the person I answer to? What, being Sheriff isn't enough for you?"

"I'm not fooling. He had a gun, or did you forget?"

"He's a teenager, or did you forget?" she fired back.

Gerard rested his hand on his hips, accentuating his solid, yet well fit, frame. "You don't make a point. Have you seen the damage teens do with guns?"

"Maybe some, but not this one."

"What makes you an expert on teenagers?"

Nothing. "To steal your phrase, 'gut feeling.'"

"My gut has had years of practice and seen things that would make your shudder."

Well, I have mother's intuition and that trumps everything else. Or so she'd experienced.

Her stomach teetered. She couldn't be thinking about things like that. It would only take a split second for that thought to slip out of her mouth, and then what?

Her phone rang. Recognizing Tate's distinct ringtone, a frantic energy surged through her as she lunged for her phone. Resting next to Gerard, he looked at the name, and then a flat expression spilled across his face. Willow moved into the break room so he wouldn't overhear.

"I know, Baby. It stings to be away from you, but this opportunity won't come around often; you have to do it. I'll be there next weekend, okay?"

"Perfect. Sounds like a plan. I love you, too."

Willow turned around and was face to face with Gerard. *Please don't ask!* Will he let this go? Being the professional interrogator he was, she was doubtful.

"I imagine Tate wouldn't be too happy if he knew his woman was putting herself in danger."

Woman? Oh, no. He thought Tate was her boyfriend. "You don't have a clue what you're talking about."

"Whatever you say. Zeke is on the hook for Randall's and Harvey's break-ins. I convinced the judge to sentence him to community service if you'll agree to that."

"That's wonderful. Any leads on who broke in here?"

"No, but we're working on it, I promise." He stepped into the small room. Feeling like a giant, he said, "The judge also stipulated that Zeke has some place to stay."

"And you're telling me that becauuuuse..." she stretched out the word and rolled her wrist around, trying to hurry him up.

Gerard wiped his palm down his face. "Your center can have boys eventually, right?"

"Haven Horizons."

"What?" he grumped.

"The name of our business is Haven Horizons."

"Okay. Boys. Can you house them?"

Grr. When Mr. Sheriff got upset, he was a grump. "Potentially." She answered just as sharply as he'd spoken to her seconds ago.

"Why do you have a boy's sweatshirt in your trunk?" his erratic change of subject caught her off guard.

"In case we get cold."

"We?" He sighed. Obviously losing his patience.

"It was on sale and it's an adult small." That was the truth. Either Tate or she could wear it if they needed.

He coughed out a laugh. "Your man fits into that? No wonder you're not interested in me. I'm the size of a full grown man."

"Whatever you say, Sheriff." He was going to regret his comments one day, and Willow couldn't wait to have a front-row seat when he realized his mistake.

Gerard crossed his arms. "Does Tate plan on coming to Haven Ridge to oversee the boys?"

She smirked. Oh, my, this could be fun; Gerard was jealous. "He plans on coming when I tell him he can."

Truth be told, Tate had been pestering her for the last seven months to just bring him to Haven Ridge and surprise everyone. His reasoning made her chuckle. "No matter how mad they are at you, they won't be mean to you in front of me, right?"

Oh, how she missed her little boy. This weekend he was going with Uncle Steve to a Boy Scout camping retreat and that's why she wasn't leaving for California tomorrow. Hopefully, spending time with the women from Big L' Ranch at their Bible study would give her the strength to come clean.

"He must be one of *those* guys," Gerard mocked, jarring her back to reality.

She caught the chuckle trying to escape. "Meaning?"

"The one who doesn't know how to make a woman happy. She has to direct his every thought because he's too incapable."

"On the contrary, Tate makes this woman elated. In fact, no one on the face of this Earth could ever replace the feelings I have for Tate. I'd die for him, and while I'm alive, I live and breathe for him, too."

He deflated faster than a tire when the nail released, but he recovered quickly. "That sounds like a challenge to single men."

A sudden jolt of shock reeled through her. "That's what you got out of what I said?" *Good grief Mr. Alpha Male Sheriff.*

He moved even closer. "I am not *that guy,* so I won't rip you from your precious Tate—"

"Darn right, you won't," she responded spontaneously.

"But you'll be begging me to kiss you before you know it."

She should just tell him that he would never win her heart in competition with Tate. Begging to kiss him might also be a challenge he lost. Willow's stubbornness ran deep. Hence, the reason her parents haven't met Tate yet.

"Right, because that went so well the first time." She slapped her hand over her mouth, humiliated. She vowed to never bring that up.

Instead of his typical grin or smirk, his lips dipped slightly and his eyes resembled sadness or regret. "That was the biggest mistake of my life."

"Oh," she said, not intending to say anything at all.

"Is that why you won't look at me for more than a few seconds?"

One reason. "I don't know."

"I think you do," his voice, husky and his eyes yearning. "I'll let that go for now, but I don't give up easily." She saw the determination in his ridge features.

He was in her bubble now. Nuclear alarms blaring in her mind: BACK AWAY! BACK AWAY! Her heart galloped and her breath panting in anticipation. Would he kiss her?

She swooned when Gerard sang the chorus to her favorite One Direction song that she was listening to earlier in the week. Did he just learn it, or had he been a closet 1D fan?

> *Baby, you light up my world like nobody else*
> *The way that you flip your hair gets me overwhelmed*
> *But when you smile at the ground, it ain't hard to tell*
> *You don't know, oh-oh, you don't know you're beautiful*
> *If only you saw what I can see*
> *You'll understand why I want you so desperately*
> *Right now I'm looking at you and I can't believe*
> *You don't know, oh-oh, you don't know you're beautiful, oh-oh*
> *That's what makes you beautiful*

She couldn't hold his gaze. Her lashes rested on her cheeks, the heat of embarrassment rising. He rejected her! The horse's hooves plowing through her stomach also made it difficult to keep his intense gaze.

"Look at me, Beautiful."

Wow. She'd spent the better part of her life crushing on this man. For him to notice her now was nothing short of miraculous, not literally, but to her, heaven had answered her prayers.

Beware of misleading men who use your skills to get what they want and then reject you. Miss Negativity, she lived on the right side of Willow's brain, and liked to come out of hibernation at just the right time, spoke with the bitterness Willow was in the habit of hearing.

"You want me to stare at you? Are you a narcissist?" *Yup.* Miss Negativity won.

He flashed her an off-kilter smile that worked for him. Her heart thumped against her ribcage, and she wiped her palms on her jeans when he cupped one cheek with his large palm. "I want your face," he whispered.

His free hand twirled a strand of her blonde waves. "I want your hair."

She gulped.

"I want your thoughts." He kissed her forehead, making her legs feel like marshmallows.

Pointing to the middle of her chest, he breathed, "I want your heart and soul."

His thumb brushed across her lower lip. "I want all of you." His eyes dropped to her lips and back up to meet hers.

Aww. Since returning to Haven Ridge, her feelings for this man had blossomed into a deep and overwhelming affection, a feeling that intensified with each passing moment. She was beyond a crush and it petrified her. Would he reject her again when he found out who Tate was? She marveled at the thought of Gerard being a mischievous teenager, but that wasn't him now.

She leaned in closer, but he pressed his finger to her lips. "Is that your way of begging me for a kiss?"

Nothing like reality to kick one in the butt.

She ripped away from his hold, ignoring his question. "Yes, Haven Horizons will house boys when we can, but for now, you'll have to help Zeke with a place to stay." She stopped in the doorway, not able to get away quick enough.

"As far as having me. You had your chance. It's Tate's turn now, and he hasn't mastered the skill of sharing."

Chapter 13

I hate you, Tate, Gerard thought as he jabbed his left then right fists into the punching bag. That wasn't entirely true. He hated himself for being a dumb twenty-eight-year-old. But let's be real, he'd yet to find an adult who said his, or her best self was before the age of thirty, at least.

Gerard thought he would've won her over with the One Direction song. Nada. Well, today was a new day and success was waiting for him after a shower and breakfast.

An hour later, he heard, "Over here, Sheriff," Myrtle called, more like shrieked, when he entered the diner.

Lord, please help me not to say anything incriminating.

"Take a seat," Hazel offered. "We have something we'd like to talk with you about."

Suddenly, the heat from the kitchen swirled around Gerard. This couldn't be a business call. Everything in Haven Ridge had been back to normal, at least for the townsfolk.

Doris dove in for the kill first. "Why are you single, Sheriff?" Without waiting for a response, she rattled on. "You're a hunk with a capital H. You have a successful job, and now you're helping with Zeke. It shows you're able to be a family man."

How did she know that? Amelia hadn't agreed to including Zeke at the ranch for schooling and working purposes, yet.

"Exactly. You're a catch," Myrtle added. "You're making it possible for Zeke to have a semblance of a real teen life." The woman shook her head and her large, blue, and yellow feathery earrings swayed with her. "I can't imagine parents leaving that kid to flounder on his own. You should be arresting them," Myrtle finished.

As she carried on with more compliments, most likely to butter him up for something, Gerard zoned them out. He imagined his heart would have swelled if Willow were the one saying these things.

Zeke hadn't told him anything about his family, but based on the teen's notebook, he could track down Zeke's parents. His mom died two and a half years ago from a self-inflicted gunshot wound. Without the father's name on Zeke's birth certification, Gerard was stuck; however, determination ran through Gerard's veins. He wouldn't let Zeke fall into the same trap he had as a kid.

"Are you listening to us?" Hazel's tender voice asked, interrupting his flow of thoughts.

He shook his head. "I'm sorry, ladies. I have a lot on my mind. What can I do for ya?"

Warning! Beware, meddlesome women going in for the kill. All three of them were smiling like a hacker who broke the code.

"It's more of what we can do for you." Myrtle rubbed her hands over each other like the Wicked Witch of the West. All he could hear was, "These things must be done delicately," that award-winning cackle roared in his ears.

Why did it seem like he was selling his soul to the devil right now? Joining forces with these women went against everything he stood for. He valued people's privacy, unless they broke the law, then he had no problem invading it within the parameters of the law, of course.

"I think Miss Willow is meeting the Valentine's Day dance committee at the church this evening—"

"Absolutely not. The last time I helped you with something at the church, I was there for hours."

"With a beautiful woman," Hazel added.

"Who acted afraid of a mouse to stay close to you," Doris included another bonus.

Acted. He couldn't see his face, but he imagined it reflected pure shock. Did Willow pretend to be afraid so she could stay close to him?

Dori's raised brows and nod confirmed it. "I wasn't supposed to say anything, but everyone knows better than to tell me things."

"The church is a scary place when you three are involved," He said, partially joking.

He stood up. "I am sorry to waste your time ladies—"

"Sit down, Gerard McDugal." Hazel rarely used a stern tone or his full name, so when she did, he listened. This time wasn't any different.

Hazel leaned forward, elbows propped on the table and her chin resting on her laced fingers. "You're thirty-five years old. Well beyond marriage age." She inhaled a deep breath. "We've tried to do this the easy way, but both you and Willow are too stubborn."

"She hates me. Something happened years ago between us and I blew it."

Myrtle scoffed. "You mean that silly little kiss before she left the town for seven years?"

Good grief. These women knew everything.

When she put it that way, Gerard felt awful. Had he driven her away? No. She wouldn't leave over the likes of him.

"How'd you know?"

"Everyone knows?"

"Even her mother?"

"Yup," they responded in unison.

Maybe that explained her mother's attention toward him the day of Randall's break-in. Maybe she really was rooting for Willow and him.

"What about her father?"

They all nodded.

He gulped. *I'm still alive. Thank you, Lord.*

The ladies laid out their elaborate plan in a whirlwind of intricate details and rapid-fire instructions.

He wondered how long it took for the trio to create this down-right scary plan. "I'll probably mess up your exquisite details, but I'll do my best to see if it makes a difference with Willow."

"It's not that bad working with us, is it?" Myrtle asked, still rubbing her hands together.

"I haven't made up my mind."

Pastor Myles didn't seem surprised to see Gerard when he arrived at the church. "Willow never gets to these meetings on time. I think she's silently rebelling against me still. She hates these kinds of things."

How did Pastor know he was here to see Willow? Had the ladies shared this plan with him?

Gerard now realized that he should have asked the trio more questions.

"Oh, Gerard, you're here. It's so nice to see you again," Cora entered the meeting room behind the sanctuary.

Gerard nodded respectfully. "Evening, Mrs. Payne."

"None of that Mrs. Payne stuff. Call me Cora."

"So, you and Willow will check out the area between the church and the dance hall to see if we can use it for some outdoor activities."

Yup. He knew it wasn't a question, more of a directive. The glimmer of hope in his eye, as well as Cora's, led him to believe they were part of this setup. That adage: Keep your friends close and your enemies closer swirled through his mind. Apparently, he was the ladies' enemy.

The fast-paced conversations filling the room surprised Gerard. All the ladies from Haven Ridge on the committee moved their bodies and mouths like a Japanese bullet train.

"It takes some getting used to it," Pastor must have recognized fear in Gerard's expression, "but the ladies are very efficient. Everyone means well and their number one focus is to give God all the glory, so how can you go wrong?"

Valid point. Gerard believed that as long as a group of people operated with Jesus in the center, everything would turn out the way He intended.

"Hey, Mom, Dad. I got caught up at—"

She lost her voice the moment she spotted him. The redness in her cheeks was adorable. The coloring might have already been there, for it was only sixteen degrees when he arrived, but Gerard would rather believe he made her blush.

"What are you doing here?" she snapped.

"Willow, is that anyway to talk to your new partner?" Cora asked him.

"Partner?" Her flailing arms and exasperated tone caused laughter to bubble in his chest.

"The committee would like to use the area between the dance hall and the church for fun activities and you're going to work with Gerard to come up with those ideas."

"How about pelting the sheriff with snowballs?" she shot him a smirk.

A tingle of attraction ripped through his chest at her sass. "I'm deeply touched, Princess."

"Willow," Cora reprimanded her. "That's no way to talk to the sheriff."

She rolled her eyes.

"Oh, look," Cora exclaimed. "It's snowing. What a perfect setting." The woman's eyes sparkled brighter than the sequins on her Christmas sweater.

Five minutes later, he was walking down the path between Haven Ridge's only church and dance hall. With the freshly falling snow, the ice patches were hidden just enough, and he offered his arm, so she didn't fall.

"I'm good; thanks."

Amused, Gerard said, "No worries, if you fall and twist an ankle, I'll have to carry you back, bridal style. We can get real close then."

She slowly slid her arm through and gripped his biceps. A surge of energy ran through his arm.

"We could see if Randall can order those lights like the ones he has at Christmas time in the shape of candy canes. They must have heart-shaped ones for Valentine's Day."

He didn't have the foggiest idea what she was talking about. All he could think about was the tingling sensation elicited by this woman's petite fingers. His entire left arm was numb at this point. *I think that's a heart attack symptom. This woman is trying to kill me.*

"What do you think about the heart-shaped lights? They would look great on either side of the path. You know, like lighting the way to an event."

"What event are we promoting deep in the woods? There are quite a few teenagers. Maybe your dad should be the chaperone."

She guffawed. "He'd be perfect. "Ah, Son, no hands below the neck unless you're married."

"He wouldn't?"

"He would. Trust me, I know from experience."

Gerard shrugged. "Nothing wrong with a dad trying to protect his daughter. I bet if I had a daughter, I'd take a different approach."

"What would that be?"

He tossed snow up in the air and to the side with the toe of his boot. "For starters, I'd lay some t-shirts over the back of the couch like I'd just taken them from the dryer. The one that says something like I have a daughter, a gun, shovel and an alibi that will be on top," she chuckled.

Yes! If Willow wants a protective man, it's me all the way.

He continued with his actions for a future daughter. "I'd be decked out in my full uniform, hand rested on my weapon."

"So, you'd intimidate him?"

"Nooo," he dragged out the word, shaking his head as he spoke. "I'd scare the dickens out of him, so he'd think twice before he even touched her above the neck."

His stomach tightened when she reached out her freehand, tears pooling in her eyes from laughing. "Okay. No more. I don't want any information if I ever get brought in for questioning."

"Don't fear that, Darlin', a wife doesn't have to testify against her husband; it's in the Constitution."

Her expression froze, and just like that, she was back. "I thought we were having a good time. Why'd you have to go and ruin it?"

Chapter 14

They reached a clearing, and a small stone circle bordered a teepee of logs. Four benches marked the cardinal directions. The south bench held a click lighter, pieces of a brown paper bag, and a personal-sized cooler.

"If this is your way of not pursuing me, I think your wires got crossed somewhere."

He didn't know what to say. This was not part of the plan he agreed to with the ladies. If he had to guess, Cora and Pastor Myles teamed up with the trio, and they had duped him.

"I mean, this feels like a GAC Christmas movie. If I were playing the role of the main female character, I'd swoon over the effort you put into this night, under the guise of a committee meeting."

Unable to ignore the overwhelming prickling awareness in his body, he took a step away from her, redirecting his attention on her suspicious features. "Swoon away. Heck, I am!"

"You didn't plan this?" She shrugged her shoulders when he shook his head as slow as a long pendulum swing. "Okay. Let's start a fire and see what's in the cooler."

"Wait a minute," he said, stepping in front of her, but putting his hands by his sides, resisting the urge to touch her. "It wasn't okay a minute ago when you thought I planned this. Now that you know I didn't, you're ready to open the cooler like it's the door to Fort Knox."

A small, barely audible sigh slipped from her lips. "Look, you are an Olympic caliber flirt. You didn't want me once, I'm not putting myself through that again. There's too much at stake this time. Can I enjoy a little food and a warm fire with you as friends catching up? Sure, but that's it."

Her nonchalant attitude was a slow poison eating away at him. He'd never get Willow to beg him for a kiss at this rate.

Her life seemed to revolve around Tate. What did he have to do for her attention?

His phone pinged four times with incoming texts. He hoped he wouldn't have to leave. Talking with Willow had become his favorite pastime, even when she was sassy. "Excuse me."

His stomach dropped when he read the first one.

Myrtle: Change of plans. Just eat dinner there. If you check under the bench, there's a blanket to keep the two of you warm.

Gee, thanks.

Hazel: Don't be mad at us. We love you!

So mad. Not really.

Raddix: The only way you'll know if there's an attraction is to kiss her.

He couldn't tell him about his stupid declaration. At this rate, Zeke will be married with grandkids of his own by the time Willow begs for a kiss from him.

What!? You're in on this, too?

Raddix: Yes, for Lily, I'm wasting my time texting you when I should be enjoying time with my wife.

Damon: We expect a full report the next time you're at the ranch.

You too?

Damon: That's from Harlyn, but if you make a fool of yourself, I'm all ears.

Thanks, Man.

"Is everything okay?" Willow's sweet voice cut through his concentration.

"Yes, thank you." She didn't to know he was talking with the culprits.

After polishing off a thermos of hot chocolate and the crackers and cheese, Gerard checked in with Jimmy. All was good in town, so he flung out the blanket left for him and covered their laps.

"So tell me about Tate." She stiffened next to him and unease trickled down Gerard's spine, wondering if he'd pushed Willow too quickly.

"Why California?" He changed his question.

Willow took a breath. "Tate's lived there his whole life. But he wants to move to Haven Ridge, so as soon as we get a few things in order, he'll live here with me."

"Do you plan on getting married?"

"No. Not all people who love one another should be married."

Gerard laughed. "I'm sure that doesn't make your parents happy."

"I've been disappointing them for years. One more won't make a difference." She hopped on the seat and rubbed her hands gloved together. "Enough about me. Why aren't you married? You've always had ladies falling around you."

"That's a bit of an exaggeration, but since you asked. I almost got engaged two years ago; saved Jennie from a car wreck. We were each other's everything for about a year. I thought I loved her, too." *But I never had half of the jolts and excitement as I do when I'm with you.* "Wrong. Neither of us loved the other enough to make the sacrifices to stay together. She moved home to Chicago, and I stayed here."

"I'm sorry for you, I think."

"You think?" He chuckled. "You are a stubborn woman."

"No, I say 'I think' because if you realize now that you didn't love her, isn't it better that you didn't marry and have kids?"

"True."

"Do you even want kids?"

"I'm not sure." A wave of regret smashed into him when her smile vanished, replaced by a tight-lipped frown.

"I'm sorry about the whole wife not testifying against her husband thing," he couldn't form an intelligent sounding sentence, but her smile told him she understood.

"No worries. I've already forgotten it. How could I not when I'm caught up in this moment? Look at the snow ground trail, quaint fire, and the food. It really is like a movie."

She wasn't wrong. The heavy snow resting on the evergreen branches added to the picturesque ambience and the chill from the night air, replaced with fire embers, burning steadily in his gut when she glanced his way.

"I get it. It's too bad I'm the pathetic single sheriff and you're the beautiful hairdresser who goes off every weekend to be with her man."

"When you put it like that..." she tapped her gloved forefinger against her lips. *What's she going to say? I hear, I'll stay this weekend and we can have fun together.*

Her face beamed. "I think you have a story. We should call producers now as long as you don't mind the pathetic side of you being on millions of people's TV screens."

Anything for you.

She bumped her shoulder into his, sending a zap of electricity through him. *It's just cold weather static.* He coached himself, but then time seemed to move at a sloth's pace. His stomach twisted in nervous knots. Did she feel that, too? Her eyes darted toward the snow covered ground. *Yes! She had to feel it.*

He leaned closer, the colors from the snow-covered trees behind her blurred in his vision. He wrapped his hand around her neck, and he gently pulled her toward him. As he stared at her beautiful eyes, her warm breath sent shivers down his spine. This was ridiculous. He'd never felt like this... ever!

A centimeter of space lived between their lips. He'd close that gap and feel how wonderful her full lips were on his. Then she backed away. "I thought you were waiting for me to beg you."

Chapter 15

Finally, quitting time on Friday. This monster of a week felt like it would never end. Willow locked the salon and headed toward Big L' Ranch. She hated snow. Why God did you make it snow now?

"Because I can, and I never give you more than you can handle." Willow answered with something she thought God would say.

She hadn't seen Gerard since their time at church. If he only knew how badly she wanted to kiss him. It took every ounce of strength she had to remind him she hadn't begged yet.

The more she thought about everything, and replayed their time together an embarrassing amount, she had to tell her parents about Tate.

Of course, she felt horrible keeping their only grandchild from them. If she hadn't been so worried about what people thought, she wouldn't be in this mess now. The longer she kept her secret, the easier it was to keep quiet.

Thirty minutes later, she turned into the driveway. Willow's mind returned to her childhood, the feeling of jubilation she experienced as a kid every time she'd visit here. The black wrought iron sign with the big L in the middle made her smile. Standing outside of her car, she breathed in the air. Somehow, it seemed cleaner on the ranch than anywhere else in town.

The picturesque mountains formed a dramatic backdrop to Amelia's seemingly endless ranch. Willow could get used to this view.

"I'm so glad you could make it." Amelia snuck up behind Willow.

"Thank you for having me. I brought my nail polish if anyone wanted a quick mani," she said, holding up her case.

"That's really sweet of you. With as much dirt and grime as I deal with, I know I could use one."

The sound of a loud bang of a vehicle door echoed through the air, capturing her attention. *What the heck? Is he following her?* Willow's body was drawn to Gerard like a flame seeking fuel. Seeing him now, she could almost feel the warmth of his breath on her neck, remembering their near kiss last night. Following her interruption of what she imagined would be a kiss to stop time, he'd kept some distance between them for the rest of the night.

Perfect. She couldn't afford more complications in her life.

"Hey, Gerard, I mean Sheriff," Amelia greeted her guest.

"This is a social visit, so Gerard is good." He turned his attention to Willow. "Hey. How are you?"

She smiled, catching Amelia's peaked interest, eyes bouncing between Willow and Gerard.

"What can I do for you?" Thank you, Amelia. Move this along, please.

Gerard fidgeted, a nervous energy radiating off him. "Can I talk with all the adults for a moment?"

Like a whirlwind, we were in Amelia's kitchen. That woman got things done. But Gerard, who wasn't with them any longer and this impromptu meeting was all, but forgotten when Katy, the woman who ran the ranch store and always gave her a piece of candy when she visited with her dad, wrapped her arm around Willow in a side hug. "I'm so glad you could make it."

"Thank you. I hated the drive, though. I forgot how awful driving in the snow can be."

"Amen, Sister!" Lily shouted. "Driving in snow is horrendous. How can something so spectacular be so annoying?" Lily came from California, moving when a stalker took a deadly interest in her. "But," she continued, "everyone knows why I put up with the snow." Her flushed cheeks and her sparkly eyes let everyone know she was referring to her husband, Raddix.

"That's what you need!" Lily exclaimed, tapping her finger against her lips, lost in thought.

"Oh, no," Harlyn warned. "Lily is the unofficial fourth member of the Troublesome Trio. We may have to change their name to The Troublesome Squad."

"If recollection serves me correctly, you're not too far behind Lily." Willow shot her with accusing eyes. Gerard eventually told her about the texts he received last night.

Harlyn fell in love with Damon while running from danger. Her family abused her and tried to kill her. In the end, her mom killed her dad. Growing up, her mom had been the most abusive to Harlyn, but it stemmed from the abuse she had taken from her husband.

Seeing both Lily and Harlyn happy gave her hope. Maybe marriage wouldn't be off the table after all.

"I'm on to something. If she had a man, he could have driven her tonight and she wouldn't sound so apocalyptic."

Willow wouldn't argue since she'd thought the same thing on the right here. "Well, there aren't that many available men flowing out of the barns and silos. You ladies have taken the good ones."

Lily wagged her forefinger like a dog's tail in front of her. "There's one man I can think of—"

"Don't finish that sentence, men entering," Quinton, Damon, Raddix, and Jeff paraded into the kitchen, hustling to kiss Amelia, Harlyn, Lily, and Katy, respectively, on the cheek.

"We're trying to think of a man for Willow so she doesn't have to drive in the snow anymore."

Jeff chuckled. "If that's all you want a man for, he's getting a short end of the stick." He gave Katy another kiss on the cheek and sat down.

"Lily, give the woman a break. She's only here during the week. I don't know a man," Carolyn, the ranch's chef, said, shaking her head, "who'd willingly stay away from his woman for that long."

Interesting. They noticed she left every weekend.

"That's right. I'm surprised you came tonight," Lily added.

"Yeah, plans changed, so I worked at the salon." Gerard appeared again, stopping her short. "I'll be here all weekend." Willow heard the sadness in her voice, and judging by Gerard's expression, he noticed it, too.

Katy was the first to say something, though. "That's the voice of a woman in love."

"Yeah." Willow wouldn't outright lie, so she needed to change the subject before Gerard and everyone else found out that Tate was her son.

She should have known better. These women would never let her out of the hot seat until she gave them answers.

"Do you already have a man in your life and that's why you leave?" Lily asked with hopeful eyes.

Why does this woman care if Willow had a man? *Dunno.* The desperate look on Gerard's face made her feel a little guilty for withholding the truth.

"Maybe let the woman breathe, Darlin'." Raddix kissed his wife's temple.

Willow's mind raced, unease picked at her already aching stomach. *This was a bad idea to come here,* she thought as she tightened the grip on her bag. She'd expected to could tell these women her situation, and they'd offer wisdom.

How can she tell her secret without telling her secret? How can she withhold the truth without lying? She could never tell her secret now. These guys were just as bad as women when it came to gossiping. If her parents found out before she could tell them, maybe a pastor killing someone wouldn't be too unrealistic any longer.

"What's up Gerard?" Raddix asked, breaking the awkward silence.

God bless that man a thousand times over.

"I needed to talk to you guys about a situation I could use your help with now that I've done my job like I'm supposed to," Gerard teased.

Willow whipped her head toward him, but was surprised when Gerard's playful taunt met her gaze. His alluring looks were chipping away at her heart, making her defenseless against all things Gerard.

"It's about time you did your job." He must not have expected her mock tone and wink because he opened his mouth to speak, but nothing came out, so he winked back.

Was it hot in here? *Eek.* Her stomach dropped and her heart raced. He wasn't supposed to have this effect on her. *Remember, I gave him up as my New Year's resolution.* Oh, well, who keeps their resolutions, anyway?

Unfortunately, that little interaction captured Lily's attention. Her eyes were sparkling like she'd won the jackpot.

Oh, no! *She **is** just as dangerous as Doris, Hazel, and Myrtle. She'll probably lock Gerard and me in a cell at the station.* Not that Willow would mind, unless it ended with her embarrassed again.

"That's great, isn't it, Willow?" Harlyn asked.

With a toss of her head and a slight frown, she asked, "What?"

"I'm sorry, are we boring you?" Gerard's playful quip elicited a round of laughter.

"No, I was enjoying myself immensely before you showed up," she said, her eyes dancing.

"Yes, I can imagine how standing in freezing cold weather and snow pelting down on you could be a fun time." Imagining snuggling into the crook of his arm while he kept her warm would have made that just perfect.

"Well, it might be fun if you had a wife," Raddix said with a grin, earning him laughs and high-fives from the other men.

See!

Gerard wagged his eyebrows at her as if he were thinking the same thing. It was definitely ten degrees hotter in here now than it had been.

"Enough Raddix. There are children in the living room," Lily ordered playfully.

"Yes, on that note, I am wondering if you can help me with Zeke?" Gerard asked everyone. He went into a detail explanation of taking in Zeke and hoping to have his schooling and work experience at the ranch, so he was among honest people.

The response was overwhelming. Everyone wanted to help. Reneé agreed to homeschool him. Jeff, Raddix, Damon, and Quinton agreed to mentor him and show him hard work when he wasn't with Gerard.

"Now that we're done with that, why don't you all join our Bible study?" Lily asked the men.

The men spit and sputtered, but we're fast to agree when they're women whispered something in their ear.

"I'm in," they responded simultaneously.

Gerard turned to leave. "Well, thank you very much for your help with Zeke. He will start school on Monday if that's okay."

Reneé was nodding her head, but schooling didn't seem to be the primary concern at the moment.

"If I have to stay with these women, you need to stay, too," Raddix declared.

"Hey," a chorus of objections filled the room, making Raddix wince.

Willow felt Gerard's eyes on her. A few moments later, he said, "No, I don't want to intrude."

If she had any game at all, her eyes would have told Gerard to stay. *You'd have to look at him and not the floor.* She hated it when her inner self was right.

"Pish posh, you're not intruding. You must stay," Lily ordered, waving her hand like a sorcerer.

What the heck! Lily even sounded like Doris now. *Thank you, though.*

"I didn't know the guys were coming tonight." Willow's statement was more of a question directed at Amelia.

Quinton spoke up. "Don't blame us. We just came for our children."

A wave of intense emotions washed over Willow; she felt dizzy and distraught. It's likely because she wouldn't be with Tate this weekend. The sheriff's presence had no effect on her emotions.

Try again. Willow's mind taunted her. A hollow ache echoed the lie she tried to whisper to herself; the truth was a bitter pill, swallowed with invisible tears.

Chapter 16

Sunday hadn't come fast enough. Life was kicking him in the can. He hadn't attempted to see Willow since Friday, when the men at the ranch had gotten his mind racing and it hadn't stopped all weekend.

"You know she's hot for you, right?" Damon laughed when Gerard had been complaining about their bantering.

Apparently, Lily, his psychologist wife, told Harlyn, and she told Damon. Raddix nodded in agreement.

"Just kiss her and get it over with," Quinton suggested. "You could be fretting over nothing. What if you don't have a connection, or spark, as Amelia calls it?"

Not this again. He had to come clean so they could help. They were all married; he was a novice in the relationship department. His fault, but still a fact. He'd only had one serious relationship, and she left him when what his former therapist called "rescue romance" and reverse Nightingale Effect wore off — Gerard no longer captivated her like he had when he saved her.

When he told them about his dumb comment, they laughed. Outright, knee slapping chortles. *Jerks*, but he'd grown to love these guys.

"You have two choices, Son," Jeff, the resident butcher, shared his wisdom. "You can either be right, or you can be warm at the end of the night."

"I choose to never be right," Jeff added with a chuckle.

"Same, Diddo, Amen," Raddix, Damon, and Quinton responded in harmony.

The closer he got to church, the faster his heart raced. Willow would obviously be there. He needed to find out how serious she and his Tate person were.

That wasn't all.

Living with a teenager was getting the best of him. When he wasn't moping around the house, he was intentionally ignoring everything Gerard had asked, at least verbally. He'd asked Zeke to take out the trash. The teen did, but refused to acknowledge Gerard before and after. Not all the time, but enough for it to irk him.

If it hadn't been for Doris visiting with Zeke all day yesterday, the kid probably wouldn't be sitting in the truck next to him.

"Now, you promised not to cause trouble," Gerard reminded him with deep authority.

"I cross my heart and hope to die."

Maybe his silence was better than his facetiousness. "Don't mock me."

"I'm not. I mean it."

Recalling his teenage years, he'd said things like that too, and the 'hope to die' part was what he meant. Was that the same for Zeke? If so, hopefully being in Haven Ridge would change that for him like it had also done for Gerard.

"You remind me a lot of myself when I was your age."

"Yeah, right," he scoffed. "You don't become sheriff by being like me."

Gerard nodded. "You're right; I didn't. I became sheriff by building a relationship with Jesus and cleaning up my act." If he'd only had a place like this before he'd gotten into trouble, Gerard wouldn't be impacted by the trauma of his past actions today.

"I'm glad everything worked out for you, but I don't have your blind faith. I haven't prayed since…" The boy didn't have to fill in the rest, Gerard understood.

Memories assaulted him as he drove. Though his mom had left him to fend for himself and most likely was still alive, unlike Zeke's, he still understood where the boy was coming from.

"Your situation isn't unique. You have a whole town willing to help," he said as he pulled into the church parking lot. "Once I got here, around the love and support of these people is when I got straight. These people care about you."

"Even her?" Zeke asked, pointing at Willow in a low voice, too low, according to Gerard.

She was shimming across the parking lot. Overnight a steady rain left driveways, sidewalks, and parking lots an ice skater's dream.

"Yes, but—"

"Yeah, I know. She's yours." Zeke interrupted. "Maybe one day, I'll get so lucky."

A boisterous laugh filled the front of Gerard's SUV. "Lucky? Her and me? You're wrong on all accounts?"

"I saw the way you looked at each other when I got brought in. She likes you. Why haven't you figured out yet?"

He'd let that comment slide for now.

"Teenagers. Think they know everything," he muttered. "Look, she has a boyfriend."

Gerard's shocked expression matched the boy's. "Really? I've never seen her with anyone."

"His name is Tate; he's from California." Gerard wanted to add that she left every weekend to see him, but Zeke's annoying laughter stopped him short.

"I hope you're better at solving crimes than you are dealing with your love life. Tate's not her boyfriend."

"How do you know?"

"She told me," he responded before jumping out of the truck and rushing as fast as he could on the ice to Willow. He offered his elbow and escorted her inside.

If he were keeping score, it would be Zeke, one; Gerard, negative fifty.

"Hi everyone." Lily's usually soft voice blared through the sound system as she tapped on the mic, causing a screech that jumped many of the parishioners.

"That's one way to get everyone's attention," Pastor Myles laughed.

The grimace on her face and shrugged shoulders let everyone know she didn't mean to cause everyone a heart attack this morning.

"It's that time again."

"OCC already?" Randall's dry humor put everyone in stitches most mornings.

"Not quite, Randall, but it's never too early to shop for Operation Christmas Child."

A chorus of "Amen," burst out behind him.

"I'm referring to Forget me Nots. If you're new to our church, we make little cards that spread the love of Jesus, reminding those who cannot come to church that they are loved. This year, Earl, our amazing mailman is going to help spread more love by getting these little babies into the mail." She held up some completed cards.

"Mailman Earl spreads the love of Jesus," a man's voice hollered behind Gerard.

"I'll be telling you more about this as the weeks go on, but please be working on them at home. Grab one or more of the coloring pages. Take them home and color them. Reneé, maybe you can make it a requirement." Lily winked.

"Noooo," Emmanuel, eyes glued to his Nintendo Switch, hollered out. No one could accuse the boy of not listening.

Gerard watched Amelia whisper into the boy's ear. He'd come a long way since arriving at the ranch. From needing Gerard's assistance to arrest any girl who liked him (Gerard still laughed at that) to trying to kiss Darlene under the mistletoe. The boy was a hoot.

"In other announcements, leadership, and anyone else interested in helping plan the town's Valentine's Day party, there will be a meeting right after church," Pastor Myles said, replacing Lily at the pulpit.

"Finally, I'm pleased to announce that Haven Horizons has officially opened. Willow, would you like to say anything?"

She stood in the pew and turned to face the congregation. Her eyes skated over his. Something had to give. He would find out why she wouldn't look at him.

"We finally moved in on Saturday. This is Chelsea. She'll be staying with us for an undetermined amount of time, so I hope you make her feel like this is her home, because it is now."

Her smile reached her eyes as she continued. "Ladies, we have a baby shower to plan and, men, I'm sure you could make yourself useful by putting cribs and whatever else that's needed together."

The pastor interrupted. "I'm sure we could be useful for more than our construction ability."

"Well, for some of you, I know from experience it's not your construction abilities that are bothersome, rather, your destruction that might require our volunteer EMT and firefighters to spring into action."

The sarcasm rolled right off her tongue, making Gerard's heart skip. Her feistiness was so dang appealing he couldn't think straight.

A voice from the back of the church warned, "Don't rile up these folks; otherwise, we might need the sheriff, too," the words bubbling with energy rippled through the congregation.

She scrunched her brows. "Who did you think I was talking about?"

A chorus of hoots, hollers, oohs, and aahs spread through the sanctuary like COVID.

When Willow sat back down, Zeke slapped her high-five. Oh, so that's how it was going to be. He should have expected they'd join forces against him. Perfect, I love a challenge.

Chapter 17

"Haven Horizons, this is Willow. How may I help you?" This was the tenth call she'd answered since she returned thirty minutes ago from dropping Tate and Chelsea off for school. She hadn't even touched the thirteen messages on voicemail.

How had they become so well known in such a short amount of time? She caught a glimpse of a golden sunlight streaming through the window, painting the room in a warm, hopeful glow, heralding the opening of the center, and she had her answer. *Thank you, Lord.*

"Hey girlie!" Val showed up with coffee and muffins from the diner. "Guess who I saw at the diner?" she asked in a sing-song tone.

Willow put her hand up, signaling she was on the phone. "She sounds like the perfect candidate for our place. I have a few voicemails to listen to and consult with my partner. Let me have your number and I can call you back in an hour." If this kept up, they'd be filled by the end of the day. "Okay. Thank you for calling. I'll be in touch."

"Val, this is insane," Willow burst out with trepidation, all but forgetting about her friend's cheery entrance. The weight of their stories hung heavy. Six girls needed immediate shelter, three mothers sought a safe haven for their daughters, and a counselor's urgent call about a pregnant teen who faced homelessness when her parents found out. "We also have messages to listen to before we decide."

Willow's heart ached for these girls; their struggles were sadly familiar, a weight settling heavily upon her chest. The lonely road ahead of them stretched before her eyes, a desolate path that the family would have to travel alone if she, Val, and Harper didn't intervene.

Seven years of whispered plans, shared via text and flickering zoom screens, left Willow elated with the joy of their newly fulfilled goal. Giving girls a roof over their heads was only the first step; they also needed support, education, and a sense of community to thrive.

"We're ready for this." Willow hugged her friend, appreciating her confidence.

A warm feeling of purpose filled Willow as she and Val organized arrival dates for newcomers. This was her chance to make a real difference for these girls. Thankfully, Lily agreed to counsel them. The emotional strain these girls were going to face was nothing like they'd ever experienced, and the thought of their young hearts breaking under such immense pressure filled her with a deep, aching sorrow.

Willow's friend, Dr. Jenelle Merriman, traded the California coastline for the rolling hills of Haven Ridge, agreeing to build her own general medicine practice there. Besides the responsibility of caring for the newborns, she knew that the residents of Haven Ridge would appreciate not having to endure the stressful, hour-long drive to their previous doctor. The thought of her arrival in just one week filled her with uncontainable excitement.

To her relief, Reneé also agreed to homeschool. This way, the girls wouldn't have to miss any of their education. Willow wanted to give them something she didn't have: the chance to graduate, most likely on time and with their peers. Willow refused to force them to make such a terrible choice between caring for themselves, caring for their children, or jeopardizing the children's future.

Thirty minutes later, the front door opened and closed. Val stepped back, eyeing the visitor.

"Is that another teen looking for shelter?" Willow asked, a little nervous now that she and Val had packed all but two of their available beds.

Val shook her head. "I tried to tell you when I came in, but things got away from us."

Nathan Roberts peered from around the corner. He took off his cowboy hat and squeezed the brim with his fingers.

An icy dread washed over her as that unwelcome face appeared in the doorway. Ice-cold fingers seemed to grip her heart, stealing her breath and freezing her blood. The audacity of this man. No, he's not a man; he's a jerk. She stared with clenched fists. The sight of him, a painful reminder of what he did. Why was he here now? The silent question hung heavy in the air. She opened her mouth to speak, but nothing came out as if her tongue wrapped around her vocal cords, rendering them useless. Nathan smirked at her. The nerve. A furious fire ignited in her belly, its scorching heat threatening to consume her with righteous rage.

"Get out, you're not welcomed here." She pointed at the doorway he'd just strolled through.

He shook his head. "No can do, sweetheart. You have something I want, and I'm not leaving until I get *him.*"

She felt her intestines knotting up like a tangled ball of yarn. A bitter bile rose in her throat, a burning rage mirroring the turmoil in her gut. She will never let him near Tate. "Over my dead body."

"That can be arranged." He smirked and walked out the door.

Val rushed to her side. "Don't worry, no one will let him near Tate or you."

Lord, please forgive me for my sinful actions. Please do not let anything happen to my baby. Her anxious heart hammered against her ribs, a frantic drumbeat against the silence, before a calm voice whispered in her mind: *Tell people the truth.*

Chapter 18

Monday afternoon, Willow inhaled a deep breath as she finished sweeping the hair from her last client, preparing herself for Hazel, Doris, and Myrtle. They'd pester her until they got answers, but if she told anyone about Nate, her secret would be out.

"Willow, is everything okay?" Harper asked.

No. "Yeah, just thinking about a lot of stuff."

Now that Haven Horizons was fully operational, she felt guilty about leaving every weekend. But was it safe to bring Tate here? Her surprise visitor this morning had her nerves on edge. The only solution was to tell her parents and Gerard. They'd help her keep Tate safe. He would be more safe with her than in California, right?

Her dad's words from yesterday's sermon flooded back. "Once God forgives, there is no reason to remain burdened by guilt and self-recrimination."

Easier said than done.

"Yoo hoo, we're here!" Myrtle chimed louder than the jingle bells on the doorknob.

"And look who we brought," Doris added.

Willow's heart flipped when her eyes met with Gerard's. He could arrest Nate for her, couldn't he? Given her state of unrest, she was tense and feared her irrational thoughts would let loose. He certainly couldn't arrest the man for showing up at her business. If Val or she had recorded his threat, that might be something, but shock consumed her, preventing her from thinking straight and as quick as he walked in to threaten her, he left. She wasn't sure how many more triggers she'd endure before having a complete meltdown.

Myrtle dragged the sheriff by the forearm toward Willow's styling station, plopped him in the chair and pressed the foot pump until his head was eye level with Willow's.

You've got to be kidding me. Is this a sign, Lord? Am I supposed to tell him right here?

"The sheriff has to relieve Jimmy soon so he can have my slot and if you don't have time for my cut, it's okay," Hazel declared.

Despite not having children of her own, she was surprisingly motherly, especially with Gerard.

Willow shook the cape in front of him, careful not to touch his skin when she draped it over his shirt and clasped the button behind his neck.

His scent was driving her crazy. She couldn't inhale like she wanted, savoring his woodsy with a touch of cinnamon scent, for he hadn't stopped staring at her in the mirror since he sat down. Her stomach rattled like the namesake snake.

"Where's Zeke?"

"School."

She tried to catch her jaw quickly, but failed.

"What, you didn't think I could handle a teenager?"

Not really. "I didn't say that. I just know how difficult dealing with a child is, er—must be, especially for someone who doesn't know if he wants kids. How are you handling all the changes?"

"Aw you care."

"Yup, as much as a porcupine. Any more wisecracks, I'll use my scissors like quills and shoot them at you."

He tsked. "Willow Payne, you're being a bad girl. Threatening the sheriff could get you six months in jail and a five hundred dollar fine."

"I'll take my chances." She winked at him and plastered on a saccharine smile so sweet it could give him a cavity.

He smirked at her. It was aggravating, sexy, and stomach dropping all at once. Ba! This man was too much.

"Hey, quit flirting with me. I can't handle all this attention." Gerard winked at her.

His wink went straight to her core. The man could charm the tentacles off of Ursula.

"Oh, puh-lease. Quit dreaming. It's messing with the rational side of your brain."

Their bantering, a shiver of pure delight, danced down her spine.

Doris interrupted. "Aren't you going to wash his hair, Dear?"

Her shoulders sagged, forgetting they had an audience. The faster she washed and cut Gerard's hair, the sooner her heart would return to its normal rhythm.

"What a fantastic suggestion, Doris." His eyes sparkled as he smirked at Willow. "I'm ready and willing if you are." He got real close and whispered in her ear. "I'm referring to the hair wash, but I'll always be ready when you want that kiss."

Jerk. With her thoughts elsewhere, she'd forgotten about that stupid comment. No matter how appealing Gerard McDugal was, she'd never be vulnerable again. She would not beg the beautifully sculpted man in front of her, sauntering over to the wash bin, to kiss her. Nope. Definitely. Not.

After their playful banter and hair washing, they finally had a serious conversation.

"I'm happy to see that Bill and his crew are nearly done with the construction of the boys' section at Haven Horizons."

She laughed. "You must be in a hurry to drop Zeke off."

"Are you serious?"

She ran a comb through his hair, thankful she resisted weaving her fingers through it. "Well, you'd said how difficult it was having a teenager. I figured you weren't cut out for having children."

"That stung."

"Uh, huh. I'm sure. Nothing stings those shoulders."

He turned himself around, now face to face with her. "You're lucky I didn't snip the same time you moved. Your hair would look pretty interesting."

"You like my shoulders?" He flexed one arm and rubbed his mountainous shoulder with the other hand.

Yes. What woman wouldn't? "They're alright. I've seen better."

"Like Tate's?"

"Perhaps." *Someday, in maybe ten or fifteen years.*

She twirled the chair back around and subconsciously weaved her fingers through his tresses. *Oo, la, la.* His thick, dark brown hair made her fingers tingle and her forearms quake. "If you stay still, I could get this done."

"I haven't moved. Maybe you're jittery from being so close to me."

She bit her cheek to keep her from smiling. He knew how to get to her.

"Have you had any blunt force trauma to the head lately?"

"Ha. Ha. How's Haven Horizons going?"

"Busy. As they say, 'there's no vacancy at the Inn' as of today."

"That's awesome, but you don't seem happy about it. Willow, your dream came true." His chest felt light and effervescent.

"One of them, anyway."

Chapter 19

"What am I doing to you?" Willow's sweet voice interrupted his musings.

Driving me crazy in the best possible way. "Short. Take all that off the top."

"If that's what you want."

He raised an eyebrow. "You think I should do something different?"

"You can do whatever you want. It doesn't matter to me." Willow shrugged.

A peaceful silence laid upon them as Willow prepped his hair.

He wished someone like Willow was around when he was getting into trouble. Even though years had gone by, he'd held on to his sins like a security blanket, impacting every decision he made, including to push Willow away years ago. He'd always found Willow Payne intriguing, but doubted her father, the pastor, would accept him if he knew about Gerard's past. He'd done too much to be forgiven. Even more importantly, he believed that Willow deserved a man better than a former criminal. Was Tate that man?

Remember the pastor's sermon, his inner angel reminded him. "Once God forgives, there is no reason to remain burdened by guilt and self-recrimination," he whispered aloud, having already memorized it, hoping it gave him the courage to share his past with Willow.

"You clung to the same part of my father's sermon as I did."

"Care to share why that stood out to you?" Gerard hoped to get her talking and bring her smile back.

Anticipation surged through him, a powerful current that lifted his spirits when the corners of her lips twitched.

"Everyone deserves second chances. Sadly, most people hold their sins over their heads because they worry about what others think instead of what God does."

If only he could tell her how deeply her words resonated with him, but the weight of uncertainty kept him silent. "What haven't you forgiven yourself for, Willow?"

A film of tears covered her eyes, dimming their usual sparkle, and her expression was one of profound sorrow. But she blinked and avoided his question.

"That's why I started Haven Horizons — I want people to get a second chance."

If she felt like everyone deserved a second chance, then maybe she would give Gerard one. Could she overlook his stupidity not only as a teenager, but a man who pushed away a fabulous woman? He hoped so, however, in his experience, people say one thing, but when they have to put it into action in their own life, they don't always live by their beliefs.

Zeke, unfortunately, was headed down the same road Gerard had once traveled. The boy needed a new path, like the one Saul found on his way to Damascus. Gerard hadn't changed his name, but he had changed his ways when he arrived in Haven Ridge thanks to people God put in his path. It was time for Gerard to do the same for Zeke.

"Have you had to give Tate second chances?"

"Of course, like he has me, but like I said before, Tate and I will be forever bound at the heart. No one will come between us, even in death."

We'll see about that.

Willow ran the comb through his hair, but before she made the first cut, he stopped her.

"If your boyfriend had hair like mine, how would you cut it?" Gerard hated that Tate was making him question himself.

"You still don't have a clue what you're talking about, yet you walk around thinking you're omniscient."

Ouch.

"Fine. If Tate's not your boyfriend, how come he isn't? Not into titles."

"I could ask you the same, but it's obvious you can't find a woman who can put up with you."

Was she still joking? Gerard had a difficult time sometimes determining where her joking ended and her wall began.

"Willow, the man is trying to have a civil conversation with you. Perhaps you could try," Hazel encouraged, obviously eavesdropping from the waiting area. Her age didn't fool Gerard. The woman could hear like a wax moth. While helping Zeke with his homework, he'd learned that a wax moth has the best hearing of any animal, even bats.

"Thank you Hazel." He never thought he'd thank the women for eavesdropping, but this time it was in his favor, so why not?

"I'll try," Willow said, her smile reaching her eyes, and the warmth of it spread through him. He started to see that her quips spoke from a wounded heart. Could he heal Willow's pain? He'd like the chance to try.

"Wait. I wasn't kidding. Cut it as if I were Tate. He's obviously very important to you. How would you want it to look?"

What am I doing? *Enacting a new military disciplinary tactic — the level of influence a woman held over a man.*

"How about I give you a haircut as if you were my man."

His heart stopped. Gerard's tongue against his esophagus, robbed him of his voice. The sight of his own stunned expression staring back from the mirror startled him, pulling him from his stupor.

"That's the greatest suggestion I've ever heard."

Twenty minutes later, Willow rubbed mousse in her hands and ran her fingers through his fresh cut. She massaged his scalp and he had to swallow a groan building in the back of his throat.

"Do you like it?" She pulled him from his dreamland.

"Woo wee, Sheriff, you're even more handsome than before," Doris shrieked from underneath the dryer where Val had placed her ten minutes ago. Hazel and Myrtle agreed.

Gerard felt his cheeks heat, embarrassed that the only compliments he seemed to get were from women in their seventies.

Willow suppressed a giggle. *Is she thinking the same thing?*

"What's so funny?" He mocked, being upset.

Willow put her arms up in a surrender. Now full on laughing.

"Did you give me a bad hair cut on purpose?"

"Never!" Willow barked. Her laughing ceased; clearly upset that he questioned her professional ethics.

Hazel stepped forward, patting Gerard's forearm. "She was giggling, Sheriff, because that's what women do when they are smitten with a man and their emotions become too overwhelming."

"Hazel!" Willow barked.

"That's understandable." He winked at Willow.

"I bet it's the new haircut with that little bit of stubble on your jaw. You are a catch!" Myrtle added.

Willow's jaw dropped, her tempting mouth forming a perfect O. She huffed and stalked toward the check-in/out desk.

"It looks like someone needs a time out," Gerard teased, loving how he got under her skin.

"Oh, Sheriff," Doris hollered and waved him over to her seat under the dryer. She tugged on his forearm, nearly bending him in half so she could "whisper" to him. The woman couldn't whisper, dryer or no dryer. Everyone in the salon heard her say, "You two are meant to be; don't give up."

Gerard chuckled. "I think you've reached a delusional state. That woman," he pointed in Willow's direction, "despises me."

"If she did, Dear, she wouldn't have given you a smokin' hot hair cut to match those delicious muscles." Doris squeezed his biceps.

"Doris, we need to find you a man," Gerard straightened and stepped away, but not quick enough for she smacked his cheeks, causing him to jump.

"I feel violated. I might have to report this to Jimmy."

"What happens in the salon stays in the salon," Doris chimed, positioning herself back under the dryer.

"Stop right there. I don't want to hear any more sorted stories of how Harper and Ryan got together here in the salon."

The newly married woman burst out laughing from her nail station, where she was giving Myrtle a manicure.

"Pish, posh." Doris waved her hands. "You're making it sound dirty."

Gerard halted. "The woman took his clothes when he was in the tanning booth."

"Try again, Sheriff," Harper sang.

His eyes bounced from one lady to the next, and their guilty expressions told him a different story. "Wait. It was you three." It was more of a declaration than a question.

Hazel, the most reserved of the three, said, "We don't know what you're talking about." The glimmer in her eyes told him he couldn't trust her anymore than the other two.

"I give up." He threw his hands in the air.

As Gerard drove away, trepidation filled his chest. He never should have left Willow with The Troublesome Trio. He could only imagine what they were scheming up now.

"Although," he pondered as he drove away. "everyone in town knows they have a knack for matchmaking," yet no one would admit that, "and I can use all the help I can get."

Bring on the shenanigans!

Chapter 20

Zeke

The quiet ride home from school pressed down on Zeke like a heavy blanket, the silence filled with the unspoken weight of his day. Was the man he saw his dad? *No.* The man he saw had a clean-shaven face and a crew cut. If his dad was in Haven Ridge, Zeke would have to leave.

That would be just like his dad — to come back and ruin Zeke's life... again. *Not this time.* The people of Haven Ridge had done everything to welcome him and teach him about God even after he put them through misery, especially Gerard. He'd taken him into his house and treated him like a person should treat a son.

In the past, Zeke had complained about doing chores and going to school. He didn't know how good he had it! Today, Damon made him muck the horse stalls and Raddix had him trudge through the pasture in snow that almost reached his waist to fill the creep feeders. Quinton assigned him his favorite job — making flyers. This spring, he was selling thirty percent of his herd to make room for the new births.

Gerard pulled into the driveway. He pushed open his door, but halted when he realized Zeke hadn't moved.

"Everything okay?"

A sense of happiness washed over Zeke. He'd never expected to live in a house again. He had his own room inside the light blue cape with black shutters. "Why have you done this?" Zeke questioned, still staring at the house.

"Done what?"

Zeke shrugged. "Let me live with you. Set up school for me." His voice got low and vulnerable. "Be my parent. You could have left me in jail."

"Come on."

Gerard rested his arm on Zeke's shoulders. Would Gerard get sick of him and kick him out? If he did, hopefully the boys' section at Willow's Haven Horizons would be ready and he could stay there, but he hoped it didn't come to that. He wondered if Gerard would let him stay until he graduated.

"It's no place for a kid." Gerard held up a hand, as if to say, "Sorry, I know you're not a kid because you remind me of that at least twice a day."

"Thank you."

Neither one of them readily shared their emotions, resulting in a swift conclusion to their discussion, yet Zeke knew the sheriff was being real with him.

"How was your day?" Gerard asked, opening his front door.

"Cash and Carolyn are the best chefs ever. No offense."

Gerard barked out a laugh. "None taken. I'm glad you get quality food when you're at the ranch."

"It sure beats the swill I got out of dumpsters on my own." Zeke would never put Gerard's cooking down. That, too, was better than the dumpster food, but just barely.

"Miss Reneé created a fun assignment for Addison and me — an escape room for algebra."

"That's cool. I heard one of the best escape rooms on the planet is in Billings. Maybe we could go sometime."

"Really? I'd love to go with you." Gerard nodded his head in agreement.

"How are you doing with Bible?"

"Did Miss Reneé talk to you?"

Gerard nodded as he set a brown grocery bag on the counter.

It was his favorite subject. He'd lost his faith a long time ago. God didn't care about him, given all the misery he'd endured. Miss Reneé told him it wasn't the way he should be thinking. Instead, he should focus on how God had provided for him. When I mentioned eating from dumpsters and stolen food, she said, "Exactly. See, He provided for you." *Say what?*

"It's hard to believe when so many horrible things happen to you."

Gerard washed his hands at the sink, pumping the blue detergent into his palm. "Can't argue there."

"One of the younger kids has so much faith, I don't get it."

"Oh, yeah. Tell me about it."

"Today, Emmanuel said, 'I am autistic and I have Chron's. Mom says that God doesn't give us more than we can handle. He cares about me and provides for me.' Did you know he lost his biological mother, too?"

"Yup. He's a pretty funny kid, too."

"He got really upset about a story Miss Reneé was reading. The kids and mother got hurt somehow and looked like he was going to cry. I've never met someone who cared about other people as much as he does."

"That's a true skill for sure."

"Any time he's asked to do something and doesn't want to, he just says, 'No, thank you' sweet and kind and he rarely has to do it. Does that really work?"

"Not always," Gerard said, wiping his wet hands on a dish towel.

"How can someone younger than me have more faith? He's had a hard life, too?"

Gerard shrugged. "That's a question for God." He laid his large palm on Zeke's shoulder before heading down the hallway.

"What's in the bag?" he hollered to Gerard, who'd disappeared into his room, probably to change. Who could blame him? That uniform must get old. He wears it every day.

Gerard's phone vibrated on the counter, and being the teenager that he was, Zeke peered over the phone. *Willow, huh? What are the chances the sheriff doesn't have a passcode?* Zeke swiped the banner to the right and tapped the open button. *Bingo!* Someone should talk to him about technology security.

> Hey, it's Willow. Sorry about the ladies fooling at the salon today. I hope you like your new haircut.

Zeke hesitated. He really shouldn't do this, but he had to repay the sheriff for all his help with the judge, school, and letting him stay here. Before he could talk himself out of it, he typed a text to Willow.

> Fooling around is my middle name. I dig my new cut, thank you. Do you think before you head home you could stop at my place? Zeke needs help with his homework, and it's out of my league. Never thought I'd say that.

He reread it quickly. *Does this sound cocky enough to be the sheriff? I hope so; it will have to do.* He tapped the arrow and almost instantly the delivered tag changed to "Read 6:10 PM".

Three dots appeared and disappeared. *Oh, no. Please respond before Gerard comes back.*

"Dinner." Gerard yelled from down the hall. "Carolyn made us a meatloaf. God bless that woman."

No joke. If he had to eat one more of Gerard's concoctions…

He tapped the phone's screen, so it didn't go black. *Please, Willow, respond now.* Gerard's footsteps got louder as he approached the kitchen. Would he throw him back in jail if he saw Zeke playing with his phone? He didn't think so, but Gerard was a no-nonsense person, unless, of course, your name was Willow.

His stomach tightened. Dinner? Who could eat? The question echoed in his mind, making his stomach lurch, as he dreaded the potential consequence if he got caught. A cold sweat filled his pores, excitement building within him as he anticipated Willow's response.

Finally!

Sure, I can be there in about five minutes.

He gave her message a thumbs up reaction, swiped up to close messages, and tapped the side of Gerard's phone, turning the screen black just as Gerard slapped his gigantic palm on Zeke's shoulder, making him startle. "Are you hungry?"

Give me a few minutes. "I could eat, but then I've got homework and lots of it."

"Do you need any help?"

"Yeah, I probably will."

Gerard grabbed two plates from the corner cabinet. "Okay. Let's fuel our brains, then we can get to work."

Just as they'd sat down to eat, the doorbell rang. "I wonder who that could be?" His voice went up an octave. It hadn't been that high since before he'd gone through puberty. *Yeah, that wasn't sus.*

"Willow, this is a surprise," Zeke heard Gerard say when he opened the door. *He really hadn't thought this through.*

Zeke jogged toward the door before Willow could respond. "Hi, Willow. Thanks for coming to help with my homework."

He wasn't sure what his eyes were doing, but he tried to convey, "Please play along."

"You're welcome. I'm happy to help."

Gerard motioned for her to come inside. "Have you eaten? We just sat down. I can get you a plate."

"I'm good. Thanks."

"Carolyn sent us home with meatloaf," Zeke offered.

"Oh, I could eat then."

Gerard gasped. "You've already wounded me earlier, so what, now you're twisting the knife?"

"You're tough. You can handle it." Willow double tapped his chest and sashayed into the kitchen.

The door clicked shut, a finality in the sound that mirrored the intensity in Gerard's lingering glare. "You have some explaining to do."

As the three of them ate dinner together, Zeke realized it'd been years since he felt happy. Back during a time when his dad played baseball with him in the backyard and mom had cookies and milk waiting for them when they finished. Then his seventh birthday changed everything. Dad lost his job and mom started waitressing to put food on the table. Supposedly, so distraught over being let go, Dad just laid around all day doing nothing.

When Mom and him got home from work and school, she'd cook dinner and help him with his homework while intermittently waiting on Dad. By the time he'd turned nine, Dad had progressed to a drunken state most often, and when he wasn't drunk, he was out trying to make money by hustling people at the pool hall. One day, he was gone.

Chapter 21

Willow was more hungry than she thought, accepting a second piece of meatloaf when Gerard offered.

When they finished, Willow gripped her plate and stood, ready to clear her place setting.

Gerard placed his hand on hers. *Wowsers!* Warmth traveled through her arm like a nomad. "You guys start his homework and I'll do the dishes."

"Okay. Thanks, Man." Zeke's excitement eased any potential awkwardness when she wasn't able to respond.

As Gerard positioned himself at the sink, Willow scanned all six feet three inches of his rugged frame. Starting with his stellar deltoid muscles to his narrowing waist; from behind, he formed a perfect V. While the polyester uniform worked for him, the low-rise jeans and blue fitted workout shirt pulling across his shoulders was intoxicating.

"What's first, Willow?" Zeke asked, eager for help.

"Excuse me, can you repeat that?" She snapped out of her ogling.

Zeke smiled, a wide, knowing grin that spoke volumes; the gleam in his eyes revealed he knew Gerard was the culprit for the burn in her cheeks.

Wise beyond his years, Zeke said nothing to embarrass her. *Thank you, God!*

"I've got it all, math, science, economics, Bible. What can you help with?"

An hour later, Zeke was packing his bag for school the next day when he said, "Thanks for your help, guys."

"Sure. I'm just glad Willow came when she did, out of the blue and all. I don't know what we would have done without her."

Out of the blue. "But you texted me—"

"No, it was me," Zeke confessed.

Gerard's jaw dropped. "You mean you tricked Willow into coming here? I am shocked you would do such a thing." Gerard laid the sarcasm on thick.

"Well, everything turned out great," Zeke rushed to say, probably hoping he wouldn't get into trouble.

Gerard threw his thumb over his shoulder. "We'll talk about this later. Go wash up."

"Yes, Sir. Bye, Willow."

Once Zeke was out of earshot. "So he's the one who responded to my text?" Willow whispered, amused.

Gerard nodded.

"That's really cute?"

"It's actually an invasion of privacy and against the law," Gerard grimaced, causing Willow to giggle.

"I should go now that homework is done." For the first time all evening, she noticed how hot it was inside the house. As she walked toward the door, Gerard's inescapable shadow followed, looming over her like a mountain. His presence, both imposing and oddly comforting in its familiarity. She still hadn't told him about Nathan or Tate. Maybe this impromptu visit was God giving her another chance.

Before reaching for her coat, she turned to thank him for dinner and instead slammed into his rock-hard chest. "Oof." Her forearms, the only thing between them.

Gerard grabbed her shoulders. "Are you okay?" The concern in his voice had her stomach doing an Olympic level round-off, back handspring. Speechless, she nodded.

With a slow, deliberate step backward, Gerard's eyes devoured her form, their intensity silencing her despite the brevity of their encounter; a palpable tension hung in the air.

What she would have given seven years ago to have Gerard McDugal look at her with such interest! *Her spot as cheer captain, her first car, her kidney? Yes, yes, and yes!*

Breath and leave. She instructed.

"Thank you for dinner," she finally found her voice.

"The pleasure was all mine." He grabbed her coat from the hook and held it open for her.

Once the sleeves covered her arms, she fastened the buttons down the front of her jacket with quivering fingers. Gerard grabbed the wool belt straps and teased her by moving at the same speed as molasses pouring from a jar to make an x and loop one end of the belt through.

All the while, she watched the pulse on his neck, a frantic drum against his skin, quickening with each passing second. When she couldn't take it anymore, he finally pulled both straps in opposite directions, cinching it at her waist. "Is that too tight?"

A little. The sheriff doesn't know his own strength.

The heat of their proximity fueled the flames of attraction burning inside her. She shook her head. "I'm good. Thank you again for dinner."

Still close enough to spy his brown eyes turn a darker shade than she'd ever noticed, he leaned in and pressed a lingering kiss to her cheek.

Her eyes closed without warning. The exhilarating scent of his cologne made her legs quake and her stomach soar. Thankfully, he was still gripping her shoulders.

"I'm patiently waiting for your plea." He pressed a second peck on her cheek.

Willow's eyes popped open. "I will not beg you to kiss me, no matter what you do."

"You can lie to yourself all you want, but the way your knees buckled when I kissed your cheek told me the truth — I bet you'll come around."

"You're incorrigible. Good night, Sheriff." Willow pulled open the door and stormed away.

"Good night, Princess!" He hollered at her back. She lifted her hand in a nonchalant wave as she raced to her car.

Settling in, she realized she missed her opportunity to tell him about Nathan again. *Lord, please continue to protect us.*

Chapter 22

One morning mid-week, Gerard visited with the men at the ranch after dropping Zeke off for school.

"I'm going to tell you the same thing I told Violet," Raddix began as he changed the bedding in the stalls. "The entire town can see you like each other, so stop fighting it. You know Myrtle, Doris, and Hazel aren't getting any younger."

"Yeah, you're just making their job harder and our lives turn into a soap opera," Damon added, emptying a water bucket and refilling.

"How so?"

"Our wives have turned into their mini-me matchmakers. Every time I turn around, Harlyn is either throwing up or telling me about some elaborate plan to unite Haven Ridge's next conquest."

"Throwing up?"

Damon's face blanched. Clearly, he wasn't supposed to say anything. "Um."

"Just tell him. People will know soon enough," Raddix urged.

"She's three months pregnant."

Gerard clasped Damon's hand and pulled him in for a man hug. "Three months, you stud! So we're talking about a honeymoon baby?"

"Yeah, but remember, say nothing. We haven't told the kids yet. Harlyn wants to wait until Lily is ready."

What is in the ranch water? Gerard's head snapped toward Raddix.

"If you get me in trouble, Damon, payback will be brutal." Raddix turned toward Gerard. "Lily is about two weeks behind Harlyn, and they want to share the news at the same time."

A longing pierced Gerard. Most people with fathers like his didn't want to be fathers themselves and that had probably been him at some point, but now that he was spending more time around Willow, the idea had floated in his mind a couple of times, especially after he'd taken Zeke into his home. Diner the other night didn't help. He'd since imagined having family dinner every night with more kids. Afterwards, Willow and he would help teach him, or her right from wrong, appealed to him. The prospect of being a father didn't look promising for him, though.

"I won't say a word."

"Everyone heard about Zeke's texting abilities," Raddix said, blowing out a laugh.

"I should have never come here."

Gerard walked toward the barn door, but Raddix tossed his pitch fork and grabbed Gerard's shoulder. "No, wait. We're sorry. I'm just shocked you fell for such an amateur trick."

"Yeah. Women can be quite persistent. Even if you were Casanova reborn, she'd die before begging for a kiss from you," Damon insisted, his tone sure.

"Like Jeff told you before; kiss her." Damon said with determination.

"Give in," Raddix agreed.

The very thought was enough to make him cringe. He never gave in. *You're not married either.*

Check out the divorce rate; it's filled with men who wouldn't give in and make their woman happy and vice versa.

"If you give in on this, you'll not only get your kiss, but you'll start racking up your points."

"Points?"

Raddix hung his head, shaking it slowly, showing his disappointment in Gerard's ignorance. "You have so much to learn."

"Women remember the things you forget, or the slips of the tongue. They sometimes forget all the good things, so you have to keep track of those and remind her every so often about how many points you have racked up."

These complications were why he hated dating or dealing with women. As if he could read Gerard's mind, Damon said, "Relax. When you marry the right woman, it's not that difficult."

"Agreed." Raddix picked up his pitchfork and finished the bedding in the last stall.

Kissing Willow would be a bold move, or deadly. Either way, they'd move past this challenge and hopefully more kissing would follow.

The longer he pondered this, the more he'd convinced himself that giving in was really a benefit to him. Ever since Willow had come to the house to help Zeke with his homework, the thought of kissing Willow's soft lips had crossed his mind more than he'd admitted. Each passing minute screamed at him to go find her and rectify this situation. So why weren't his feet moving?

Fear.

Willow was the type of woman who made him want to be a better man. Despite his resistance, her feistiness lit him on fire, making him want to banter with her every day, like in a real relationship. Yup, he'd said it. A once broken man due to a bad relationship with his family and Jennie now wanted to convince Willow that he was worthy enough to be her man. He might be more successful at persuading her if he could sell the lie to himself.

"I'm not good enough for her," Gerard admitted, feeling vulnerable, but honest.

Damon nodded his head. "You're ready for this. Once you realize you're not worthy, but she makes you want to be, then she's the one."

Hopefully, these guys were right. If not, he knew Willow would let him know.

Chapter 23

Willow spent the rest of the week in a whirlwind of activity, helping the ladies plan the Valentine's Day dance. If she didn't know better, Gerard had been phishing for information, trying to find out if Tate was taking her to the dance.

Ironically, that happened the day after Myrtle's shriek at the last planning party. "I'm so glad you and Gerard are going to the dance together."

That was news to Willow. "I think you've got the wrong information." At that point, Gerard hadn't even mentioned the dance in her presence.

Willow had too many pressing matters to worry about the Valentine's Day dance. She still had told no one about Nathan. Willow took it as a good sign when she hadn't seen him around town, so that was something, but she had a feeling her time was running out.

That's why Friday morning, despite the slippery sidewalks and still fuzzy head from the evening she'd spent with Zeke and Gerard, Willow trekked out to take in the clean Montana air. By nightfall, the smog-filled California air would envelope her.

Yes, Willow always felt better when she could clear her head. Between the girls pouring into Haven Horizons daily, Nathan reappeared and then disappeared, and keeping Tate a secret, her loaded brain needed air.

"Oh, Willow." She cringed at the high-pitched, annoying voice. Slowly turning around, Willow plastered on a smile — a facade to avoid getting on this woman's evil side, though Willow wasn't sure the woman had another side.

"Hi Selena, what can I do for you?"

She pointed to the door. "I was hoping to get a cut and maybe we could chat a little."

Warning bells thundered in her ears, drowning out every other noise around her, including Selena, whose mouth was still moving.

This woman had consistently and pointedly ignored Willow, never offering her even the slightest bit of attention or acknowledgement. One day, when Willow first returned to Haven Ridge, Selena tripped over the worn rug, its edges frayed and caught on the diner door, and screamed at Willow, accusing her of being stupid and causing the mishap.

"Willow. What do you have to say for yourself?"

"Excuse me, I didn't hear anything after you wanted to chat and get a cut."

The woman let out a heavy, theatrical sigh, her breath expelled with exaggerated force. Willow worked not to roll her eyes.

"I wasn't going to say anything out here on the sidewalk, but I don't have time for your games." Selena's tone changed.

Now dark and sinister, Willow said, "Well, don't let me keep you, then." Willow turned and started to walk away, but Selena grabbed her arm.

"You better listen to what I have to say."

Willow ripped her arm from the woman's claws.

"You have some nerve—"

"No, you do, Willow Payne. A pastor's daughter who racks up the sin. Premarital sex, an illegitimate, fatherless son…" Willow tapped her pointer finger on her lips. "That's right. He's not fatherless. You just chose not to tell the boy Nate Roberts was his dad."

The acrid taste of bile filled Willow's throat, a burning sensation that made her want to vomit. The evil woman standing in front of her could ruin her.

"It would be a shame if Sheriff McDugal found out that you were trying to hook him so he could become the child's daddy." Willow rarely thought of violence. The woman's snide remarks and false accusations fueled her anger, making her want to rearrange her face.

"That's a lie and you know it."

An evil smile pulled at the woman's lips. "And who do you think they'll believe, a lifelong resident or the woman who's been lying to them for years? I wouldn't take my chances if I were you."

Lord, what is wrong with her? She is worse than the serpent in the garden.

"I'll keep quiet if…"

Willow shook her head. "I won't let you blackmail me."

"Don't think of it as blackmail, but more of an investment."

You're going to tell everyone the truth. Just walk away.

"You'll regret walking away from me!"

Willow ignored her. She felt the woman's eyes on her back, like daggers searing hot, pressing into her skin. At the end of the street, Willow turned right and pressed her body against the building, her jacket catching on frayed splinters in the rough wood. *Figures!* The frantic beating of her heart had her chest heaving with fear.

Why is that woman so cruel? *It's my secret. I deserve to tell people the way I want, when I want.*

Taking multiple deep breaths, Willow calmed herself and continued with her walk.

The peacefulness of the park, a stark contrast to the interaction she'd just had with Selena, was exactly what Willow needed. The few birds perched on a nearby bare branch chirped in response. Apparently, not all birds fly south for the winter.

Lord, please give me the strength to follow through with telling my parents and Gerard about Tate. Please don't let anyone else tell them.

Earl and his wife Loretta were sitting bundled up on a bench, gloved hands laced together throwing bird seed to the small flock at their feet. One day, she wanted a man who loved her enough to just sit and feed the birds with her.

The evergreen in the middle of the park in town still had Christmas lights wrapped around it that shone blazed at night. In the daylight, the bright winter sun reflected off them, showcasing a bright case of sun glitter.

"Gorgeous."

As she moved further down the path to give the couple their privacy, she slipped on a patch of ice hidden by freshly fallen snow. Her arms circled back like airplane propellers and her feet scrambled like Shaggy from an episode of Scooby-Doo. *This is going to hurt*, she mused, thinking about her rear meeting the hard ice in an unwanted introduction.

"Oof." Though her back hit something hard, it was more organic and welcoming instead of the ice, and apparently she'd grown an extra set of hands. Ones that stuck out from under her arms freakishly close to her chest.

"Whoa there."

But the warning was too late. Willow's panic over the extra set of hands, she knew weren't hers, proved to be too much, and she ended up taking both her and the owner of the hands down. He got the brunt of the impact on the hard cold ice and then Willow on top of him.

"Are you okay?"

That deep voice in her ear sent shivers down her spine. Willow scrambled to her feet. She may have inadvertently elbowed him in the ribs in her haste, but she would never admit it, and he was too much of a gentleman to point it out.

"If you wanted to make out, all you had to do was ask. I would have picked somewhere warmer. It's only in the teens today."

She hadn't noticed the cold the last few minutes. She harrumphed. "You're so full of yourself, Sheriff. Where did you come from, anyway?"

"Patrolling," he said evasively.

His cologne made her mind fuzzy, reminding her of what she already knew — Gerard was her ice cream. Hey, Superman had his weakness; she had hers. Willow had been mesmerized by him since she was a teenager. A crush that she thought she'd outgrown. Even seven years away from him, she couldn't erase him from her mind, but she'd never try to trick him like Selena suggested.

Some people have a conscious and are ashamed of their actions, so they don't want them on display for everyone to judge.

"Oh." Words escaped her. Precisely what she didn't want to happen had — Gerard had taken her heart again. She liked the way they bantered. He sang to her. If he didn't think she had a boyfriend, she imagined he would comfort her more in those brawny arms.

"And Willow," Gerard's tender voice made her heart melt.

"Yes."

"When can we work on the making out?"

Goodbye melting heart. Welcome to reality. "To take a line from one of Tate's favorite movies, 'The fourth of never-ary'."

Much to Willow's chagrin, Gerard continued "patrolling" where she traveled. Since Zeke was caught, Haven Ridge returned to crime level zero. It wasn't a bad thing, except now. Her resolve was weakening the more time she spent around Gerard. Kissing him was something she'd always wanted, but wouldn't beg him. He'd never let her live it down. She needed to make him kiss her first.

"I know you have a man in your life. It's plain to see why you keep him hidden. He's so ugly you don't want to be seen with him."

She laughed. "You watch too many movies."

"If I'm wrong. Tell me about him and then I won't have to guess."

"Fine. He's funny, sweet, and dreamy. He's tired of living apart and frankly, so am I, so I've decided to bring him back with me. I just have to find a way to break it to my parents."

He swallowed and nearly choked on his disappointment. "Wait. They don't know?"

She shook her head. "I left the moment I turned eighteen, telling them I'd be safe living with my Aunt Clarissa and Uncle Josh, my mom's sister and brother-in-law."

"Is he that bad they won't accept him?"

Heavens, no. "It's me they'll be mad at, rightfully so. Nothing is Tate's fault."

"It takes two to tango," Gerard offered a stupid cliché that didn't fit the situation, but he didn't know that, so she couldn't be that upset with anyone except herself.

"He will exceed their wildest expectations, that much I can promise. How my dad deals with me: Please pray."

As they reached the back entrance of the park, he caught her off guard. "Why are you flirting with me if you have a man in your life?" His silky voice slithered throughout, wrapping around her like a python trying to take dominance by invading her entire system.

"If anyone's flirting, it's you" She hadn't flirted with him first or on purpose. It just happened.

A curve adorned his tempting lips.

No, not tempting. She will never beg him to kiss her. Even though the idea of his lips careening across her warmed her body, she wouldn't give him the satisfaction.

"I'm teasing. I have been flirting with you. Are your sassy comebacks your way of flirting, or do you really hate me?" His voice was unshielded, yet filled with passion. He stuffed his hands in his pockets.

He had the strength of Sampson to continue studying her features, she did not. His eyes were too intense, even now when she could also see a glimmer of vulnerability as he awaited her answer. She could never flirt with him until he knew the truth about Tate. That would only be fair. Would she get her chance? Once he knew about Tate, he'd probably stop flirting with, knowing she didn't have a boyfriend. Some men only wanted what they couldn't have. Then when they got it, it wasn't all they desired and toss it out like garbage.

That's not a man. Nathan fluttered through her mind. She needed to tell him now before she lost another opportunity.

Her eyes landed on their snowy footprints. Man, he had big feet, compared to her miniature ones.

"How tall are you?" she asked, avoiding answering his question.

A soft chuckle escaped him, and he rocked back on his heels. "Six-three."

"Wow. No wonder your prints look like Bigfoot."

He stepped closer, and her breath hitched. At least he kept his hands in his pockets. "What are you afraid of, Willow?" His voice, so tender she almost hadn't recognized him.

When she hadn't responded, Gerard swooped in, his hands cupping her face like she was a porcelain doll in danger of smashing against a concrete floor. "You can tell me. Let me help you."

Aw. Her eyes pooled with unshed tears. His concern coursed through her veins. Where should she start? At the present moment, Nathan was frightening.

"Not being enough," her honesty slipped out. Their eyes met, but hers darted away. *Please don't make me elaborate.*

"You're enough for me."

She scoffed quietly. "Right now, maybe, but how long before you lose your interest?" She murmured. "Besides, what happened to not being *that guy?*"

Willow hated her insecurity. She knew that men found it a turnoff, but she didn't have anything from her past to be secure about. Living up to her dad's expectations and trying to make sure she conformed to every statement in the Bible as if it were black and white proved to be too much when life was a dismal shade of gray. That's when Nathan showed just the slightest interest in her and she gave in to one moment of passion because he loved her. Yuck! She'd been a conquest for him, and then he dropped her like an anchor.

Fortunately, she found her way back to God and had never left him again.

"I'll never lose my interest in you. In fact, my interest has only grown for you. Willow, I was interested in you when you kissed me seven years ago. I never thought you'd be interested in my, so when you kissed me, I was shocked. If you knew my past, you wouldn't want me, nor would your parents want you to be with me."

Never again would she fall for the charismatic words that once weakened her. At least now she had a solid relationship with Jesus. Time to pick up her shield and block the sweet words that rolled off his deceitful tongue. If the shield doesn't protect, beware of the sword. No one could mess with her again.

"I can't believe that."

"I'm not sure where your insecure feelings come from, but if it's a man, I pray it's not Tate." She shook her head. "You need to know that whatever man made you feel this way is stupid."

Hello, Stupid number one!

"Not all of us can be a saint sheriff in a small Montana town. Some of us live separated from God and have to crawl our way back to Him.

"I understand more than you think," he muttered.

Chapter 24

Pandemonium roared in Gerard's bones. Zeke needed spiritual guidance; that's how he'd left his life of crime behind. That, and becoming friends with the people of Haven Ridge accepting him. With enough time in their presence, he'd lost the thrill he once had from committing the transgressions that would have landed him up to twenty years in a penitentiary.

Thankfully, Pastor Myles agreed to meet with Zeke and him tonight. Gerard wasn't qualified to offer spiritual advice. Yeah, he'd changed, but would people still see Gerard, the sheriff, or the criminal if they found out? Gross. He would never let that happen. Gerard couldn't risk it. Pastor Myles was more qualified to share the right road with Zeke. End. Of. Story.

By the time he picked Zeke up from school, Willow was thirty thousand feet in the air, returning to her man. The crushing weight of disappointment pressed against his ribs, a heavy, icy weight of failure suffocating him. Willow believed nothing he said.

"Hey, how was school?" Gerard asked when Zeke exited the ranch with a joyous grin reflecting only one thing; the boy had a crush. *Please God, no.*

"Bye, Zeke, see you Monday." Rocco and Reneé's oldest daughter, Addison, wiggled her fingers and smiled at Zeke. The little red tint to Zeke's cheeks told Gerard all he needed to know.

"School was great. I asked Addison to the Valentine's Day dance, and she said yes. But then she said I had to ask her dad, so Miss Reneé let me find Mr. Rocco during lunch and he said he'd think about it."

Think about it? What was there to think about? Gerard noticed he'd become protective of Zeke, but he had to remember that Zeke was still new in town and he was a criminal they were trying to reform, so he could understand Rocco's hesitation.

"What's for dinner? I'm starving?" Zeke changed the subject.

"We are heading to Willow's parent's home for dinner. Pastor Myles and Cora are serving pizza, french fries, and broccoli."

"What'd they have to ruin it with broccoli for?" Zeke scrunched up his nose. "Do you know if they believe in no thank you helpings?"

He laughed. "Since I don't know what that is myself, I can't say."

"A no thank you helping is where you get a really small portion and have to eat it. So in this case, maybe one little tree."

Another laugh burst from Gerard. "It's not a tree."

"It looks like one," Zeke defended his position.

Gerard wasn't sure when this happened, but he'd taken a real liking to Zeke. Even when the Haven Horizon's Boy's Center was complete, he hoped Zeke wanted to stay with him.

"I'm sure Cora will oblige, if you ask politely."

An hour later, Gerard could see why people opened up to Pastor Myles. He shared his testimony with people; didn't preach to them. So far, he'd learned that Pastor Myles used to swear like a sailor, speed everywhere like a Nascar driver, and he used to judge other people for a million and one reasons.

"Without my relationship with Jesus, I would still be separated from him, doing those things, digging myself a deeper proverbial hole I couldn't get out of that would ultimately lead me to Hell."

Zeke's eyes bugged.

"No one likes to hear that word, Son, but it's a real place and people need to accept that if they don't have a personal relationship with Jesus, they will go to Hell. People cannot earn their way into Heaven with good deeds or being a good person." He used finger quotes to emphasize one of the strongest misconceptions out there.

Gerard got as intrigued as Zeke and started asking his own questions; the first one directed at Cora. "Did you know all of this about him before you married him?"

She smiled. "Yes. God had already worked on him before we got married. Throughout our marriage, we've continued to remind each other of those things that God is helping us through. It's easy to judge someone when we don't know the entire story, or speed around the annoying car putting in front of us, but Myles uses his relationship with Jesus to manage those situations."

"No one will ever be perfect this side of Heaven, so don't let them fool you. Everyone has to examine themself and make sure they are working every day to please God with their words, actions, and thoughts, so that way when we meet God one day and when he judges our sins, he will say welcome home faith servant."

Pastor Myles pulled open his Bible and turned to a tabbed section. "I shudder to think of the people who hear these words: 'Not everyone who says to Me, 'Lord, Lord,' shall enter the kingdom of heaven, but he who does the will of My Father in heaven. Many will say to Me in that day, 'Lord, Lord, have we not prophesied in Your name, cast out demons in Your name, and done many wonders in Your name?' And then I will declare to them, 'I never knew you; depart from Me, you who practice lawlessness!'" Pastor Myles shut his Bible.

"Wow." Zeke was more engaged than Gerard thought he would be. "My mom used to take me to church, but then things got bad with my dad. I think he killed her, but that's not what the police said."

Gerard remembered reading the report stating it was a self-inflicted gun wound that killed her, but another detective questioned the statement. The case was closed anyway. Maybe he could get it reopened. At least it might help Zeke have closure.

"Are all sins judged the same?" Zeke asked, resting his forearms on top of each other, resting them on the table.

Yeah, I'm interested in that, too.

"In my humble opinion, sin is sin from the human perspective, meaning you should not judge someone else's sin as a worse or lesser offense than our own. The book of Romans tells us that we are all sinners and fall short of the glory of God. However, all throughout the Bible, especially in the Old Testament, God shows how He judges sin differently. Some sinners were executed, while others were exiled. So I'd say sin is judged differently."

Interesting. Where does that leave me, Lord? The more Gerard listened to Pastor Myles, the more he wondered if he would ever be worthy of Willow, or if he should back off and give Tate his chance, like Willow said.

"So we carry that sin forever until we die."

Pastor Myles sat up straighter in his seat. "This is the best part," he said, clapping his hands together. "When someone asks Jesus to forgive them for their sins and welcomes Jesus into their heart, all is forgiven. It's truly miraculous. Only God can forgive like that. He forgets that sin—"

"What if you keep doing it?" Zeke asked earnestly.

Myles tipped his head to the side and pursed his lips. "Then, that person needs to examine their heart and see if they truly have a relationship with Jesus, or if they are just professing they do."

Zeke sat, lost in thought, nodding his head as if he was coaching himself. *If only I could read minds,* Gerard thought, thankful that no human could read his.

"You obviously believe, but how do people who don't believe, or lose their faith, start believing?"

"Son, that is an excellent question. Let me say first and foremost, you need to read the Bible. This is God's word breathed into the prophets or apostles, sharing their experience. Hebrews says that 'having faith is the assurance of things hoped for, the conviction of things not seen'. But I have seen things. I've been at the bedside of dying people I know had a personal relationship with Jesus and they were happy, ready to go, and I've been with people who didn't have Jesus and it was dang frightening for me and the person leaving this earth. He screamed for me to help him and not let the man take him. I had nightmares for months after that. It's something I never want to see again, nor do I want anyone to experience that."

Gerard needed to know where he stood with the pastor. "So, if Willow brought home a man who had a past of crime and sordid stuff, but he'd changed, would accept him as good enough for your daughter."

"Remember, I told you one sin I fought was judging others, but I like to think after building my relationship with the Lord for thirty years, I've learned a thing or two and would look at the heart of the person and not his past."

Gerard's racing heart slowed. *If I can get Tate out of her mind, I may just have a chance.*

"Is there something you know, Sheriff, that we don't?" Cora asked, with a glimmer in her eye, letting him know that she was keenly aware of his reason for asking. But how? *The diner and the Troublesome Trio.*

"No." Turning his attention to Zeke, "Do you have any more questions for the Pastor, Zeke?"

He shook his head. "You've given me enough to think about. Do you think I could borrow one of the Bibles from the church?"

"I can do better than that," Cora said before leaving the room. When she returned, she handed Zeke a Bible. "Here, this is yours to keep."

He opened the box and his eyes went big as saucers. "This is a brand new Bible." He gingerly took it from the box and fanned the pages using his thumb. "Thank you so much. I've never had one. I mean, when my mom took me to church, I used the Bible there."

Gerard felt Zeke's appreciation. He remembered the first time he'd experienced someone's love after being on the streets. Doris and Hazel found him behind the diner, and they marched right up to him. They've always been tough women. Hazel brought him into the kitchen, where Frank stuffed more food into him than he'd eaten in the two previous years. They said he was going home with them. He lived with him until graduation day, when he rented Violet's apartment above the flower shop. He stayed there until he purchased the home he lives in now. Gerard worked at the diner from the day Hazel and Frank took him in until he became sheriff. He never accepted a dime from Frank until he graduated. His service was all he had to offer for their generosity. It changed his life forever. Would this Bible do the same for Zeke? *I certainly hope so.*

For a small town, it always amazed him that his story never got out. These people have never treated him like the criminal he had been. They've accepted him from the moment they found him.

Chapter 25

After dropping Zeke off at school Monday morning, he stopped in the salon, eager to see Willow. She'd been gone all weekend. The number of times he tapped out a text and erased it was embarrassing.

He wanted to believe Lily's professional opinion that Willow was attracted to him, but if she was, she was better than Houdini at hiding it.

"Hey Val. I didn't see Willow's car out front," Gerard greeted the woman, getting straight to his reason for visiting.

The woman worked to set up her station, obviously expecting a client soon.

"And you won't either. Not today anyway. She texted, asking me to clear her schedule today and tomorrow."

"Oh." he said, trying to hide his disappointment. The smug look on Val's face revealed how unsuccessful he'd been.

"You should text her," Val's sympathetic eyes rested on him. "Don't accept a broken heart. Put on your big boy vest and try to woo her."

"Woo her?"

Val shook her head. As Willow's only friend from high school, she'd be the only one with a deep knowledge of the woman he couldn't stop thinking about.

"Have you met Tate?"

"Yes. He's such a cutie."

Always the rescuer, never the keeper. "So he's good to her. He won't hurt her, will he?"

A perplexed look had Val's brows scrunched at the bridge of her nose. "Sheriff, who do you think Tate is?"

"Her boyfriend."

The volcanic eruption of laughter that filled the salon plastered Gerard with a grimy feeling akin to the ash and soot that would explode from a real volcano.

"Did she tell you that?"

He recalled all their conversations that included Tate, though he'd tried to forget them. He didn't think she'd ever confirmed his suspicions. In fact, she always answered with something about him not knowing anything.

"So he's not her boyfriend?"

Val shook her head. "I plead the fifth, Sheriff. You have to get your own answers. If you want some advice, convince her to tell her parents first, then you might have a chance at knowing the truth. Ask her if she has had any visitors lately. It's about time you know if you don't already."

Dang! Gerard hit his palm on the steering wheel when he returned to his truck. He saw red. How could Willow lead him down the wrong path? To be fair, she didn't lead him down the *wrong* path, but she certainly didn't guide him to the right one. And what was Val talking about some visitor? Her face was the most serious Gerard had ever seen. Who visited Willow and why hadn't she told him if there was a concern?

"Come on, Woman. Give a man a break," he said aloud, hitting his palm on the steering wheel.

As if his words traveled directly to God's ears, his phone alerted him of a text. Willow's name splayed across the banner. Like an eager teenager, he tapped in his new six-digit passcode thanks to Zeke's sneakiness, and saw her message.

> Val said you were looking for me. Did you need something?

This town! He shook his head, realizing for a bunch of God following individuals, news traveled faster than the Creator's lightning. At the same time, relief flooded him with waves of peace and serenity. Now he could get some answers.

Not in the mood for small talk, he started with his first question, going straight for the jugular.

Who's Tate?

Three dots waved on his screen and then disappeared, and again. That happened four more times. He wished Willow would just say what she's thinking instead of perfecting her words. Thoughts were messy, just like love. When one messed up and their blunt thoughts come out wrong, they could spend quality time making up for their blunder.

Willow's perfectly shaped, full lips came to his mind.

Why are you so concerned with Tate?

She was testing his patience. When people answered a question with a question, they were avoiding the answer. Everyone knew that. Why didn't Willow want to answer questions about Tate?

You've told Zeke and Val knows. What's the big deal?

Are you jealous?

Maybe a little, but he wouldn't tell her that. She'd already turned his stomach into mush when she was around. Heck, even when she wasn't with him, he found himself thinking of her. The feeling, a suffocating void, left him with a relentless ache.

Do you want me to be?

Ten seconds of silence passed. No waving dots. Thirty seconds later, still nothing. After a minute of silence, Gerard smiled, knowing the answer.

I'm just looking out for you. That's all. Oh, and who visited you?

Why, Sheriff, I didn't know you cared.

Well, duh! He would never say that to her, but he thought he'd been clear.

Don't let it go to your head.

Too late, it's already taken up residency. LOL.

Good. He wanted to be on her mind twenty-four seven like she was on his.

I've been wanting to tell you about Tate since our first conversation, but it was fun to watch you squirm. Sorry. Tate and I will be at my parents' tonight at six, so I can introduce him. Please show up at 6:15 if you can, so in case your official presence is needed, I'd appreciate it.

You think it will be that bad?

With my dad, it could go either way.

Okay. In the meantime, will you give me a hint?

Like I've been saying, it's not what you think. You don't have to compete with Tate. You guys are in different classes and you're at the top of yours.

I hope your parents feel the same way. You think they will?

That was the nicest thing she'd ever said to him. It evoked feelings in him that screamed Willow was more than just a friend or an acquaintance. When his phone buzzed again, he glanced down and his smile faltered as he read her response.

They have extremely low standards, bordering on nonexistent. You're all set.

He saw the emoji and the sound of her laughter echoed in his mind, confirming she was kidding. The teasing, light and easy, filled him with a joy that he'd never experienced before.

In return, he sent her a selfie of him pouting with his bottom lip puffed out, hoping she'd send him a selfie. Nope. She gave it an exclamation reaction, though.

Your dad met with Zeke and I. He made a great first impression on Zeke and I feel a little more at ease around him too. He's human and makes mistakes. Give him the benefit of the doubt. Don't go in with a preconceived notion of what you think he'll say or do and you might be surprised.

More dots. Now she sent the emoji face with a single tear drop. Hopefully, he hadn't been too bossy.

Gerard! That was the most serious, sweetest, and helpful thing you've ever said to me. Thank you. I guess I should thank you for the flowers you sent to. Honestly, I thought they were a joke.

He saw the dots working on her end, but he was too impatient to wait.

You're welcome. Does that mean you'll look me in the eye for longer than a split second, or am I still too handsome for you?

That was short-lived. You never cease to disappoint.

She sent the emoji heart kiss. *Whoa!* That was real progress, but then she unsent it just as quick and sent the upside down, closed-mouth smile emoji instead.

> It doesn't have to be, especially if you keep sending me heart kisses.

> I'll see you later tonight. Tate and I are boarding our plane for MT. See you soon.

> Do you need me to pick you up at the airport?

Why would he offer that? *Because you want to spend all the time you can with her.* She'll be with Tate. The last thing Gerard wanted was to feel like a third wheel.

> No, I parked my car there. Thanks though.

> Of course. See you tonight.

Anticipation rushed through Gerard's veins. Tonight, he'd meet the man who filled Willow's heart in some way. His heart threatened to beat out of his chest. At least it was still in his chest. After tonight, it might be shattered into a gazillion pieces. He sucked in a deep breath and let it out slowly. Would he ever be able to tell her what she does to him?

Just then, a final text came through. She'd sent a picture of the flowers along with the typed note:

```
I'm sorry for anything and everything.

    Can we please start fresh?

            - G
```

Who sent those to her? He sighed, realizing she never told him who'd visited her and then a call blared through his radio.

"Dispatch to Sheriff."

"Go ahead," Gerard pressed the button on the side of his radio.

"Peace disturbance at Big L' Ranch."

"10-4. I'm on my way."

Zeke better not have anything to do with this!

Chapter 26

Montana is coined "Big Sky Country." This morning the sky was bright blue and welcoming, but now gray clouds have eaten up the joy that once beamed over Gerard's town.

When he arrived at the ranch, a cacophony of angry, adult voices pierced his ears the moment he stepped out of his cruiser. Not in the mood to yell over people, Gerard pulled out the handheld microphone to his public address system and gave directions.

"Everyone stop talking. People from the ranch move back to the porch. Selena, stand in front of my vehicle. Blake, you go to the side you choose."

"I'll wait right here, if you don't mind."

Smart man. Gerard felt bad for the rancher. He got more than he bargained for when Amelia hired him and then loaned him out to Selena to learn how to run her dad's ranch when he's gone. Everyone was surprised he'd made it to the new year.

Once everyone followed his orders, he returned the microphone and slammed his door shut.

Judging by the shade of red blooming on Raddix's face, Gerard decided to let Amelia start first.

"Why are you asking them first?" Selena barked.

"Don't start, Selena, or you'll be sitting in the back of my car until I can figure out what's going on."

She started to speak, but Gerard cut her off. "Don't try my patience."

Selena let out an exaggerated puff and crossed her arms over her chest, mirroring a two-year-old. *Yikes! Blake better ask for a new assignment soon.*

"Amelia, tell me what happened."

She pulled her jacket sleeves over her bare fingers. "Selena came here with Blake accusing someone from the ranch of shooting her cow. I came out when I heard all the yelling."

"First of all, Selena, is the cow okay?"

"Finally, someone with a heart. No. All the shot did was wound her. Blake had to shoot her to take her out of her suffering."

Rocco stepped forward. "I told her she should have called me and I would have tried to help save the cow, but that's when she started swearing telling us we are all bad people and this is our way of getting back at her for being such a menace."

"You are. Amelia pretends that she doesn't hold a grudge from high school over my head by giving me Blake to help at my ranch." Her eyes darted to Blake. "You're probably working for them. Oh, I can't believe this. I feel so violated." She threw her hands up in the hair.

"Give me a break," Damon sputters, but Tanner is right there, putting his hand up to silence him. *Good. I'm really not in the mood for this.*

"The narcissist strikes again. You think everything is about you," Raddix added.

Gerard raised his eyebrows and glared at Raddix with a look that hopefully said, "Really, Man. Don't make this worse."

"Where is Reneé? The kids?" Gerard asked, scanning the property.

"Downstairs, in school," Quinton answered. "Why?"

"The sheriff probably wants to make sure his boy didn't do this," Selena said, with a high-pitched tone and smug look. "Or maybe you should ask your girlfriend what trouble she brought from California."

Gerard's chest pricked when Raddix gave him a look like, *take that* and *I told you so* wrapped into one.

"If you have something to say, Selena, go ahead." *If Selena thinks she can get me angry with her silly antics, she is wrong.*

Doubt scrapped the back of his mind. What if Selena's comment had something to do with whoever visited Willow? Val was concerned enough to drop the information. Too bad Selena couldn't be trusted. He could tell she was itching to share what she knew.

Gerard knew he was a big man and could be very intimidating with jovial facial expressions, so he could only imagine how much people feared him at this moment with his pursed lips.

"Come on, Sheriff, we all know you took that boy Zeke in and he's the one who held a gun to Randall's head." *That's a bit of an exaggeration.*

He could react to her ridiculous statement. Instead, he chose to play it safe. "Rocco, could you call Reneé and have her send Zeke out here, please?"

"Look, this is more of a domestic issue between the two of you. I can certainly look into the killing of your bovine, but if they want you to leave their property, you need to, so peace can be restored."

"Ah, Sheriff, could you come here?"

"No, everyone here should be privy to the information you found out." Selena's voice was as annoyingly squeaky and high pitched as everyone always complained. He didn't know how he'd missed that in the past.

Gerard put his hand up to stop her from speaking any further. "Since dispatch sent me here, I call the shots until I leave." She huffed, pressing her lips together, offering a precious moment of quiet respite. *Thank you, God! Keep her mouth shut like you did to the lions in Daniel's story.*

"Um, Reneé said that Zeke told her he was coming out to help us because he was caught up with his work, but none of us have seen him."

No, it can't be. "All that glitters isn't gold, so I'm not going to jump to any conclusions."

"When was the last time anyone saw him?"

Rocco turned his attention to his phone when it dinged. "I'll kill him!" Gerard had never heard that level of disdain drip from Rocco's tone before.

"Addison is not on the couch. She told my wife she wasn't feeling well and needed to lie down for a bit."

"We'll find them, don't worry."

"If he's done anything to her—"

Gerard's stone expression stopped Rocco in his tracks. "We can't just assume he's done something awful because he's guilty of a different crime. Think back to being a teenager. Was it always your idea to run off and make out?"

"Like I said," Rocco repeated, his face as red as Mars and the corded vein in his neck pulsing.

Gerard slapped his hand on the man's shoulder. "Settle down until we have answers."

The ranch door flung open and Reneé peered through a pair of binoculars. She scanned the ranch from east to west.

"Don't you guys have cameras?"

Quinton pulled out his phone. "On it."

After about ten clicks Quinton announced, "I found them. They are by the orchard."

"I'll go get them," Raddix offered, and he was gone.

"See, he's not even attending school like he's supposed to and he taking these good people's daughter down the tubes with him."

Gerard spun on his heels, ready to lambast this woman with words he hadn't even thought through yet. Thankfully, Reneé came to his rescue.

"Why are you here, Selena? I thought Damon banned you from the ranch?"

"I came here because while Zeke was supposed to be in *your* care, he escaped, shot my cow, and apparently, took your daughter with him."

"Is that so?!" Reneé was off the porch faster than a peregrine falcon going in for the kill and slipped past Rocco, but Gerard blocked her path to the woman, antagonizing her.

"First of all, my daughter has never caused an ounce of trouble in her life. Second of all, Zeke didn't escape; this isn't jail. Third of all, you have no proof Zeke did anything. What we probably have here is a case of two teenagers running off to make out."

"I'm going to—" Gerard held up his hand to stop Rocco's repeated threat.

"You better hope nothing happens to them. You'd be the first suspect with the threats you're flying around."

"We'll see about that. The person left the gun next to my prize cow that was going to bring me a lot of money."

"Is that the cow that Amelia *gave* you?" Damon asked.

Please, Lord, don't let him add to this muddled mess.

Selena just narrowed her eyes and threw him a snarky smirk.

That must mean yes.

"Here Sheriff," Blake said, stepping forward with a plastic bag carrying the weapon.

"You shouldn't have touched this."

Blake shrugged like it was no big deal. Hadn't he ever seen a police show? Never touch evidence. *Good grief.*

Gerard placed the evidence on the hood of his SUV just as Raddix returned with the teens.

"You need to start talking," Gerard said to Zeke.

"Technically, I don't by law."

Gerard growled.

"But I will because we did nothing wrong," Zeke added quickly.

Zeke gave Reneé a sheepish look. "I planned on coming out to find Damon to work with the horses, but then..." he looked at Addison and then back at Reneé, "I thought it would be fun to explore the ranch, and now we're back."

He recognized Zeke's tells. The only thing he wasn't completely honest about was Addison's part in the charade.

"Addison, did Zeke whisked you away when your mom thought you were resting on the couch?" Gerard asked, hoping the teen would tell him the truth.

"Actually—"

"I really had to beg her. I'm sorry," Zeke interrupted.

Addison shook her head. "No, you didn't. It was my idea."

Gerard gave Rocco an *I told you so* look, which didn't help ease the man's anger any, but it made Gerard feel a little better.

"Addison Marie, you are grounded until you turn eighteen," Rocco exclaimed.

Zeke held up his hands. "I didn't touch her below the neck, just like the pastor told me."

Addison's face turned cherry red as she avoided eye contact with her dad.

The adults were biting back grins, Gerard included, appreciating the boy's moral compass finally pointing north.

Reneé ordered her daughter into the ranch's main house and told her husband to go down into the exercise room and punch the bag until he calmed down.

"I'll see you tomorrow, Addison," Zeke smiled as she walked past him.

"Zeke, zip it. Not the time," Gerard instructed.

Gerard held up the gun. "Has anyone seen this before?"

A chorus of nos all around helped him breathe a little easier. "I'll send it to the state lab for fingerprinting and let you know what I find. In the meantime, if anyone sees anything suspicious, please call immediately."

"Your boy looks a little guilty, Sheriff. He's fidgeting with his hands and his eyes are fixed on the ground. Is that your gun?" Selena's voice, a venomous hiss, spat accusations, scorching the air with its intensity.

Zeke looked her straight in the face. "Look, I just got caught by my girl-friend's dad for making out with her behind the barn. You'd keep your head down, too. Although, you probably don't have to worry about anyone wanting to make out with you. You resemble the serpent more than Eve."

Raddix and Damon caught their laughs, but not quick enough.

"Sheriff, I suggest you do your job and catch the person who killed my cow."

He shook his head. "Yes, in the meantime, you need to leave the property and not return."

She huffed and turned on her heels, barking at Blake to follow her, and he did. *Dummy.*

"If one more woman tells me to do my job…" He muttered, moving toward Zeke.

Harlyn, Lily, and Amelia all giggled as he walked by them. "Keep up the good work, Sheriff." Amelia said.

"Only listen to one of those women," Lily said in a singsong voice and waved at him.

Even though he was mad, Gerard wrapped his arm around Zeke's shoulder and led him to the truck.

When they settled in the cab, Zeke turned his attention to Gerard. "That's my gun, but I didn't kill her cow."

"Explain how the gun got there, then."

"I don't know. When you scared me off that night. I must have dropped the gun or left it behind, but I haven't seen it since that night."

Gerard ran his palm down his face. He might just head home and text Willow that he'll see her tomorrow; not sure if he could handle much more of this day.

Chapter 27

When she pulled into her parent's driveway, the presence of Gerard's truck felt like a chunk of lead in her stomach. Would he be mad at her when he met Tate?

"Come on Sweetheart. You'll wait right inside the door until I prep them," Willow choked out the words.

Tate shook his head. "Mom, you're worrying too much. I'm the grandchild; they're going to love me. Who wouldn't?"

She wrapped her arm around her son, who was nearly as tall as her and he was only seven. "You're right."

Willow's stomach twisted, and her lunch threatened to reappear. To be fair, she'd left this way since lunch when she received a text from an unknown number.

I'm coming for you!

"Hello. We're here." Willow froze in the entryway when her mom and dad walked in with Gerard. Her heart raced out of control. Willow put her hand over her mouth.

"Honey, are you okay?" her mom asked.

"Yeah, you look like you're going to be sick," her dad added.

Cora stepped toward Willow. "Oh, no, did something happen between you and Tate?"

Willow swore she saw the slightest twitch in Gerard's lips. Would he really be happy if Tate was her boyfriend, and they'd broken up, breaking her heart? *Focus, Willow. That's not the case, so it doesn't matter. Introduce your son!*

"No, nothing like that." Willow put her hands up, preventing her mother from moving any closer. If Cora did, she'd see Tate and Willow needed to prepare them and give herself more time.

"Some of you may be really mad at me when I introduce you to Tate and I know you'll have a gazillion questions, but for the sake of the situation, can you avoid asking questions and blowing up at me until Tate is not around?"

The three agreed. Willow inhaled, counting for seven seconds, and then blew out her breath. By the time she got to five, Tate stepped out of the closet area and said, "Hi I'm Tate."

Willow's remaining breath blasted through her mouth and mingled with the room's air, which turned chilly instantly. Her heart raced again, faster this time, as she watched the mouths of three people drop. Her mom rushed to her grandson. "Well, hello young man, I'm Cora."

Her dad moved next to his wife. "And I'm Pastor Myles," he said, sticking out his hand for Tate to shake.

"Tate, that is Gerard," Willow said, pointing toward the sheriff.

Her son moved back next to her and did his best to whisper. "He's a big dude." Everyone chuckled, letting them know that he still needed to work on his whispering skills. Maybe he and Doris could get lessons together.

Willow's heart skipped a beat when Gerard took up residency in front of her son and knelt down to eye level with him. "You're going to grow up big one day, too, but between now and then, you don't need to be afraid of me. I'm a big teddy bear, right, Willow?" he asked, looking up at her and winking. Her dad scoffed a little, but stifled himself quickly when her mom elbowed him in the side.

"Just like the bear from Five Nights of Freddy." She winked back. Not that she'd seen the movie, but that bear looked scary, and she had to tease him a little. Surprisingly, it calmed her nerves to joke with Gerard.

Tate seemed to ignore the interaction between the adults, though her mother was giving her a suspicious eye. Almost as if she were questioning what the little monologue between them meant. Time would tell if it meant anything or not.

"How do you know I'll be tall? Do you know my dad?"

Willow's heart seemed to stop. She sucked in a breath, wishing this moment never came. She felt moisture building underneath her arms. *How is this going to end, Lord?*

"I don't know your dad, but I know you'll grow taller than you are now, so don't worry."

Tate laughed. "As long as I'm taller than my mom, that's all I care about."

"How tall is your mom, Dear?" Cora asked, oblivious to the clues in the room. Maybe things weren't as obvious as she thought, but since Willow knew the truth, it seemed like it would be evident to everyone.

He shrugged his shoulders. Then she saw it coming with the twist of his shoulders. He turned, pivoted around and gave her that innocent smile; the one where his eyes sparkled adorably, and said, "I don't know, Mom, how tall are you?"

No one pressed Willow for answers during dinner, but they all engaged with Tate.

"So, Dear, where do you and your mom live?" Cora asked, taking a small bite of mashed potatoes.

"In California with Aunt Clarissa and Uncle Josh. But I want to move here with Mom, or she needs to move back to California, but these months apart have been awful."

"Aw. It's been rough for me too, Buddy."

Her dad cleared his throat. "Have you decided on a plan, or are you going to just run off again?"

"Myles," Cora warned.

Heat crept up Willow's neck and into her cheeks. As usual, she avoided eye contact with Gerard, but she could feel his intense stare. Did he want to throw the book at her, or was he relieved that Tate wasn't her boyfriend?

Not that it mattered, anyway. Gerard had his own hangups, so could either of them embrace anything more than harmless flirting?

She let out a little breath, feeling sad at the potential answer. When she caught her dad's expression, she remembered he was expecting an answer.

"I haven't decided yet, but I will in the next few weeks. Reneé was nice enough to add Tate to her schooling, so he won't miss school and he can get a feel for Montana. I'm not making the decision alone."

"I get a say?" Tate's eyes, big and bright like the high sun.

Willow smiled and nodded. "I have the final say, but I want to hear your opinion."

Cora clapped. "We need to spend time together, so I can persuade you to stay." Her smile turned to a frown. "And if I can't convince you, at least we had time together."

"That sounds great."

Myles stood abruptly, pausing when he must have realized he made a spectacle. "I'm going to clear the table, if you'll excuse me."

"Come on Tate, let's help your grandpa while your mom and the sheriff talk. I think they have a lot to discuss."

"Thanks, Cora," Gerard said as he stood and walked toward Willow, helping her with her chair.

Once Tate and her mom retreated to the kitchen, Gerard spoke. "Should we head outside to chat?"

She felt a tingling sensation down her spine, leaving her feeling on edge.

As they bundled up and strolled outside, they ended up in the backyard inside the gazebo. All the while, Gerard informed her of the action that took place earlier in the day.

"I'm not going to change my life because that happened to Selena's cow. I'm sorry it happened, but it doesn't have anything to do with me or Tate."

"No one is safe until we know who did this," he retorted with his authoritative tone.

That worked enough to make an icy chill slither down her spine, but she refused to shudder. Instead, Willow shoved the creeping feelings rising in her chest down into the depths of the Earth. She had a sickening feeling that Nate was behind the death.

"What danger could I be in? You know, with the Rockies bowing down to you and all!" Her lips curved into a smile that hinted at mischief and flirtation.

His expression softened. "You do know that Zeke isn't the one who's killed Selena's heifer, right? There's someone out there, without a soul, killing just because, and I don't want you or Tate to get hurt."

Her body stiffened against the wooden rail inside the gazebo. He still hadn't acknowledged Tate as her son. He must be really mad. "Then go out and do your job. Arrest the person or people terrorizing our town before they kill people next." Her tone, sharp.

He leaned in and whispered in her ear. "You're hot when you're angry."

"Shut up," she flung back, playfully pushing against his arm, but he wouldn't budge.

"You know, I could do my job much better if I could focus all my attention on the problem."

She scoffed. "Are you insinuating that I'm taking all your attention? If that's the case, it's on you. I haven't asked for your attention at all."

"I know," escaped his lips, the short utterance punctuated by the lack of space between them.

A sudden stillness settled over Gerard's usually animated demeanor. She feared he might crack a tooth if he clenched his jaw any tighter. The seemingly insignificant comment hung heavy in the air. A dull ache settled in her chest, knowing it'd upset him.

"I'm confused. You sound sad or disappointed."

"I am."

He is? He is what? Willow's breathing picked up. Her mind raced with more questions than answers. "Please elaborate."

"I'll make it crystal clear." He crowded her space, forcing her back up against the wood. Placing his hands on either side of her hips, gripping the wooden railing, he leaned even closer, and she felt the heat radiate off his body, making her temperature rise at least ten degrees. "Now that I know Tate is your son. I'm going to chase you and I won't stop until I catch you."

She swallowed hard. *Is he playing games with me?* "I-I'm ten years younger than you, though."

"Does that bother you?" Gerard asked, still not leaving her any room to breathe.

She shrugged. "It never has, but it obviously bothered you before and I won't gamble with my heart or Tate's."

His warm breath ghosted her ear as he leaned closer. The soft rasp of his stubble against her jaw mixed with his words caused a shiver to ripple down her spine. "I'm a guarantee win, not a risky gamble."

Breathe. She coached herself.

Arrogant confidence radiated off him in waves, creating a unique cocktail of amusement and a nervous flutter within her stomach.

"Mmmhmm." This close, his manly smell stimulated a memory of them when she was eighteen. She'd leaned in and kissed him right after he won his election for sheriff, but he pulled away and she ran off, right into the arms of Tate's father. Since then, whenever she'd caught that unique woodsy scent with a touch of cinnamon, it left her heart longing and sad. Tonight, it had the opposite effect. She wanted him to kiss her, but that could be more dangerous than dealing with whoever killed Selena's cow.

She escaped under his arm and plopped on the wooden bench. *Could she trust him?* The last thing she'd ever do was put her son in a position where another man would disappoint him.

He sat next to her, their thighs touching, and the warmth of his hand on her leg was a stark contrast to the cold winter air. A pleasant heat bloomed even through his glove and her jeans. Tracing lazy circles just above her knee with his thumb, he leaned over and whispered, "Is this okay?"

Nothing has ever been more okay.

This whole situation was mind-numbing. She nodded as she stared at his hand on her thigh. "It's fine. At least you're keeping my leg warm."

"I'll do more than keep your leg warm if you let me make you mine."

He gently squeezed her leg, robbing her of air. She tried to ignore the horse's hooves running ramped in her stomach, and the shiver that caused her whole body to jolt, which likely was the result of the heat within meeting Montana's freezing temperature. In fact, her insides were on fire. Warmth spread throughout her core, igniting her heart. Gerard has pushed past her walls. She trusted him, and felt safe with them, but was that enough?

Chapter 28

Outside the diner the next day, Willow and Tate were heading to the front door when she spotted Gerard jogging toward them. "Let me get that for you."

She looked away with a nervous flutter in her stomach. *Just open the door and escape into the thralls of community gossip.* That sounded ominous, even for her. However, it'd been almost twelve hours and she couldn't help but wonder what the folks in town were already saying about her, Gerard, and Tate. Even her parents asked. Her mom gushed and pressured her for answers — ones she didn't have — all morning, while her dad asked in a *I want to know because I'm dad* type of way.

They still hadn't asked her about the past seven years. Like doting grandparents, they talked about how wonderful Tate was and hoped we decided to stay. She needed to tell them about Nathan before things exploded and she took Tate and ran again.

Willow spent too much time in her own head that Gerard was now in front of her.

"Hi Mr. Gerard. How are you?" Tate stood in front of his mom. Was he protecting her or just excited to see the town sheriff? Either way, it made Willow feel special. "Mom, this is perfect. He can have breakfast with us."

"Oh, I don't think so, honey."

"Aw, Mom, why not?"

"Yeah, Mom, why not?" Gerard teased.

She let out a loud, quick sigh; frustrated that they were ganging up on her, but the idea of having breakfast with Gerard did sound like a great idea.

"I'm sure the busy sheriff has work to do, so he can't waste his time on us."

Gerard crossed his arms over his chest. "You two are never a waste of time to me."

Oh, my! Her heart pounded and her stomach did a cartwheel as his gaze raked over her with affection and longing. His words from last night skipped through her head like a carefree child. 'Now that I know Tate is your son, I'm going to chase you and I won't stop until I catch you and make you mine'.

The door crept open and Myrtle stuck her head out. "Hey, Buddy, why don't you come in with us and let your mom and the sheriff talk?"

"That would be wonderful, thank you," Gerard stated at the same time Willow said, "Oh, that's okay, but thank you."

Tate looked between both adults, but his eyes landed on his mom. "Can I please go inside? It's cold out here."

"That's fine," she conceded, rubbing her son's shaggy hair. "Thank you, Myrtle."

Once they were gone, Gerard said, "I see why you were reluctant to cut my hair. Does Tate like it long or you?"

"It's mutual."

An awkward silence swirled around the chilly air between them.

"How are things with your parents?" he asked, concerned.

She shrugged. "As I expected, Mom is not talking about the obvious. She's gushing over Tate and hoping we choose to stay here. This morning, she had a candid conversation with her sister, but thankfully Aunt Clarissa didn't blame me. She knew my mom would fight with her once the details were out."

"Your mom is scary."

"Aw, the big bad sheriff can't handle the mama that barely comes to his belly button?" She teased in a mocking, baby tone.

He eliminated the gap between them. Staring down at her with the most intense brown eyes she'd ever seen, he said, "Do you want to see how I handle women who barely come to my belly button?"

Gulp. She had to fight hard not to fan herself. *Dear God, thank you for the heat wave in the middle of January, but feel free to cool it a little before I have a stroke!*

"I come above your belly button, so I know you weren't insinuating me." she jutted out her hip and lifted her chin, showing more confidence than she had.

"Mmmhmm. I think we should walk and talk." Gerard placed his hand on her back, branding her with his palm.

"Let's go around back. I don't want to leave Tate here alone."

When they turned the corner of the diner, she saw a flash of someone entering the building, but the back door slammed before she could determine the person's identity.

"Why'd you let me believe Tate was your boyfriend?"

She didn't like his serious side. At least when he was joking around, she could laugh and brush it off. Instead, her intestines were strangling her stomach. He lifted her chin, forcing her to look at his handsome face. *This isn't helping.*

The Lord spoke to her. *The truth will set you free.*

Willow let out a big sigh. "I didn't want to get hurt again, so if you thought I had a boyfriend, then I wouldn't be available."

"Who hurt you, Willow?"

She scoffed. "You were the first one."

"Me?"

She stepped back, and his hand dropped. "Your rejection scarred me."

His tempting lips curved into an irresistible smirk. "I'm sorry. For the record, the kiss was the best moment of my life."

She rolled her eyes and replied, "Oh, you." The words hung in the air as she shoved his arm, but he didn't move. "Don't mock me."

Instead of letting her go, he caught her wrist and the slow deliberate trace of his fingers up her arm and neck sent a delicious shiver down her spine; his touching, leaving a path of warmth.

"I also remember the stupidest decision I ever made in my life, too. But in my defense, I'm a much better kisser when I'm not ambushed." A playful grin spread across his face, assuring her it was a joke.

Ambushed? Okay. Maybe she did just spring it on him.

He curled a strand of hair behind her ear and leaned down so close all she had to do was lift her chin and make eye contact and their lips would meet. A glorious reunion awaited.

From his body, she felt a wave of heat radiating from him, a palpable warmth that was intense and caused her to feel flushed.

In a low silky voice, he breathed, "If you give me another chance, I promise I won't make the same mistake again." Gerard waited for her to respond.

Drowning in his gaze — a sea of milk chocolate — she inhaled his cologne, a wave of intoxicating scent washing over her, her breath catching in her throat.

"I won't kiss you unless you tell me I can. So you might want to try breathing first, then we'll work our way up to talking." He offered her a reassuring smile, the crinkles around his eyes softening the jest.

Willow shook her head. "I can't be hurt again. I have Tate to protect now."

"Then I won't hurt you, or Tate. Let me in, Willow." He leaned in even closer.

It's now or never.

"I need more time," Willow stepped back. "I'm sorry," she said as Gerard straightened himself.

"Don't be sorry. I respect you for wanting to be there for Tate. Does that mean I can't even take you to dinner?"

She smiled. It would be nice to know more about him. The apprehension in his eyes caught her off guard. "Should I be worried if I say yes?"

"No, Ma'am. I'll be an open book for you." Gerard gently laced their fingers together. "Will you do the same for me? We didn't exactly get to discuss how Tate came along."

She couldn't resist. "Well, Gerard, when a man and a woman—"

"You're really funny." He shook their linked hands. "Please, that's not a picture I needed in my head."

"Sorry. Come on, let's get inside, so Tate isn't corrupted by the ladies."

As Willow turned to walk away, "Ow!" A rope tightened around her ankles, jamming her feet together. When Gerard jumped into action, he too got caught and they descended toward the snow. Despite having a big frame, Gerard was quick. Somehow, he turned in the air and landed on his back in the snow. Extending his arm, he guided Willow toward him, letting him break her fall.

Something wasn't right. Had Selena planned this to oust her?

"If you had changed your mind about dinner, a simple text would have sufficed. Although I must admit, I am quite content with this situation and harbor no objections whatsoever."

She was starting to appreciate his playfulness; it was quite endearing.

The snow must have been cold on Gerard's back, but he didn't complain. In fact, he wrapped his arms tighter around her back, pressing her closer to his chest.

"Thank you for breaking my fall," Willow said as she rolled off him, now feeling the cold powder on her backside. "Who put this rope here?" she asked, wondering if he knew and she was worrying for nothing.

It seemed like a trap, one someone might see in the movies. She whispered, "Gerard, do you think whoever killed Selena's cow put this here?"

Gerard gave her an incredulous look. "Why?" He struggled with the knots to release their feet.

"I'm not sure, but it seems odd that a trap would be set up back here, out of sight from the road and other customers."

He followed the rope to its end. With his back against the dumpster, Gerard paused. If he was trying to make her even more nervous, it was working. She couldn't imagine whoever set this up was still around, but clearly her racing heart missed the memo.

Gerard slowly peeked around the green, smelly monster before walking nonchalantly into the opening, crossing his arms over his chest.

What did he find? Willow was on her feet, rushing over when she heard his next words.

"This is endangering a police officer. That could land you in jail for years."

What am I, chopped liver?

When she was nearly beside Gerard, she heard a small, familiar voice. "It was just a little shenanigan."

Her mouth dropped, and she froze like Frosty without his hat when her eyes landed on the culprit.

"Tate William Payne, you get up here right now."

When he stood, Willow wiped the snow off his jeans. *He must be so cold. What the heck possessed him to do this?*

"Please don't be mad, Mama. It was supposed to bring you two together. You were supposed to kiss...GROSS...and I was supposed to get a daddy."

Willow's mouth dropped. She's not sure how long she stood there staring at her son with a gaping hole in front of her face, but Gerard placed his thumb under her chin and manually closed her jaw.

What in the world had gotten into her son? Everything around her seemed to be moving at normal speed, but she felt as if she were moving in slow motion, each movement agonizingly slow and deliberate, as if time had decreased just for her. Willow's head turned toward Gerard, whose shrug and smile spoke volumes, while his eyes held a hint of mischief.

"So I guess a date isn't out of the question then."

She back handed his biceps. "Ow!" She shook her hand and pumped her fingers a couple of times.

"Pure steel, Baby. Are you okay?" She waved him off, getting back to her son.

"Explain yourself more. How'd you get the rope and the ideas?" She wanted to say crazy ideas because they were, but she didn't want to hurt her son's feelings.

"Well, Doris gave me the rope, but Myrtle helped me set it up."

Of course. She must have been the person entering the dinner right as Gerard and she came around the corner.

"What else did those *lovely* ladies tell you, honey?" Willow asked, wondering how mad she should get.

"Who sounds like a scary teddy bear now?" Gerard quipped.

She turned her attention back to Gerard. "You're okay with all this?" When he didn't answer, she crossed her arms over her chest and pierced him with what felt like daggers coming from her eyes.

"Are you hurt?" he asked.

"No."

"Then, I'm not mad."

"Phew." Tate let out a loud sigh. "Does that mean you'll be my daddy, too?"

Gerard's face blanched, and though she shouldn't, Willow felt vindicated. With what she hoped was a smug look and extra sparkly eyes, she said, "Go ahead sheriff, Tate's waiting for your answer."

"Tate, it would be an honor to be your daddy."

Willow's jaw hung slack once more, marking the second time this had happened in a matter of minutes, leaving her with a silent expression of utter disbelief and annoyance.

"Yay! Thank you, Gerard." Tate jumped into the sheriff's arms.

"I didn't agree with this," Willow objected.

"But you did agree to a date," he reminded her with a hint of satisfaction.

"One date," she said firmly.

He leaned down, kissing the top of her head. "Perfect, that's all I need."

Chapter 29

"This is nearly impossible," one of the newly hired ranch hands groaned as they searched for any clues.

Gerard shared another look with Damon and Raddix as if to ask *how long is this guy going to last on the ranch?* Their eyes responded with what Gerard assumed was *not long.*

"What time do you think this happened, Raddix?"

Raddix shrugged. "When I came out at a little after four, she was already gone. Rocco gave me his best guess that she'd suffered her last breath about three hours before that."

"He better not touch Yoshi, or..." Emmanuel's voice trailed off. "I'll kick 'em in the—."

"Emmanuel!" Quinton hollered, stopping the boy from finishing his new favorite saying he'd learned during a lesson on kidnapping and human trafficking that Reneé had taught.

Those crimes have become big businesses, and it made Gerard want to puke and go Jason Statham on the scumbags. *Focus on the situation,* Gerard ordered his brain.

Something suspiciously warm bloomed in Gerard's chest, thinking of how passionate Emmanuel was about his horse. Not that he'd make this comparison in his out loud voice for fear of Willow smacking him, but Tate had that same lovingness with his mom.

Pride swelled in Quinton's eyes when he heard his son's declaration. Gerard imagined the pride also had something to do with his son, a mere tween helping without a single complaint, while the new, thirty-something-year-old ranch hand hadn't stopped complaining.

Damon checked his phone. "Tanner's ready with the tractor if we're okay to move the bovine."

"You better hurry before Amelia catches him using that in the dead of winter," Quinton ordered.

Everyone understood her concern. Jack Lawrence, her dad, died one winter when the tractor got stuck in the snow and ice and flipped on him, trapping him underneath. That was the worst call Gerard had to respond to until lately. The break-ins, robbery, and cow murders — still not nearly as bad as losing Jack, but Gerard was beside himself.

He chuckled. "Afraid you'll get in trouble with the Missus?"

"Yup. If a husband knows what's good for him, he keeps the Missus happy. Then she keeps him happy." He wagged his eyebrows.

Gerard shook his head. *Good grief.* He needed to stop talking to these married men. Did married women talk this same way?

Just when they thought that finding any evidence was futile, Emmanuel hollered, "What's this?"

All the men ran in the boy's direction. There in the snow was a matchbook from The Red Mill. Gerard pulled out an evidence bag and shook it open while his gloved forefinger and thumb picked up the square. One of these had been found at the robbery, too. Zeke said he'd never been to the restaurant or even knew where it was. Did that mean someone else was at Randall's?

Lord, please don't let Zeke be playing us. The idea of Zeke working with someone else would crush him. Gerard had grown so fond of the boy.

The men were chatting by his truck when a car screamed up the drive. He knew it was Willow, but he couldn't imagine what would warrant her driving like that. If Emmanuel had been standing there... he shuddered at the thought.

She rounded the hood of his SUV. "Maybe you need a ticket to remind you how to drive," he joked. The men almost laughed at his joke with him, but they were stopped short by Willow's harsh words.

"Shut up, Gerard. I'm not in the mood. If you want to give me a ticket, leave it in my seat. I don't care." Willow looked at Quinton — or maybe Rocco. "Is Tate with Reneé?"

Her no-nonsense tone had everyone stunned. Rocco muttered, "Yes," while Quinton pointed toward the house. "Through the kitchen, turn left, head down the stairs."

"Thanks."

It wasn't two minutes later, Willow returned, almost dragging Tate behind her.

"Stop, Mama. I don't want to leave."

"We have to. It's not safe here."

Gerard's chest flurried with concern and by the men's faces, they were wondering why Willow thought the ranch wasn't safe for Tate.

"Willow, hang on a minute." He stepped in front of her, and every time she tried to dodge him, he side-stepped, blocking her way. "Will you please stop? Breathe for a moment and tell us what's wrong."

He was surprised that she did heed his direction. But she remained silent until she wasn't.

"Unless you're arresting me for something, officer, kindly get out of my way."

A cold shiver trickled down Gerard's spine, unease settling in as he wondered if he'd pushed Willow too far the other day; her silence now amplifying his worry. Her trembling body spoke volumes, while the fear in her eyes shone brighter than the gold buckle Tanner brought home from Nationals.

Before he'd let her run off, he said, "Look around you, Willow, all these men will protect you and Tate. If you run, we can't help you."

She let out a long sigh. *Fabulous.* He'd convinced her to tell him what had happened since they'd last talked. He tried not to let it bother him that this was the first time they'd even interacted since.

She'd ignored all his texts after agreeing to a date. That same day, he told Tate that he'd love to be his daddy. Did she think he was lying? Because he wasn't. The idea of marrying Willow and adopting Tate had fallen upon him as easily as the angel spoke to Zechariah, Mary, Joseph, and the Shepherds.

She looked toward Quinton, Raddix, Damon, along with Tanner, who joined us after we finished the burial. "Thank you, gentlemen, for allowing him to offer your protection services, but I've taken care of myself for the last seven years. I will be fine."

He wondered which of them would be the bravest to speak first.

"But you don't have to be fine. We are happy to help you with whatever you need," Quinton's voice was tender and diplomatic.

She smiled in appreciation, but didn't take the offer. "I need to be going."

The chaos of a three-ringed circus rang through the air when another vehicle pulled up. Blake and Selena stormed across the snowy gravel, slapping a note to his chest.

"What's this?" Gerard asked, peeved that she had the gall to slap him with the paper.

<pre>
Tell your loser sheriff to stay away
  from my son. He can take Willow if
  he wants her, but the boy is mine!
   You only have a few cows left.
   Imagine what I'll move onto when
          those are gone.

          Get it done!!!!
</pre>

"Willow, you'll want to see this before you leave." Gerard showed the men while he waited for Willow and Tate to return to his side.

As she read the note, the blood drained from Willow's face and she fell limp into Gerard's arms.

"Mom!! Are you okay?" Tate screamed, gaining Katy's attention from inside the store.

She hollered into the store for Jeff, then ran over. "What can I do to help?"

Just then, Willow's eyes popped open. Her eyes met his. "What are you doing?"

"Y-you passed out. I prevented you from bouncing off the ground." He righted her, holding onto her shoulders, steadying her still wobbly frame. "Are you good?" He slowly removed his hands, palms up, guiding away from her.

A heavy, stagnant air pressed in on him, laden with unanswered questions and a host of unspoken worries that clouded his thoughts and added to his burdens.

"Who typed this?" His tone, more gruff than he intended, leaving him with instant regret when her eyes flinched. A white-hot rage, a righteous fury, filled him at the thought of anyone harming Tate; he was consumed by the need to make things right.

"Willow!" he exclaimed, again frustrated with the situation.

"Don't snap at me!" Her fierce tone, cutting him in half.

That's about right. She decided to speak when she could yell at him. Well deserved, he had to admit, but still.

"Neutral corners." Jeff stepped forward. "Willow, hun, you need to tell us what's going on so we can keep you and that little man of yours safe."

Gerard didn't miss how she tugged Tate closer and held on for dear life. She was one mama bear he wouldn't mess with.

"I can tell you what's going on," Selena cooed in a mean-girl way.

"You're not welcomed here," Damon stated aloud. "Can't you arrest her for trespassing at this point?"

"Sheriff, you've been duped. Little miss, I'm the pastor's daughter has been living in sin and she's trying to pull you into it."

His head spun. What was Selena talking about? He couldn't trust her.

"Has he agreed to be Tate's daddy yet?"

"You don't have a clue what you're talking about and if you don't get out of my face right now, you won't have one." Willow lunged at the woman, but Gerard caught her with his arm. If he wasn't so stressed, he might have laughed at her little legs running in the air to get away from him.

"Selena get out of here now!" Gerard ordered, setting Willow down.

Panting, Willow paced back and forth, her chest heaving.

"Willow, please let us help you," Katy begged.

Willow stopped. "Nathan Roberts," she whispered so low he almost missed it. When the name registered in his brain, he wished it hadn't.

The guy was a loser in high school. Gerard's ears burned with the stories of the slimy coward's manipulative ways — he'd lure women in with sweet words, take what he wanted, then vanish without a trace, leaving behind a trail of broken hearts. If rumors were true, he'd fathered at least ten babies, but then he fell off the map and Gerard had all but forgotten him.

One look at Raddix and he could tell he wasn't the only one remembering the loser's past. He wanted to hear the entire story, but now was not the time. Keeping Tate and Willow safe was his first priority. Capturing the dirtbag, equally important.

"Is that my dad?" Tate's fragile whisper, barely audible, carried the weight of the world. The boy's youthful voice pierced Gerard's heart and clawed at his soul. Nathan Roberts will pay for his mistakes.

"No." Willow said, sternly. "A dad is someone who loves you and raises you to be a man. Nate Roberts would never be a dad."

The boy didn't seem to fully understand what his mother was saying, but the adults did.

"Is that why Officer Gerard offered to be my dad? He wants to make sure I grow up to be a man."

Tate smirked and stuck his tongue out at Selena, who had only moved back to the sheriff's cruiser.

Shock factor times one hundred was the only way to explain the assortment of hinged jaws and smirks on those surrounding the boy. The vulnerable expression on Willow's face was what kicked him in the gut. Today, her eyes were nearly a bright blue. He noticed her eye color changed based on her clothing. It was as if they were begging him to protect her. He gave her what he hoped was a look of endearment and confidence. He'd take care of her and Tate and then eliminate the threat from their lives.

"Something like that," Gerard answered, hoping the moment passed and the heat growing on his neck and cheeks dissipated.

"You're not going anywhere," Quinton interjected. "Amelia and I have hired security for the ranch. They started today and are out patrolling right now. I'll check with them; to see if they've seen anything sus, as the kids say," Quinton laughed at his own use of teenage lingo, encouraging the rest of us to laugh at him, too.

"Will Grammie and Pop Pop be okay?" Tate asked, obviously referring to Willow's parents. It was great that they'd connected so quickly.

Second ticked by without a response. Then Selena broke the sound barrier with her shrieking.

"What about my cows? Nate Roberts is doing this just because I wouldn't date him in high school. It was easy to see he was a loser, so *I* stayed away."

Gerard sent the woman a glare and said, "Really?"

"What? This is the second cow that monster has killed of mine. I have it hard enough. I don't need this right now."

"Right, because this world is all about you." Raddix quipped, and she tossed him a snarky smirk.

Gerard faced Selena. "You head back to your ranch. I'll send Jimmy there to check for evidence. Don't touch anything. As soon as Nate is apprehended, he'll be charged with animal cruelty and you can then sue him for compensation for your cows."

"Obviously, Raddix, the same applies for you as it's likely Nathan is responsible for your bovine's murder as well."

"We haven't had any of these problems until *you* returned to Haven Ridge. Trying to redeem yourself by opening a home for wayward teens is honorable, I guess, but you should have done it wherever you've been."

Too bad she didn't open a home like that for adults like you who don't have an ounce of human decency and haven't grown up. Gerard reigned in his professional side and opened his mouth to speak, but Tate beat him to the punch.

"I don't know you," Tate started and the dense woman actually smiled and attempted to introduce herself. "And I don't care to even know your name. You're mean and nasty and if you say another mean thing about my mom, you'll regret it."

Willow tugged on her son, resting his back against her chest. "Don't waste your breath on worthless chatter."

"Did you hear that, Sheriff? He just threatened me," Selena squealed.

Gerard sighed. "Perhaps you should leave now, like I ordered you to do ten minutes ago."

"It was a promise, not a threat," Tate added, his red face revealing how protective he was of his mama. This boy is well on his way to being a man.

As for the men watching this unfold, their lips were twitching and slightly curving at one end. In order to prevent himself from laughing, Gerard bit the inside of his cheek. Tate would fit in nicely here.

Gerard sent Jimmy a text with all the information. An almost instant reply let him know Jimmy was headed to Selena's now. "Jimmy is on his way. You need to be there to direct him."

Selena stocked off, her hair almost flicking the speechless Blake in the face. "Quinton, how long do I have to deal with her?"

"I'll talk to Amelia."

"God bless you!"

"Blake, let's go," Selena shrieked from the car.

"Amelia is nicer than anyone I know," Willow said, and the men agreed.

Tate turned and faced his mom. "We should say an extra prayer for that man."

How profound. Tate was wise beyond his years. That probably had to do with being an only child. Willow spoke tenderly to him, but not babyish, and that probably made the difference.

"I'll go call Cora and let her know what I know, then we can make a plan," Katy said as she headed toward the main house.

"Thank you," Willow called.

Katy looked over her shoulder and smiled. "Of course. That's what we do."

"For now, I think Tate should go back to school. Quinton will check with his security. Everyone else, go about your day. Keep your eyes wide and your ears open." He looked at Willow. "You and I have to talk."

Chapter 30

“**H**ow could you keep this to yourself, Willow? Do you know how much danger you put yourself and Tate in?”

She halted on the snowy path leading toward the back of the ranch. Her fiery eyes steeled on him. This was not what he meant when he said he wanted her to make eye contact with him.

“You have no right to judge decisions I make in my life. I do the best I can with what I have. As a matter of fact, I think I’ve heard that somewhere, right *officer*, I mean sheriff?”

So this is how the conversation was going to go. “I wasn’t judging, just pointing out the obvious.”

“Oh, so now I’m an idiot?” She stormed off. But at least she was still heading in their intended direction and hadn’t retreated.

Who said anything about her being an idiot? Those words never came out of his mouth.

"Why would you call yourself an idiot—"

She spun on her heels again, but this time she poked him in the chest. "I didn't. You. Did." A poke for each word was not too bad, thankful she didn't use a whole sentence.

"I never said that."

"You said you were pointing out the obvious, meaning everyone can see it and anyone who can't must be an idiot."

"You got all of that out of the word obvious?"

She crossed her arms, evidently not any more pleased with his most recent words. Damon and Raddix's advice about giving in came flooding back.

"I never would have gone to that conclusion. I apologize for saying it was obvious." At this point, he couldn't even remember what was obvious. *Good Grief.* "Let's start over. Tell me your story from the beginning. I'm not going to shame you or judge you. I just want to protect you and Tate."

Willow turned and continued walking. "After I kissed my long-time crush, and he pushed me away..."

She's never going to let me off the hook for that.

"Val and I planned a graduation trip, but she had to back out at the last minute. That's when I met Nate at our summer carnival. Long story short, he made me believe he actually loved me. I fell for his lines and let my body do the talking. Shame and regret filled me right away." Tears pooled behind her eyes as she relived the misery. "He disappeared without a word."

Gerard's gut twisted. How could anyone treat another person like that, but especially his beautiful Willow? She wasn't exactly his, not yet, but he was hopeful. He clenched his jaw and fist, hating that Willow's first experience wasn't the loving, tender moment it should have been with her husband. He wanted to break every bone in Nathan's body for manipulating her.

"I don't even know how Nathan knows about Tate. I never told anyone except my aunt and Val. The father's name is blank on Tate's birth certificate."

As they neared the river, he tugged on Willow's arm to stop her. "I am so sorry you interpreted my shock as rejection so many years ago. I was and still am dealing with my own ghosts, which were and are my problem. It was never you."

"Well, like you said to me, you don't need to go through it alone. I'd love to listen."

Had Gerard just heard her right? She had Tate's dad threatening to take him and she was putting herself out there to listen to his problems? It shouldn't surprise him. She opened an entire center so she could help teens have a safe place.

Something within compelled Gerard to move closer. Their visible breaths mingled together, and he rubbed her arms when she shivered. With a tender touch, he draped his vest over her shoulders, his scent of cinnamon mingled faintly with her citrusy fragrance as it wrapped around them. His eyes never left hers, and she finally held his gaze. *Thank you, Lord!*

With everything going on with Nate, the last thing he wanted to do was push Willow into kissing him. Ten minutes ago, a cocktail of fear and anxiety splashed across her face. Now, as his fingers trailed down her arms, he laced his fingers with hers and the pulse in her neck sped up when his thumb began tracing lazy circles on his knuckles.

Releasing one of their linked fingers, he found her heated cheek. "Is this okay, Willow?" *Please say yes.* They deserved their chance. The whole town agreed. Myrtle had even called in Tate for help.

She nodded. "But please don't do this just because you feel bad for me or Tate. Do this because you want to."

"You have consumed my thoughts and my desires for months." Then the space between them vanished and the outside world faded into a blurry, indistinct background.

Their lips rendezvoused in a frenzy of emotions. His arms wrapped low on her back, securing her at his chest, desperate to feel her flush with him.

She kissed him back with her persuading lips, encouraging him to deepen the kiss.

His surroundings melted away. Only their urgency and passion existed as he trailed kisses along her jawline and down her neck. She rewarded him with a gentle shiver.

Everything about this moment was perfect — the way she fit like a puzzle in his arms, the chilly January breeze on his neck, cooling him down, her soft lips caressing him with equal parts tenderness and desire.

He kneaded her back, and their kiss intensified as she gripped the front of his uniform. Oh, how she fit perfectly with him. They'd finally figured it out. At least *this* part. Kissing her would never be a challenge.

Soft snowflakes whispered down, landing on their shoulders, but all he could focus on was the happiness burst in his chest and how Willow was exactly what he needed and wanted in his life.

For the first time in years, he felt like he could be enough for a woman, for Willow, until a version of his younger self flashed through his mind. The stolen cars, running from the police, and robberies. He clung to Willow like she was his lifeline, realizing that she was his missing piece. She made him want to be a better man. Whatever this was between them, he didn't want it to end.

In fact, he needed to know more, feeling utterly invincible as she clung to him. She wanted him as much as he did her. He'd cherish her from this day forward.

At least he'd try. Thankfully, he had role models like Jeff and Katy on the ranch. God knows his parents had taught him the opposite. That was probably why his relationship with Jennie hadn't worked out. That and because God was preparing Willow for him.

Not wanting to pass out, he trailed kisses down Willow's neck to recapture a little oxygen. She was all he needed.

"Gerard," she gasped, his name a ragged, breathless whisper. Then he felt it. Her body stiffened against his hands. Had he pushed her too fast? *Stupid, stupid, stupid.* "Why are we doing this?"

"Excuse me?"

She stepped back. "Nothing is going to come from this."

Her hazel eyes staring up at him with what he'd describe as despair. *Come on, Willow, don't lose hope.* But it was too late. Before he could convince her to stay, she ran back toward the main house. He could have sworn he saw her wipe at her eyes.

Apparently, they were on completely different pages. For him, that kiss whispered her secrets against his lips. She couldn't hide the way she felt about him now that they'd kissed. Even more, it made him want to tell her his secrets. He wanted to share everything with her. Evidently, now was not the time. Would it ever be his and Willow's time, or would he have to live with the memory of that kiss?

Chapter 31

Though the temperature was an unusual forty degrees for the third week of January, a warmth that should have been comforting, Willow felt only the crushing weight of despair. In the last twenty-four hours, so much had changed.

Gerard enlisted help from two of the same officers who assisted with the break-in at Randall's. Their chief offered the men's services for a month. This allowed Jimmy a bit of a break from full-time duty while Gerard played security at Haven Horizons.

Can you imagine the sheriff downgrading himself to a security guard? She wasn't insinuating anything was wrong with being a security guard, she just didn't know how long she could handle having him around. He informed her this morning that he'd be at the center 24/7. Tate and Zeke were sharing a room, as they were one bed shy of full capacity.

"Okay. Thank you. I'll give them a call." She'd spent all morning on the phone with other centers, looking for placements to help out the girls they couldn't take in until Bill finished the other building, or different security companies.

"No luck?" Gerard asked when she hung up the phone.

She let out a loud sigh. "Nope." Amelia's company couldn't help and directed her to a different company. She was passed along four more times. This next company was fairly new — opened within the last year. Looking at the scribbled name, G & G Security, on the pad of paper, she said a quick prayer. *Lord, if it's your will, please let a full-time security team be available and let it be enough to keep Tate and me safe.*

Everyone had decided that Tate should remain at the ranch for school. With an entire security team there, he would be safe and with Gerard keeping watch over Willow, she would be safe. There were at least two officers patrolling the town all the time.

"Do you want me to call some places for you?"

Aw, Gerard's offer was touching, but she was still torn about being with him and didn't want to lead him on or get herself hurt. In her mind, him helping her with the center or with Tate seemed domesticated, intimate even.

Despite spending the same amount of time on her morning routine, she felt drab — her dark, puffy eyes were hard to conceal and now her eyelids felt heavy, her body a vessel on the verge of collapse from the relentless blows of rejection.

"No, thanks, I only have one more to call."

Alright Mr. Grady Gunderson, please have the answer I want to hear.

Gerard gave her some privacy, or so it seemed that way, as he slipped outside to survey the property. Now alone, she was hyperaware of his missing presence. The unease prickling at her chest taunted her as she thought, *he's the one, don't let him go!* Her heart soared when she captured him in the window to her right. The sunlight illuminated his sleek silhouette and intense eyes as he peered in the window — a vision she wanted to see every night before she drifted off to sleep and again when she woke in the morning.

Yikes! Where'd that thought come from? If she had to guess, the unparalleled and unforgettable feeling stemmed from the most extraordinary kiss, forever etched on her mind. The memory of the kiss left her lips warm and buzzing.

"G & G Security, this is Olivia. How may I help you?"

Perfect. She sounded nice and open to taking on more work, slightly relieving Willow of the frenzy of emotions swirling within.

After Willow explained the situation to one of the nicest women she'd ever encountered on the phone, perhaps even in person, she remained silent while Olivia explained how payment worked. "I'll have Grady call you and discuss how the security part operates when he's finished with the client he's working with now."

"So, you can help us right away?" She didn't mean to sound so shocked, but all the rejection kept her guarded.

"Based on what I'm looking at, yes, but Grady and his partner Gunner make the final decisions. They have warrior minds and know how many guys are necessary for a job to run smoothly. Then I schedule it."

"You sound like a perfect team." Willow wasn't sure what their status was, so identifying them as a team worked for anything.

"Thank you. I think so, too. Grady will contact you shortly. It was a pleasure speaking with you, Willow. Thank you for contacting us."

"I look forward to speaking with him. Thank you."

Willow pushed back her chair and danced a little jig, excited that she no longer had to call around to look for help.

"I could get used to seeing this more often," the humor in Gerard's tone froze her hips.

Already feeling the heat creep into her neck and cheeks, Willow slowly turned, held her chin high, showing more confidence than she felt. "I imagine, but don't get used to it. Lack of sleep makes me do crazy things sometimes."

"Why didn't you sleep last night?" The glimmer in his eye told her he already knew the answer; dang him.

Willow steeled her voice. "It's hard getting used to sleeping in a new place."

"Or maybe you were thinking about that kiss all night like I was. Imagining meeting up right about here to reenact it to see if it really was as breathtaking as you imagined."

The already present heat turned into an inferno. She resisted the urge to fan herself, knowing that would give her away. Where did this man come from? Sheriff, guardian for troubled teenage boys, incredible kisser, and mind reader. What was next?

She opened her mouth to answer, but snapped it shut. What could she say after that? *Yes, you're right.* Kissing him every day multiple times a day for the rest of her life was her new resolution for the year. She couldn't put herself out there like that.

"It's okay to tell me," he said as if he were reading her mind. "Would it help if I told you I had the same dream? All. Night. Long!"

The air between them sizzled. His eyes... to say intense, would be an understatement. All-consuming was more appropriate. It was like he saw her, the real her — sinful mistakes and all — yet he still wanted her. *Unbelievable.* She thought she'd convinced herself that this wasn't real. He really didn't care. Maybe it was a ploy or a harsh joke to see... she didn't know what. His declaration to be Tate's dad still stirred a raw emotion in her chest that if she thought about it too much right now, the waterworks would come flooding back.

She wasn't so sure of anything anymore. His mouth curved into a sheepish smile, clearly waiting for her to answer. "Maybe a little," she said, tucking a strand of hair behind her ear for the sole purpose of distracting herself to calm her nerves.

Shock or hope, perhaps both, flickered in his expression. He recovered quickly and his trademark smirk returned. "Maybe we should capitalize on this moment?" he said low and husky, leaning closer, just as she found herself doing. Now inches from her lips, he whispered, "Would that be okay, Willow?"

Yes, please. Totally fine.

As her name, breathed in a low husky whisper, reached her ears, a shiver cascaded down her spine followed by a wave of warmth spreading like a sunbeam through her body.

In a swift impulsive movement, she pushed up onto her toes and captures his mouth, fusing their lips. The kiss transcended a simple kiss; it was a claim, a staking of territory, leaving her breathless and trembling.

The heady scent of his cologne intoxicated her as his tender, unhurried movements deepened the kiss, making it feel as though they had forever.

His kiss was possessive, a delicious brand of ownership that sparked a fire within her. She weaved her fingers into the hair at the nape of his neck, igniting more fire within her when he groaned, a desperate hunger... for her.

The steady thump-thump-thump of his heart against hers calmed her, each beat a soothing balm against her worries as she melted into him.

She pulled back, and he rested his forehead against hers. Their ragged breaths mingled as if they were hoping for another round. "Nothing will be the same between us, you know that, right?"

"I was hoping you'd feel that way."

Chapter 32

The week flew by, probably for the mere fact that he and Willow had kissed twice now, and the second time was better than the first. In the middle of the night Friday, he woke with a jolt to an ear-piercing scream. Footfalls and Willow's rapid speech set off alarms in his mind.

"Thank you, Dr. Merriman. Harper is with her now. We'll see you when you get here."

"What's going on?" He asked automatically, already having a good idea of the situation.

Willow turned and her sea-green eyes were pools of longing as they raked over him. Maybe he shouldn't have leaned there, ankles crossed and arms folded, but he needed to capture her attention somehow. He knew it drove women crazy, and she didn't disappoint.

"Liz's water broke. Dr. Merriman will be here in about twenty minutes."

Gerard stood to his full height. "Hopefully she gets here soon; that doesn't sound very comfortable. Poor Harper, she has to endure everything. That's what a husband is good for — squeezing his fingers and yelling at him." His short-lived chuckled caught in his throat.

A wave of regret smashed into him when her smile vanished, replaced by a tight-lipped frown. Recognition washed through his mind. Willow had been one of these girls.

"Seriously?"

Oh, no. He should just go back to sleep, his brain not fully awake, and he didn't have any business trying to hold a conversation with anyone, especially Willow.

He stepped forward with arms reaching out, but halted when she put her hand up like a stop sign. His arms dropped to his side. "I'm sorry, Willow, I wasn't thinking."

"It's fine. We're tired. Let's just avoid saying anything else until we're truly awake."

He couldn't believe she'd given him such an easy out. There was always a first time for everything. But what she didn't realize was that it made him want her more. Nodding slowly, he tried to smile, but could tell his lips formed a straight line, his guilt stretching even further. His fingers itched to reach for her, wrap her in a hug that showed he was sorry, but he knew she needed her space. He'd get his chance to show her soon.

All day, that poor girl writhed in pain. Harper was amazing. She was a nurse and doctor all in one. Willow ended up being her assistant until Dr. Merriman arrived and Gerard had never been more thankful to be the sheriff. He patrolled the property, still void of any sign of Nate. The snow made it easy to detect footprints or other signs of an invasion.

Too many times his mind flash backed to Willow and the hurt on her face. The hurt he'd put there. She'd let him in, telling him everything she'd gone through, at least the short version, but he still couldn't imagine the physical and emotional pain she'd endured.

The crunch of gravel underneath car tires captured Gerard's attention, and he rushed back to the front of the house. Willow beat him to the driveway, greeting her parents, Tate, and Zeke. Gerard checked the time on his phone. He couldn't believe the day had got away from him like that.

"Thank you so much for bringing the kids here." Gerard seconded that when he reached the car.

As of right now, the plan was for Myles and Cora to transport the kids home every day. He didn't tell Willow this, but it was the easiest way to make sure her parents were safe. A missed pickup would signal a problem.

"Are you guys going to come in for a little while?" Gerard would love more males in the house. The estrogen to testosterone ratio was significantly unbalanced.

The mature couple made their decision with a simple look into each other's eyes. Gerard wanted that one day, where he could look into his wife's eyes and know what she was thinking.

Once they unbuckled their seat belts, his gaze drifted toward Willow. How long had she been staring at him? Was she thinking the same thing? The longing in her eyes led him to believe so, but would she ever look at him like Cora looked at Myles?

"How was school, Zeke?" He rested his hand on the teen's shoulder.

"Fine."

Gerard grunted inwardly. *Here we go with twenty questions again.* Why couldn't teenagers elaborate on their answers? Then parents wouldn't seem like they were nagging. Not that he was Zeke's parent. Not yet, anyway.

"What happened with Addison today?"

Zeke shrugged as they walked into the house. "Not much. Mr. Rocco gave us permission to go to the dance together. Miss Reneé said we could date if we didn't go off without telling where we were going."

"That's progress. How'd Rocco feel about that?"

"He told me if I touched her below the neck or broke her heart, he'd break my legs and arms to start."

Gerard laughed. "Take it. He's going pretty easy on you."

"He sure is." Willow offered. "Why don't you ask my dad how he kept the boys away?"

"Come on, Son, let's chat," Myles chortled.

"Can I come too, Pop Pop?"

Myles wrapped his arms around Tate. "You betcha."

As they walked away, he swore he heard Cora say, "That's the best group of men I know." Did she mean him, too? Gerard wasn't a good man. In fact, he was going to clear the air right now; tell Myles all he'd done and been through.

"Has she been screaming like that all day?" Tate asked when he heard Liz.

"Unfortunately, yes." Gerard checked the time on his phone. "It's been thirteen hours so far."

Tate shook his head. "I'll never cause anyone that much pain."

Gerard, Myles, and even Tate, smirked. "You most likely will be to blame for the same pain one day, Little Man," Pastor Myles chuckled.

"Speaking of sins, I'd like to talk with the three of you," Gerard began, leading them to the back enclosed porch. He sat on the loveseat, leaned his elbow on his knees and fumbled with his fingers before clasping them together to stifle his nerves.

"Tate and Pastor, I need you to hear this because I'm interested in Willow, but I've wrestled with a lot in my life and it kept me from pursuing her years ago. I don't want to lose her again, but I want your blessing."

"Myrtle was right," Tate interjected. "Did she and her friends really lock you in a shed?"

Gerard nodded.

"And you didn't capitalize on the situation then?" Zeke shook his head. "She's a babe."

Pastor Myles cleared his throat, giving Zeke a glare that would probably be shot toward Gerard by the time he finished.

Gerard's stern tone held a clear warning. "Be respectful, Zeke."

In an effort to move away from the boy's comment, Gerard continued. "When I was sixteen, like Zeke, I was mad at the world. My dad was always criticizing me. I couldn't do anything right. When you hear it enough, you start to believe it."

Gerard stared at the ground, getting closer to the part where he messed up. His pulse raced. Fear etched his entire being. What will Pastor Myles say? He couldn't look at the Godly man. Yeah, Gerard had recently learned of the man's faults, but Gerard knew he'd done worse. The walls around his heart were reinforced with tungsten steel. It was the only defense mechanism he had, designed to keep people from seeing in and to prevent Gerard from getting hurt.

"One day my dad hit me and I'd had enough." Gerard wiped his palm down his face. "As angry as I was, I couldn't bring myself to hit him back. I wanted to, though. Instead, I packed what I could carry, and I left."

Tate looked scared. That was the last thing he wanted to do, so he wondered if he should stop there, but the boy asked questions.

"What about your mom?"

"She'd already ditched us."

"How'd you live?"

"That's where it gets bad, Tate. I don't want to scare you, but it's important for you to know because you love your momma and I know you look out for her." Gerard smiled at him when he nodded, full of pride.

"I'd never do anything against your wishes, or your mom's," he looked at Myles, "or yours."

Gerard told him about hot wiring and stealing cars, breaking into abandoned houses to escape the cold, stealing from the grocery store to eat, begging for food. The last car he ever stole was the one that brought him to Haven Ridge. He told them how Hazel and Frank took him in and protected him from himself, a life of crime and the town's gossip.

"Frank did more for me than the officer who was supposed to be running a program to prevent boys from acting like I was."

"Do you blame the cop for not doing more?" Zeke asked.

Gerard shook his head. "Not really. The responsibility to change was always mine, not his. Yeah, as a kid I felt like he should have cared more, but as an adult, I have to give him the benefit of the doubt that he was doing everything he thought he could at the time."

"Is that why you took me into your house instead of putting me in a foster home?" Zeke's earnest question hit him square in the chest.

Gerard nodded. "Yeah, I wanted to pay it forward. Help you out and hopefully help you leave the life of crime behind."

Zeke rushed Gerard and hugged him tight. He initially guarded himself and then returned the hug. As a cop when anyone rushed you, especially a criminal, regardless of age, one must think of protecting himself. However, he no longer saw Zeke as a criminal.

"Did your dad ever get better?" Take asked in a timid voice, breaking Zeke's hold around Gerard's neck.

"Don't know. I'd heard he died a few years back, but I never looked into it. I'd grown so much thanks to Hazel and Frank that my life before didn't mean anything to me."

Throughout his confession, Myles was quiet. Too quiet. Lately, Gerard had been successful at reading Willow's mind, but her father was a different story. He had a poker face.

Despite the below freezing temperatures, his dampness, a suffocating weight from each band of sweat coating under his arms, mirrored the icy despair that settled deep in his bones as he waited for Myles to say something. Anything.

"I've always known." Myles only said two words before he was interrupted.

"Would you boys like to meet Liz's baby girl?"

"Aw, a girl," Tate groaned.

"You won't always say that, Buddy." Zeke put his arm around Tate and led him from the room. Gerard's heart leaped at the connection the boys had made.

"Gerard, can we talk?" Willow's sweet voice filled the room, capturing his full attention. How long had she been there? Was this the time she told him to get lost?

Wanting Myles to elaborate on his statement, Gerard pleaded with the man to stay and give his approval or tell him how horrible he was, but he didn't.

Instead, he stood and clasped his hand on Gerard's shoulder. "You're a good man. Don't let your past ruin the progress you've made. If you've asked God to forgive you, you are forgiven and man's opinion does not matter."

He leaned in, lowering his voice obviously so Willow couldn't hear. Great. Now he was going to get the threat on his life, just like Rocco had given Zeke. Here, Myles would tell him how he would use his connections to make sure Gerard suffered if he hurt Willow.

"Cora and I would be honored to call you our son-in-law one day if that's how things turn out."

What?! He hadn't expected that. Nor had expected the prickling of tears at the corner of his eyes.

Chapter 33

Her dad had a way of evoking people's emotions. When Gerard met her in the middle of the porch, she watched him wipe his eyes in a way that said he didn't want anyone to know he had real feelings.

The man in front of her seemed different. Vulnerable. The boyish look donning his face pulled her in. "I heard your story. How come you never told me?" She put her hand on his forearm.

He inhaled a breath, long and slow. "You already hated me. I couldn't imagine losing the little connection we had. Besides, it's embarrassing."

Willow's brows lifted. "Really? Nothing's more embarrassing, regretful, and shameful than giving someone your body. Not that this is about me, but I'm just trying to let you know that I understand. I'm really proud of you for turning yourself around."

"You did the same thing. I'm proud of you, too."

Willow let out a huff of breath. "For sure. I'm never doing *that* again until my husband carries me over the threshold."

A lopsided grin grazed his face. "Is that an invitation? I mean, I accept, whole-heartedly. I'd always imagined getting down on one knee and being the one to propose, but I won't let little details ruin a lifetime with you."

She playfully shoved his chest, but he didn't move. The man was solid. "Can't you just let me have something?"

He leaned in real close, guiding his finger through the side of her hair, sending a tingling sensation down her spine. "You can have my everything."

That may not have made complete sense, but her heart skipped a beat. She drew in a breath, hoping to ease the tension in building in her neck and behind her eyes. "I wasn't expecting that since I'm damaged goods."

He reached his hand up and cupped her face. Instinctively, she leaned into it, embracing the warmth his hand spread through her body. Was it possible that love was sneaking up on her?

She enjoyed their playful bantering, but now it had blossomed into something more. Each teasing exchange intensified their connection, silent promises of an adventurous future.

"I have a confession," Gerard hung his head.

Willow's eyebrows peaked. "Nothing good has ever come from a conversation started with those words."

"Can I explain?"

"Or those," she giggled.

The corner of Gerard's lip twitched as if he was trying to stifle a smile or work that heart sinking smirk. "This is a no-giggling zone, Ma'am."

"My-my officer. That law has never been strictly enforced before. Are you saying I'm getting a ticket?"

"Absolutely," he said with authority, handing her a ticket.

Confusion filled Willow. "Wait, what is this?"

"Open it." Gerard's voice sounded weak, something she wasn't used to hearing.

Her fingers trembled, trying to open the envelope, wondering if this had to do with his confession or if their silly flirting had side tracked something very important.

Finally, she'd opened the envelope and pulled out a ticket, her eyes watering as she read and reread the words before looking up at him.

"You made this for me?" Her pulse roared in her ears as her heart thumped like the bunny from Bambi thumped his foot.

The slight pink hue on his cheeks was adorable, and she had to chuckle when he said, "Not exactly, but I can explain that, too."

"You better start explaining, Mister." She feigned being upset when his features softened, making him even more appealing.

As if he was nervous, he blurted out, "I didn't send you the flowers, but I wish I had because I could tell they made you happy and I'd send you flowers every day for the rest of your life if that made things progress between us." He inhaled a quick breath and then finished. "Addison made the ticket. I didn't know anything about it, but Zeke brought it home. They said it was a cute and sure way to get you to go with me and I had to give it to you." He exhaled and covered his eyes, as if expecting her to yell at him or something.

Internally, she shouted, *"Aw, that's the sweetest thing anyone has ever done for me."* Externally, she said, "I'm alarmed about the flowers and wonder why Addison would create this lovely ticket out of the blue."

"As for the flowers, your aunt brought the card to the police station where I've already arranged for them to dust for prints, so don't worry your beautiful head about anything."

"The ticket; that's different. Something fishy is going on and I think there are three elderly people who will blame memory loss when asked about that," Gerard said, pointing at the ticket still between Willow's fingers.

He stepped closer, and her pulse was erratic. His intoxicating cologne pulled her in, wiping her mind of any concerns. "What would you say if I said I appreciated their intervention?"

She swallowed a lump the size of the Rocky Mountains. Willow had never expected anyone pure to be interested in her. Wait. She was making an assumption, which she'd learned never to do, but she also couldn't ask him that either. Frankly, it was none of her business.

What was his question again? Willow's pulse roared in her ears while her heart hammered against her ribs. All of this attention was bad for her health.

"Willow, I'm sorry things happened the way they did. If I hadn't pulled away seven years ago, you probably wouldn't have gone through what you did."

She put her hand on his chest to create a little space between them, but mostly so she could look him in the eyes. "Please don't do that. It's no more your fault for my sins than it is anyone else's fault for your sins. We have free will and we made bad choices, but hopefully we're both over that now."

The corner of his lips curled up, almost like he didn't want to get too eager until he had the answer to his next question. "Does that mean you'll give us a chance and I'll get my date?"

Before she could answer, a knock on the door and an unfamiliar, deep male voice requested to meet with her.

As she made her way to the foyer, Gerard trailed closely behind until they neared the area. His large hand came down on her shoulder, gently nudging her to the side, and he moved in front of her. "Get behind me," he ordered, not giving her an opportunity to argue.

Following orders, she placed a hand on Gerard's back like Willow saw on television shows when a line of police officers was on a mission. He shivered, and she removed her hand. "I'm sorry."

"It's okay. I just wasn't expecting it. Put it back," he insisted, his voice firm and alluring. She'd never tell him that, though, not wanting him to think he could boss her around at other times.

As promised, he remained steady when she placed her palm on his shoulder blade. The urge to massage the tight muscles beneath her fingers warred with her need to address the potential threat at her door; she chose the latter.

"Cora." Gerard's deep voice echoed off the walls in the entryway.

Willow couldn't see anything over his broad shoulders and the idea of her peeking around his arm made her feel like a child hiding behind her parent's body when a stranger came around.

"Oh, Gerard, this is Rudy Watson. Mr. Gunderson sent him as the lead security."

Willow stepped out from behind the wall, referring to Gerard. "Hi, I'm Willow. Nice to meet you. Are there others coming to join you?"

The smirk that grazed the man's lips needled her nerves. *Why are all men so cocky?*

"If more are needed, they'll be here, but I'm not expecting that. By the looks of your man there, the two of us can keep you and your son safe."

Gerard's chest puffed out as he wrapped his arm around her. "See, Darlin', Rudy has only been her for a few minutes and can already see the love you have in your eyes for me."

While Willow was thinking of something witty to say, Rudy spoke up and she exhaled a burst of laughter.

"I could actually see it in your eyes, not hers."

Gerard put up his hands. "What about the bro code?"

"I learned long ago when a special woman is in the picture, the bro code needs to be modified."

Interesting. Mr. Tough Muscles has had his heart broken. If he was here long, Hazel, Doris, and Myrtle would figure out how to rope him into dating here. *Who would he date, though?*

The doorbell rang and Rudy stepped aside, peeking out the sidelight of the solid oak door, and his face froze.

"Is it okay to answer?" The trepidation stained Willow's voice.

Rudy still didn't respond. Looking to Gerard for her answer, he shook his head and moved toward the door. A broad smile emerge on Gerard's face as he took a quick glance outside.

When he opened the door, and Annika walked in with Jackson, realization struck her like a thunderbolt. The best part was their introduction.

"Jackson, Tate is outback that way, holler out and you'll find him." The young boy took off, screaming for Willow's son. Then Gerard turned to Annika. The pink hue on her cheeks revealed either windburn from the brisk January weather or the proximity to Rudy affected her. Willow believed it to be the latter.

"Annika, this is Rudy. He's head of security here. Rudy, Annika is one of the newest members of Haven Ridge. Maybe you two can explore the town together."

Willow and Cora slapped their respective palms to their foreheads. Did this man know the meaning of subtle?

Rudy's eyes dropped to Annika's left hand and then met hers. "I think that's a great idea. You?"

Annika shrugged. "Sure."

Leave it to Willow's mom to bring reality back to the room. "As long as you keep my baby and grandbaby safe, I'll leave you alone."

Willow wanted to roll into a ball like one of the trolls in the movie Frozen and turn into a rock.

I am not a baby. She yelled in her mind. As a mom, she understood Cora's use of words. Tate would always be Willow's baby, but Willow would never say that in front of his prospective girlfriend, especially if she was older than Tate.

Gerard announced, "Rudy and I are going to talk strategy."

When he walked by Willow, he paused, forcing her to make eye contact before he spoke. "I expect an answer when I return." The feather-like kiss he brushed close to the corner of her mouth caused her stomach to plummet. The man knew he was her weakness. "Now, you and Annika match. Pink might be my new favorite color... on you, anyway."

Chapter 34

Flurries fell from the sky as Gerard and Zeke left Haven Horizons. The new fallen snow was starting to stick to the asphalt underneath his tires.

"Think they'll be a snow day tomorrow?" Zeke asked, his tone full of hope.

Gerard chuckled. "As I understand it, they don't have snow days on the ranch, so you'll be heading to school either way."

"Can we go to the diner for dinner?" Zeke asked as Gerard pulled out of the driveway.

He wasn't interested in cooking tonight. "Sure."

When they arrived, the guys sat themselves just as Hazel exited the kitchen and joined them in a booth. "Where are your partners in crime?"

When she raised a brow at him, he shriveled. "Ma'am."

She let out a meek laughter. "No offense; just giving you a hard time. If I don't, who will?" This was Hazel's way of telling him he needed to find a woman.

He hadn't had enough time to figure out Hazel's present angle before he was thinking about Willow.

Gerard couldn't believe simply telling Willow that he wanted an answer about whether she'd give him another chance or not could make her turn a few shades of pink. She was adorable.

Want to know the opposite of adorable? Still not having an answer. After Gerard listened to Rudy's plans for security, a sigh of relief escaped, lifting the weight off his shoulders at the same time. This man could keep all of Montana safe if need be.

Not wanting to push Willow, Gerard reluctantly left the Haven Horizons with an aching hole in chest. He could have stayed and forced her to answer him, but where would that have gotten him?

Every time he thought of Willow, he imagined his future with her and Tate. Coming home to her after a long day, cuddling on the couch or calling it an early night and engaging in pillow talk... *Get a hold of yourself, Man.* If Jimmy or the men at the ranch could read his mind, they'd revoke his man card for sure. *Oh, well.* They could have it, if he could have Willow.

"How about you, Sheriff?"

He shook his head, then looked around to see who was talking. Annika. Her notepad and pencil were in her hands. *When did she get here?*

"He's been like this since we left Willow." Zeke drew out her name, teasing Gerard like a typical teen.

Annika's eyebrows were raised and if they didn't have an audience, he might have asked what she was thinking. After he and Rudy left, Annika and Willow chatted while the boys played. She had to have some insight.

"That's enough." Gerard ordered, feigning being upset.

Once Gerard ordered and Annika disappeared, the diner door opened and Addison walked in with her mom. *Perfect time for payback*, Gerard thought, trying to keep his mind off Willow.

Zeke shifted in his seat. Gerard leaned over and said, "Don't look now, but Addison is coming." He held out the girl's name just as Zeke had done with Willow's moments ago.

"Please. I'm begging you. Don't embarrass me." The teen had the clasped praying hands, begging eyes, and almost whiny voice as he plead for mercy.

"Hey everyone," Reneé greeted everyone in a cheery tone.

Knowing this would make Zeke's night, Gerard invited the ladies to join them. When they accepted, Hazel stood. "I'll go have Annika come back and take your order so we can eat together."

"Thank you," Reneé said as she took off her jacket and slung it over the back of her chair.

Gerard stood. "Addison, take my seat near Zeke, so us adults can chat." The teen took the seat without hesitation.

When Hazel returned, her eyes pierced Gerard's. "We are getting a big snowstorm overnight, and we have some planning to do." Hazel's words rang with anticipation.

"Sounds like I arrived just in time. Is this Willow related?"

"When isn't it?" Zeke's laugh rang out as he teased Gerard.

Chapter 35

Tate whipped open the door and stood mesmerized. "Close your mouth, Buddy."

"Oh, Mama…" he ran out the door before finishing his sentence.

The first week of February and we were surrounded by an ocean of winter white dazzle, and she was excited to play with Tate his first time in the snow.

Unaffected by the ten pounds of winter gear he had to wear, Tate ran and jumped into the fluffy cold crystals, leaving Willow's heart to bloom.

It would have been better if Rudy hadn't come along for this experience, but she'd endure the intrusion to make sure Tate was safe. In her opinion, it was too cold for the man to be wearing just a spring time jacket, but to each their own.

"What was that thing you called when you lay on your back in the snow?" Tate asked, with already rosy red cheeks, oblivious to the temperature. Thankfully, the sun shined brightly, almost making her wish for sunglasses as the sun reflected off the snow. She'd endure single digits to make her son happy.

After making snow angels and attempting to make snowballs, Willow tried to bribe Tate into going back into the warm house.

He looked around a little and then at Rudy before he exclaimed, "No, way. This is awesome."

Looking over her shoulder, she saw her mom's face peering from the window, a soft smile gracing her lips as she watched them. But suddenly, despite the bright sunshine, a heavy silence fell, and the air grew colder, creating a stark contrast to the cheerful day.

"Come on, Tate, let's go inside," Willow's eyes darted from one end of her parent's yard to the other.

"But, Mom."

"No buts."

Tate looked around her. "Rudy, a little help here."

"Sorry little buddy, that's not my lane."

Tate's brows pinched together, clearly not understanding the statement, but Willow offered a grateful smile at her new security guard. In the three weeks he'd been there, she'd grown to like him. Willow believed Annika might like him a lot more than she did, but that was another story for another time.

When they turned around to go back into the house, a snowball flew seemingly out of nowhere, hitting Willow in the chest and her upper body innately dipped forward. An onslaught of spherical, frozen crystals pelted her. It'd been a long time since she'd been attacked like this.

"What the heck?" Straightening up, panic seized her as she scanned the empty surroundings. At least Rudy was with Tate to keep him safe, right? A sense of urgency flooded her when she heard Tate scream.

"Mom! Out front."

With her heart racing, Willow ran with high knees through the deep snow, sinking to her knees in some spots the more she hurried.

A few more steps and she'd be on the walkway that led to the front. Thank goodness her dad was an earlier riser and had already cleared that and the driveway. Her left foot sunk in a little too far and the snow trapped her boot.

"Mom, hurry."

Ripping her foot from the boot, Willow ran unevenly toward the front yard. If Nate hurt her little boy, she'd kill him. It might sound ludicrous for a pastor to kill someone, but don't underestimate the daughter if someone messed with her son.

Once she reached the front yard, she froze, her eyes deceiving her. What were Gerard, Zeke, and Addison doing? Her head swiveled toward the front door, where her parents remained behind the glass storm door, smiling. She gave them a befuddled look, but they just smirked and shrugged their shoulders. They knew whatever this was, but of course, they wouldn't give anything away.

"Where's Rudy?" Willow asked, concerned.

"Using the bathroom," Gerard said as he sauntered over with an out-stretched hand. He asked, "Where is your other boot?"

"It got stuck," she pointed toward the backyard. "Tate was calling and my anxiety jumped."

"I'll go grab it," Tate hollered.

Willow inhaled sharply to regain composure, but the only thing that happened was her happy hormones did a little jig when the warm cinnamon scent of Gerard's cologne mixed with his normal smell hit her hard.

"Milady, your ladder awaits." He gestured toward a small step ladder she'd missed among the confusion swirling around in her brain. He looped her hand through the crook of his elbow. Resting her fingers on his biceps, her happy hormones broke out into a hip hop rhythm.

"Wait!" Willow froze. "Tate can't be by himself." Gerard dropped her arm, and they all took off running toward the backyard. Willow saw her dad turn and run toward the back of the house. He'd probably get there first.

"I'll go this way," Rudy hollered, heading in the opposite direction of the couple, having just exited the house.

"Lord, please help Tate be okay."

"We'll make sure he's okay," Gerard hollered back in her direction. She hadn't even realized she prayed that out loud.

When they reached the backyard, it was empty, void of any sign of Tate. "Where is he, Gerard?" She heard the intensity in her own voice.

"I don't know. Look for footprints. We're in the middle of town; it's not like we're on a ranch. He couldn't have gone far."

Chapter 36

He stuffed his phone in his pocket and bit down on his tongue to stop a curse word from escaping. How could he have let his guard down?

"Jimmy and the men from the ranch are organizing a search party now."

Gerard rarely got emotional in a case, but this was different. It was Tate. The son of the woman who'd captured his heart. The boy who put smiles on his grandparents' faces, along with the teens, especially Zeke.

Willow still hadn't retrieved her boot from the snow, so he tugged it free and brought it to her.

"Thanks." Her voice clipped. Was she mad at him that this had happened? If he had to guess, she was just worried. He'd never known Willow to blame others.

He'd been so excited to show her the message they created for her in the snow, but none of that mattered now. With each passing second, the need to find Tate grew more desperate. It was obvious to anyone that Nate Roberts had figured out a way to reach the boy.

After yanking her boot on, she met his gaze, eyes slightly softened, and she gave him a rueful smile. "Gerard, how could this have happened so quickly? We hear the stories about watching our kids in public — look away for a second and they can be gone, but in our own backyard?"

Halting in front of them, Rudy reported, "I found a honeypot about a quarter mile into the woods."

Willow furrowed her brows and tilted her head. She was adorable.

"It's a term tracker's use when they see the environment disturbed," Gerard explained, letting Rudy continue.

"He can't be far. Are you up for a little hiking?"

Gerard looked at Willow. "We'll bring Tate home to you." He kissed her on the cheek and ushered her inside.

Ten minutes later, he and Rudy were trudging through the woods. This man was an excellent tracker. They'd stayed in close communication with Raddix, Damon and Quinton, who led three separate search parties through the woods, and Jimmy who patrolled on the road.

Uncertain what they were up against, Gerard prayed. It had been a minute since he'd truly relied on God, so he apologized for that first and then silently asked, *Please help us find Tate unharmed. Thank you for all the manpower. Carry them through this unscathed as well. Amen.*

As they approached a bend, fresh blood dotted the ground. The sight made his stomach twist in revulsion. "Blood," he alerted Rudy, and both men pulled their respective guns from the holster on their hip.

Gerard's phone rang, and he jumped to silence it, surprised he'd forgotten.

He froze. Glowering at the message from an unknown number, he alerted Rudy. "Hey, check this out."

Handing his phone to Rudy, the man read aloud.

> Leave the woods now, or I'll go back for Willow, too. She can't have Tate.

Cold chills raced down his spine, worry filled his mind. He couldn't be in two places at once. Would Willow and her parents be okay? Zeke had refused to stay with them, so he joined the men in the manhunt, while Addison stayed back at the pastor's house.

The retired SEAL released a half chuckle. "This guy doesn't know who he's dealing with."

Another message came through on Gerard's phone. It was from Pastor Myles. Gerard ran his hand down his face and his stomach dropped when he read the text.

> Willow left to search for Tate. Please keep her safe.

"Rudy, Willow is out here somewhere."

The man used some colorful words to express his objection to her being involved. Gerard felt the same, but stayed in his determined, focused state of mind and quickly sent a text to the group thread he'd created for the people in the search parties.

They hadn't gone more than three hundred yards when he heard voices. Bile crawled up this throat when Willow's plea fill the empty air space.

"Let him go, Nathan, please."

He wanted to run in and save her, but that would be a rookie mistake. If Nate had a gun, which Gerard always assumed his assailants were armed, that could be fatal for Willow or Tate.

Rudy instructed Gerard and Zeke where to go and what to do.

As they moved farther into the woods, Gerard now had a clear view of Willow. Her voice trembled as she begged Nate to let her son go. Tears stained her cheeks, frozen streaks of pain and fear that Gerard wanted to erase from her life.

"Let him go," Willow screamed as Nate held Tate off the ground with one arm, while pointing a gun at his own son with the other.

"He's mine son, too, you worthless—" Nate flung a string of curses at Willow; ones he would regret soon.

"You left us," Willow argued.

"No, I left you. I didn't know about Tate. I would have stuck around for him," Nate barked, with a venomous tone.

Gerard noted the look on Willow's face. It was as if Nate had slapped her. Did she still care about Nate? How could she respect a man like that? He wondered if there was more to the story Willow hadn't told him. *Focus.* He'd get answers later.

"Ow!" Tate hollered out.

Willow pleaded, "You're hurting him. You're claiming he's your son, but you're hurting him. That doesn't make sense."

"Good point." Nate dropped Tate to the ground in a heap.

"Run, Tate," Willow hollered, but the boy, probably stunned, didn't move.

As he inched closer, he noticed how Willow's body shook. If he had to assume, it was more fear as the freezing temperatures had probably numbed her body, like his, at this point.

About fifty yards west of Gerard, Rudy positioned himself behind a tree, giving him a thumbs up; their signal that he had a perfect view of Nate. Gerard continued to move in toward the assailant. He could get to him the easiest.

"You're damaged goods. You kept my son away from me, and you'll pay."

Tate rushed toward Nate. "Leave my mother alone, scumbag!"

Nate shoved Willow on the ground. She screamed. Trying to scramble toward her son, Nate grabbed her leg and twisted it like a pretzel. He pointed the gun at Willow. "You'll learn to never cross me."

Then a shot rang out!

Gerard yelled, "Willow!" At the same time she roared, "No!" She pulled her leg free and rushed to Tate. All Gerard could see was Nate's still body on the ground.

"Willow, stop!" Gerard yelled, running toward her, to no avail. This woman was going to be the death of him!

When they reached the bodies, he barked, "Don't touch. Get back."

"That's my son," she retorted.

"And that's my criminal." He tried to soften his tone, but arguing with her in this situation could be very dangerous.

Gerard nodded to Zeke, and he led Willow away about five feet. Rudy and he rolled Nate's limp body over to find a wide-eyed, frightened Tate. "Am I dead?"

They all chuckled. "No," Gerard said, assessing him for any visual injuries. "But we'll have an EMT volunteer check you out if that's okay." Gerard looked at Willow, who agreed with a single nod.

"Is my mom okay?"

Gerard helped Tate sit up and Willow was at her son's side in an instant.

She wrapped her arms around Tate's shoulders and pulled his head to her chest. "I'm so glad you're okay. You were so brave to go at him like that, but you could have been hurt."

"It's my job to protect you," Tate said with all the authority a seven-year-old "man-of-the-house" could muster.

"No, buddy. It's my job to protect you."

"Actually, you're both wrong. It's my job to protect the two of you." Gerard winked at Willow and Tate.

"Are you bleeding, Tate?" Gerard asked, scanning the boy's body.

"No," he said with a smile. "I'll have to thank Emmanuel when I go back to school."

"For what?" Willow ran her fingers through her son's hair.

Tate spoke with his entire body. "Emmanuel taught me to kick him in the... well, you know." Tate mimicked the movement to match his words. "Then, Miss Reneé said to knee him in the face or scratch his eyes out. I did both." The boy's pride radiated off him.

"You must have some sharp nails."

"Well, yeah. You've met my mom, right?" Gerard ruffled the boy's hair, brushing Willow's hand.

Their gazes locked. She mouthed, "Thank you." He smiled and kissed her forehead.

Gerard moved to Rudy's side. His eyes confirmed that Nate was dead. Gerard stepped away to send a quick text to the search parties. Using his radio, he requested dispatch to send EMT volunteers to his location. "The assailant is dead on scene."

Meanwhile, Zeke had gravitated toward Nate's deceased body. "Zeke, you don't want to get any closer." But as if tunnel vision had taken over for the boy, he didn't acknowledge Gerard.

Kneeling next to the body, Zeke said, "This is my father. That's why you had my gun. He followed me. He stole it." Silence fell among them.

It seemed like a plausible explanation, but until Gerard got Nate's fingerprints taken to see if they were a match, he couldn't say one way or another.

In the distance, snapping twigs under foot and branches slapping back.

Soon Raddix, Damon, and Quinton's search parties appeared from the south, west, and east, respectively.

"You've been destroying my life this whole time, you loser!" Zeke yelled at the man's dead body, but no one stopped him. As hard as this was on Tate and Willow, Gerard imagined Zeke had a tsunami of emotions flooding him right now.

Everyone looked at Lily, asking with their eyes if they should intervene. She shook her head. Then he watched Willow and Tate kneel in the frozen snow next to Zeke. Willow wrapped her arm around the teen's shoulders and rested her head on his shoulder.

"You must hate me," Zeke said to Willow, barely above a whisper, but, based on everyone's eyes, they heard it.

Willow placed her hands on either side of Zeke's face. "How could you think that?"

She was lucky he didn't push her away. Gerard usually rested his hand on Zeke's shoulder, and most of the time, he shrugged it off. But in all honesty, what teenage boy or adult male wouldn't like Willow's hands on him?

"Because he's my father. I won't call him a dad. Gerard has been more of a dad than he has."

Don't do that, Zeke! Gerard's chest zinged with pride and contentment. He'd grown close to Zeke in the past weeks. Gerard felt the eyes of many on him, so he strained his eyes, staring at the trio kneeling on the ground, hoping to keep his tears at bay.

"With that reasoning, should I hate Tate or myself?" She visibly shuddered. Gerard felt bad things happened the way they had, but they could fix that now.

Recognition flashed in Zeke's eyes. "Wait! This means that Tate and I are brothers."

The ecstatic smile on Tate's face brought warmth to Gerard he'd never known. His idea would be even better now.

Later in the evening, Gerard, Willow, Tate, and Zeke had eaten dinner with her parents and now the boys were playing video games, and he and Willow were in the gazebo again. As they approached it, he prayed silently that things would go better than they had the last time they met here.

"Are you doing okay?" Gerard rested his hand on her knee.

"I'm not sure."

At least she was honest. "I am here for you, whatever you need, especially that date." He winked at her, but the sorrow spread on her face, sat like a pit in his stomach.

"I'm so sorry. I'm damaged goods. You can't possibly want me."

"You're the woman I'm destined to marry." How does she not see this!? Gerard's anger started bubbling beneath the surface.

"You can't tell me what I want and don't want. Only I can tell you that, and I want you more than air to breathe."

The doubt in her eyes nearly tore him in half. He pulled his hat from his head and rested it on his knee. Raking his hand through his hair, his gaze fixed on her. "Why do you choose to believe that dirt bag over me?" He didn't mean to speak ill of the dead, but the guy had stolen Willow's self confidence.

"Where's the woman who took a chance and kissed me seven years ago?"

"She doesn't exist. I know you blame Nate for my loss of self-esteem, but I lost a lot of it the night you pushed me away." She inhaled. "I'm not blaming you. I promise, but I wouldn't have fallen for his sweet talking words if I hadn't let myself... it doesn't matter, it's in the past."

"You say that, yet..." He couldn't push her or she'd run again. "You never saw what we created for you this morning. Can we go look?" She nodded.

Gerard held out his hand, and she stared at it for a moment before she let her fingers lace with his. "Is this okay?" He offered these small moments to help her realize how serious he was about her and hoped she would trust him.

When they reached the front lawn, he placed her hand on his shoulder. "Use me to balance." He shined the light on his phone as she traversed the few steps. Then he handed her his phone while she scanned the lawn from left to right.

Her breath hitched.

"Are you okay?"

Slowly, she descended one step at a time, and her glassy eyes locked onto his. *Progress. Thank you, Lord.*

"How can you want me?"

He thought that was a funny question, but he understood what she meant. "You're beautiful. We tease each other easily. You're an amazing mother. You will be the perfect wife." Her questioning expression made him smile. "I can just tell."

Her eyes pooled with tears. "Please don't cry. I can handle criminals cussing me out, or coming after me, but what am I supposed to do with you when you cry?"

She blew out a laugh and sniffled as she wiped her eyes. "You could hold me."

"I thought you'd never ask. Holding you for the rest of my life wouldn't be long enough." He opened her arms, and she fell into them.

After a few minutes, he dared ask her to answer the question he'd written in the snow. "So, does this mean you'll let me take you to the Valentine's Day dance?" The ring in his pocket would have to wait for another time. He wouldn't do anything to push her too fast.

"You've downgraded me from wife to a date?" The twinkle in her eyes let him know she was only teasing him.

With his knee nearly touching the ground, he said, "I'm trying to respect the time you need to process everything, but if you're ready…"

She laughed, and he let her pull him back to his feet. "The invitation to the dance was perfect and I accept." She linked her fingers through his, sending a warm zing up his arm. "I want you to take your time on the proposal."

"Great. Now the pressure is on. Thanks." Little did she know, Gerard already had a plan and an entire group of homeschoolers to help.

Chapter 37

Time seemed to accelerate as the next few days passed in a rush of activity and fleeting moments. Willow and Val split their time between the salon and Haven Horizons. Harper spent every waking moment helping Liz adjust to motherhood, who named her baby girl Haven in honor of her new home.

It didn't take Harper long to realize that she didn't care about cosmetology. She wanted to work at the center full-time and stop working at the salon. That way, she could still have time with her own family.

Val and Willow couldn't have been more happy for the woman. She found what she loved to do. It would make them more busy at the salon as word continued to spread and more people from neighboring towns traveled to their business, but that was a good problem to have.

Rudy ended up taking a few days of vacation to explore the town, like Gerard suggested on the day the man arrived. She saw Annika with him yesterday and wondered about their connection.

Tate and Zeke saw each other every day at school and every night asked to spend more time together, *since they were brothers and all*. She chuckled inwardly, thinking of the line the boys used to manipulate her into giving them more time. When Gerard wasn't on call, the four ate dinner at Gerard's.

Tonight Willow took the boys to the diner, so she could help put the finishing touches on the Valentine's Day dance.

"Dearie, have you secured your date yet?" Doris asked in between bites.

Willow hated to think about the day Nate had taken Tate, but there was good that came from that.

Besides Tate and Zeke finding out they were half brothers, Gerard had asked her to the dance and even attempted to propose to her. Something she chuckled at whenever she thought about him, almost kneeling in the snow on a whim.

"My dad and her should be married by now," Zeke said offhandedly.

Willow swallowed wrong and went into a coughing fit. Tate slapped her on the back. "You okay, Mama?" She nodded and took a sip of water to clear her throat when the fit subsided.

"Why do you call that man, dad?" Hazel asked Zeke.

"Gerard?" Zeke pinched his eyebrows together.

The water Willow hadn't swallowed yet sprayed out of her mouth and onto the floor, coughing more violently this time.

"You call Gerard your dad?" Myrtle asked, sharing a look with her side-kicks.

As Zeke nodded, Willow wiped her mouth. "So you call him Dad, not just in passing, but for real? Does Gerard know you call him Dad?"

"Yes. He's the closest thing I've ever had to a dad. He likes me and wants to help me be a better person like him. I believe that's what a dad should do, so I figured the name fit. Besides, he's already looked into adopting me."

Hazel's face filled with pride, like a mother's love. Gerard had finally told Willow about the reckless choices he'd made as a youth and the unwavering support Frank and Hazel provided through guidance and refuge.

As a teen, she was clueless of his situation. That made her love this town even more — realizing any gossip she heard came from love, unless it came from Selena. *I wonder if we could vote her out of the town like they do on that reality show when they vote people off an island.*

Her parents never let on that they knew about Gerard's past, yet they had. No wonder Gerard thought they hated him.

A wave of sadness washed over her, thinking of Gerard's failure to tell her that he would be adopting Zeke, but they could discuss that later if they progressed any further as a couple. Maybe he'd already changed his mind and things wouldn't progress for them after the dance.

"That's very profound, Zeke."

"What can I say?" he shrugged.

Willow gave him the what-aren't-you-telling-me look, and he spilled it. "Addison has been reading the Bible your dad gave me, who I'd call grandpa if you and Gerard ever got married, but anyway, Addison was with me when I said my salvation prayer yesterday."

"Oooh, that's wonderful." Willow clapped her hands and hopped out of her seat, hugged Zeke, and kissed him on the top of the head.

The ladies welcomed him into the sister and brotherhood of Christ. "It's an honor and a joy to be in the same group as you, young man." Doris cooed.

"We've already got this figured out, Mom," Tate began in a quick change of subject. "If you and Gerard, who I'd love to call Dad, too, get married, then Zeke and I will live in the same house, and we can be a family. Would we move in with Gerard or would we have to stay at Haven Horizons?"

Overwhelmed, a wave of dizziness washed over Willow, making her head spin uncontrollably.

"You know, Willow, the kids have a point. Your little apartment would be great for Annika and Jackson to move into. She could be the manager at the center and she wouldn't have to be on her feet all day, here at the diner." Hazel proposed a wonderful idea, but things were moving exponentially fast. "She could be the house mother or whatever you'd call her and then one day there might be a house father, too, and he could help with the boys' section that is now ready."

"Where is all this coming from? How do you know if Annika would even consider this?"

"Do you plan on keeping Rudy on as security?"

Willow hadn't thought about him staying on, but now she understood the woman's angle. They were always thinking of others' happiness.

The very notion of the cliché putting the cart before the horse was a metaphor for her past life that she wouldn't repeat. However, she now realized impatience boiled just beneath her surface. "Gerard hasn't even asked me to marry him."

"Yet," Myrtle added.

Scanning the boy's plates, they were finished with dinner, and Willow's nerves had stolen her appetite.

"If we're all set for the dance, I'm going to get the boys home." Willow stood standing.

The ladies nodded. "Please think about what I suggested," Hazel urged.

It wasn't an awful idea. Though the current threat was over, having security at the center would be beneficial. Angry parents, boyfriends, or husbands could pose a problem in the future. "I will. We will probably need security eventually, and Rudy seems perfect for the job."

Chapter 38

The dawn broke grey and heavy, a stark contrast to the sunshine flooding her soul.

All three stylist chairs are bustling the afternoon of the town's Valentine's dance. Thankfully, Harper helped today while Katy from Big L' Ranch and The Troublesome Trio aided Liz and the other girls at the center to get ready for the dance. The stylists had already done the girl's hair first thing this morning.

Grady Gunderson, from the security company, had called, letting her know that someone had paid for Rudy's services for the rest of the year, which was basically an entire year. Willow was eternally grateful and perplexed since Grady refused to tell who the benefactor was, but his chuckle led her to believe The Troublesome Trio or their protégé were involved. Willow had grown close to Harlyn and knew she had the means to do something like that. Though it burned her brain wanting to know, she just thanked God for whomever made it happen.

Addison sat at Willow's station showing her a carousel of photos, one cut and style after another.

"Which one do you think would work best with my face?"

"Your face is beautiful and Zeke is going to love your hair anyway you decided to style it," Willow assured her with a little squeeze of her shoulders. The girl's rosy cheeks were cute. Zeke had the same reaction anytime Willow said Addison's name. He and Tate were at home with Gerard, who would bring them to the dance.

"Mom, how should I do my hair?" Darlene hollered across the aisle to Harlyn.

Harlyn thought for a moment. "What about a side French braid or one that starts at the base of your neck and then you fan out a bun type thing at the top?"

"I like both those ideas. Surprise me, Miss Val." Darlene said, settling back in her stylist's chair.

An hour later, Val and Harper had already finished with Darlene and Harlyn and they were just waiting for Willow, who was putting the finishing touches on Addison's double waterfall braid with big bouncy curls. When she finished, the ladies left, promising to meet at the dance.

"Sit down, girlie." Val pushed down on Willow's shoulders, plopping her in the chair. "It's your turn now."

"I'm going to head home and get dressed," Harper declared, checking her work in the mirror.

After they said their goodbyes, Val turned to Willow. "What can I do for you?"

"I'm too tired to care," Willow sighed.

"Just sit back and relax. Let's give the sheriff something to drool over." The sound of their laughter, bright and bubbly, was exactly what you'd expect from a pair of giddy teenagers.

The dance hall looked like cupid moved in, cluttering the place with hearts. They hung from every beam, while streamers looped around every wooden column. Rohan was at the DJ table, catering to the kid's requests.

Willow had arrived late since, after Val had styled her hair, Willow returned the favor. When she couldn't find Tate, Zeke, or Gerard, she called him, but it went right to voicemail.

Fear was of the devil. Her boys would be okay. Boys? She chuckled at the idea of anyone calling Gerard a boy, but she was using that term loosely to group them together in a cute, *they're my boys* kind of way. Right now, she mingled to preoccupy her mind, so she didn't freak out. They should have been there by now.

"Hey, Willow. You look amazing," Annika said, resting her hand on Willow's forearm. Behind Annika, Rudy towered over her.

When Rudy scanned the premises, Willow leaned closer to her new friend and whispered, "Are you and Rudy dating?"

"No," Annika said, shaking her head, her face not giving anything away regarding her feelings on the subject.

"If you'd like to date him, you're in the right place. Stick with Hazel and her friends, and you'll be married before you know it."

Annika let out a little breath.

"That said, if you don't want it, you best move, but please don't do that before I can find a replacement."

"I'd never do that to you, Willow. Thank you for this opportunity. Not that Violet's apartment was bad, but this allows Jackson to have his own room and a backyard."

Willow hugged the woman. "Thank you for accepting the position. I think you're the perfect fit."

When Annika and Rudy wandered off, Willow scanned the room again. Her boys were still not there. A cocktail of fear and anxiety threatened to suffocate her. What if Gerard changed his mind, and she wasn't worth the time?

"I'm so glad I moved here," Dr. Merriman snuck up behind Willow.

"Jenelle!" Willow hugged her friend. "You look amazing, and I'm thrilled you're here."

"I'm even closer to Haven Horizons now." When the doctor arrived a few weeks ago, the only available housing was thirty minutes away, considering what the people of Haven Ridge endured before she'd arrived.

"What's changed?"

"I moved into the apartment above Violet's flower shop," she squealed with excitement. "I can walk to work."

Haven Ridge seemed to be growing in the best possible way. She'd missed the last seven years, but in some ways, it seemed like time stood still until she'd returned.

"Who is that man in the cowboy hat over there?" Jenelle asked.

"Ah, doctor, you'll need to be a heck of a lot more specific than that since every man over there is wearing a cowboy hat."

The woman tilted her head to the side. If Willow could read minds, the doctors most likely said, "Duh, you're right."

"The tall, stocky one with the gold belt buckle."

"That's Tanner Brooks. He just won that belt in December at Nationals. Or maybe he's wearing one of his other gold buckles, but he was an amazing bronc rider. He retired after Nationals and now works at Big L' Ranch."

Jenelle winked at Willow. "I'm so glad you talked me into coming here. I think it will be the best decision I ever made."

Willow was happy for her friend as the woman sauntered off, no doubt to introduce herself to a famous cowboy. If Willow was the shy sheep, Jenelle was her polar opposite.

As her gaze swept across the room, her stomach dropped, alerting her of his presence before she spotted him.

In a moment of perfect synchronicity, their gazes finally connected, conveying a depth of meaning that no words could ever capture.

She maintained eye contact with him, her gaze unwavering as he advanced. His eyes traveled the length of her body in a slow appraisal that ended with a playful wink that ignited warmth and excitement within her.

She melted into him when he pressed a quick, intense kiss on her lips, leaving her breathless. "Hey, beautiful. Are you looking for a dance partner?"

"Just a dance partner?"

"I don't want to rush you."

She heard his trepidation. "We're beyond that. To be honest, I'm getting a little impatient." he smiled at her and pressed a hard, lingering kiss to her lips.

"Before this goes any further, where are our boys?" Willow asked, leaning back.

For the most fleeting of seconds, Gerard glanced behind him before turning his attention back to face her. "Did you say *our* boys?" His index finger wagging between the two of them.

She nodded with a broad smile that she could tell was lighting up her face.

"Do you really mean it?"

Willow responded, "I'm ready to give us a chance. You can have your date."

Gerard lifted her off the ground with a "Woot, woot," grabbing everyone's attention. But then his expression shifted. "You just ruined everything?"

Chapter 39

"Excuse me," Willow said, her voice dripping with the sassy tone that always kept Gerard in line.

He wrapped his arms around her lower waist and rocked her side-to-side as she gripped his biceps. Pulling her into his chest, his nose nuzzled her neck.

Suddenly, the banging of the microphone pierced their ears and Willow lifted her shoulders to her ears as her hands covered them.

"Ladies and gentlemen. Sorry for the interruption, but some of the kids from Miss Reneé's homeschool have a quick game they'd like to play, but need a few more participants. Is anyone willing to help them out?" Hazel asked, shielding her eyes with her hand, scanning the room.

Gerard placed his hand on her lower back, trying to guide her toward the stage, but she dug her heels in.

Now, he could have moved her, but he preferred she participated willingly. "Let's go see what the boys are playing."

She nodded in agreement.

"We'll help," Gerard hollered.

"Thank you, Sheriff and Willow. Anyone who wants to watch is welcome. If you don't, you're encouraged to find my friend Violet at the flower bouquet station. She will help you make a small bouquet for that special someone for a donation that will be used to fund our volunteer EMT and firefighters. Or you can take the path outside, where a firepit is burning and s'mores are calling your name. You can also visit with Lily at the candle making station, or Carolyn at the cookie decorating table. Both places have heart-shaped products, again for a donation to help our town."

Hazel handed the microphone over to Reneé, but pulled back quickly. "Sorry. One more thing. If anyone has completed the scavenger hunt, bring it to Amelia and she has a special prize for you to redeem a free horse riding lesson at her ranch."

The couple made their way up the stage steps as Reneé took the microphone and explained the rules the students created for musical charades.

In short, the person who gets out has to act out a phrase that Reneé placed in a bucket. If someone who had been eliminated previously guessed correctly before anyone else, that person would reenter the game.

After five rounds, Addison, Tate, and Damon's two boys, Dean and Dominic, were sitting on the sidelines. Zeke had been eliminated, but reentered the game after winning a charade.

When the music stopped this time, Willow plopped down on Gerard's lap. "Well, I like this game a whole lot more now."

She laughed as she trudged over to Reneé, who held out the bucket and Willow reached in, pulled out a piece of paper, and her eyes bugged out.

She tried holding up her left ring finger, and the kids hollered, "Wedding ring." She shook her head. "Engagement ring!" Another shake while doing the "safe" hand motion an umpire uses in baseball.

Holding up two fingers, the kids yelled, "Second word." Willow nodded.

She pointed at Addison. A child called out, "Loser...of this game."

Willow shook her head again. Trying something else, Willow pointed at herself.

One child yelled, "Willow," while Tate yelled, "Mom," and another kid chortled, "Bad at charades."

Willow laughed, pointed at her nose, and nodded.

"Is that the phrase?" Gerard asked.

Willow shook her head, clearly getting frustrated. Gerard lifted his chin toward Tate.

"Mom, come here. We'll help you," Tate ordered from the edge of the stage.

Gerard moved into place swiftly, then nodded at Tate. "Would people guess if you did that?" Tate pointed behind her and Willow pivoted.

With tears pooled in her exquisite hazel eyes and her hands over her mouth, everyone around them melted away. She stared down at him on one knee, and all Gerard could see was her. His love, his future. He realized he hadn't told her that yet, nor had she. He'd spent so much time trying to show her how a man should love a woman, he'd forgotten to say it. No time like the present.

"Willow, I feel like I've known you forever. You know how to keep me in line, and I'm sure the entire town appreciates that." Laughter spilled throughout the dance hall. "You make me want to be the best husband and father I can be for you three."

"Yeah, if you say yes to him, you're stuck with me, too," Zeke used the microphone to heighten his voice.

"We have spent too much time away from each other, but thankfully God knew how to bring us together because you complete me. Willow, will you make this cowboy sheriff happy and become my wife and Zeke's mom and let me be Tate's dad?"

A vigorous nod accompanied her whispered, "Yes."

Gerard placed the ring on her finger, then, sweeping her into his arms, kissed her soundly as the joyous shouts and cheers of the entire town filled the air.

As her body slowly descended, her palms gliding along his shoulders and chest, a shiver ran down his spine. He whispered in her ear, "I told you I'd only need one date."

"You're not getting out of dating me that easily. You consider yourself booked every Wednesday and Friday for the next, well, forever!"

"I like the sound of that." He kissed her again.

Long after Willow accepted his proposal, a sunbeam seemed to burst inside him, warming him from the inside out.

They were basking in their happiness when Willow snuck the Valentine's heart brownie that Katy made from Gerard's plate and took a bite while he wasn't looking.

A slow grin builds on his face when he stared at the half moon now donning his treat. "And you didn't get your own because…"

"I didn't want a whole one."

Her cuteness overwhelmed him; she was absolutely adorable.

"You could have fooled me," he said, teasing her and taking a monstrous bite.

He held out the last piece for Willow. She opened wide, and he gently dropped the brownie bite into her mouth. She wrapped her lips around his finger, trapping it there.

"Ahem. Are we interrupting over here?" Raddix and Lily pulled out a couple of chairs to join them.

Once Willow freed his finger, Gerard wiped the pad of his thumb over the corner of her mouth, clearing the renegade brownie crumb.

"No, of course not." Willow's sheepish look matched her crimson cheeks.

"So, finally, the sheriff is joining the rest of us men in wedded bliss." Raddix slapped him on the shoulder and shook his hand.

"When are you two getting married?" Lily asked with an eager tone.

"We just—"

"Don't say it, Man. Just sit and let them talk. Trust me." Raddix winced when Lily playfully backhanded him in the stomach.

"At least a year or two. Doesn't it take that long to plan a wedding?" Willow almost had him with her attempt to keep a straight face, but she lost it when Gerard protested.

"I'm kidding. I think Gerard would get married tomorrow, but we'll see."

"Tomorrow? Your dad is right over there. He could marry us right now if you wanted."

"Nice try," all three echoed each other, and Gerard shrugged.

A slow song echoed through the speakers, and Lily tapped Raddix on the thigh. "Will you dance with me before I'm too big and swollen to move?"

"You're going to look so cute, pregnant," Willow gushed over the petite woman.

"Thank you, Willow. I tell her that all day long, but she doesn't believe me," Raddix said, shaking his head.

"You and Harlyn both."

Gerard was thrilled when the ladies announced their pregnancies, as it was less pressure for him to keep it a secret.

"If you hurry the wedding along, you could have a little one with our crew, too."

"Don't rush them, Raddix," Lily said, dragging her husband away.

Would Willow want to have more children? He hoped so, but that was something they could discuss later on.

"Dancing sounds perfect. What do you think future Mrs. McDugal?"

"I'd love to."

They chose a place toward the edge of the dance floor, hoping to be inconspicuous after all the attention they'd received with the proposal. Gerard couldn't wait to marry this woman and have her all to himself. Sort of. They'd be starting off with two kids and Gerard wanted more, so they wouldn't be by themselves, but he'd hold his wife to the dates twice a week.

She rested her hands around his neck. The trail of warmth blossomed in his chest, encouraging him to pull her flush with him. He'd never felt more connected to a woman before. She was the first thing he thought of when he woke up and the last thing he thought of before he drifted off to sleep.

"You know, I'm not opposed to a fast wedding either, but I do have a condition or two."

With no delay whatsoever, Gerard's gaze locked with hers. "I agree."

Willow blew out a laugh. "You don't even know what they are."

"It doesn't matter. I agree." He chuckled.

She rolled her eyes. "First, you can't make important decisions without consulting me. Zeke told me you'd already started the adoption process, but I didn't know a thing about it."

"I apologize. That won't happen again. I was just so excited. I wanted to surprise you about that with the proposal. Can you forgive me?"

"As long as you don't do it again, yes."

"What's the other condition?"

She pulled him closer. "That you'll never push me away again when I kiss you," she breathed, her lips brushing his ear, a shiver of anticipation running through him.

"Oh, Darlin', you never have to worry about that."

She arched up and covered his mouth with hers in an earnest passion. He adored this woman, especially when she was in his embrace. The surrounding people seemed to vanish. One of his hands swirled through her hair while the other pressed against her lower back, tugging her impossibly closer to him; he warmed instantly with her soft body against his. Moving his other hand up her back, her golden hair tickled his forearm, feeling like mini jolts of electricity rushing through his arm.

The feeling of invincibility washed over him as her fingers dug into his biceps, his heart pounding with joy. Gerard scooped her up from the dance floor, twirled her, and gave her a deep, lingering kiss.

He'd escaped to another universe, a place where the air hummed with alien energy and the ground vibrated under his feet. Her strawberry-scented perfume filled his senses, kindling a burning desire within him.

This kiss was more than a promise; it was a cascade of emotions pouring over and enveloping him. He'd finally found his forever woman. She wouldn't leave him in a year, claiming she only loved him because he'd saved her. She wasn't his lifeline. He and Willow were bonding together in a way he'd never experienced before, nor expected.

"Keep it PG, would ya'?" Damon and Harlyn danced by them.

He jolted back to the present and slowly let Willow sink to the floor. The warmth of her body lingered on his chest like embers.

Gerard pressed a hard kiss to Willow's lips. "Sorry. I guess I got carried away."

"Me, too," Willow admitted.

"Thank you for agreeing to marry me despite my past."

"I could say the same thing to you. Gerard, we are all sinners saved by grace. God brought us together here and now. If we've asked Him for forgiveness, then we shouldn't let it follow us like a black rain cloud the rest of our lives. If our almighty Savior can forgive and forget, then perhaps we should, too. I can't wait to start our lives together without worrying about the mistakes we've made in the past."

"I love you, Willow."

"I love you, too, Gerard."

Epilogue

The sun rose on their wedding day, painting the sky in soft pastels, the air alive with the cheerful buzz of anticipation, something unheard of during the spring months in Montana.

In fact, they'd planned their wedding indoors because of the high levels of rain the state received this time of year. To say Willow was a little disappointed that her event wouldn't be outside in the sun, with the gentle chirp of birdsong and a light breeze rustling through the trees, would be an understatement.

Val opened all the windows in the salon while she took care of Willow's hair, make-up and nails. "You're getting the best of both worlds. All the warmth and sounds of spring and none of the snow and mud. Where could you logistically get married in those heels?"

Valid point. "I know you're right. I think my nerves are just getting to me."

She was already a mom, but now she was going to be a mom to a teenager; one who is way smarter than her. They'd be filling out college applications over the next few months. Thanks to Reneé's help and Zeke's over ambitious drive to succeed, he will graduate next year. With his desire to be a reporter still strong, he'd been throwing around the idea of following in his dad's footsteps and becoming the sheriff of Haven Ridge someday; joking how funny it would be to beat Gerard at an election. Going to seminary school was also a topic of interest, but nothing had seemed more important to Zeke than Addison.

After the Valentine's Day dance, Rocco allowed them to date, and Willow had spent a lot of time traveling to the ranch, which worked out well for Tate. He made wonderful friends. He and Emmanuel had grown close. Though Tate's new obsession with video games was a bit much for Willow, their friendship benefitted them both.

"You're already an incredible mother; you're going to be an amazing wife. What's there to worry about?"

"Nothing." She meant that, too. She had her Lord and Savior with her every second.

"Thank you, Val, for everything. You've been my best friend since high school and you've never let me down."

She blew out a breath. "Don't jinx me. I haven't gotten you to your wedding on time yet."

"How are Zeke and Tate doing with therapy?" Val asked, continuing her work on Willow.

"Lily is amazing. I have to say that first. Zeke had a harder time at first because he'd interacted with Nate for years before Nate abandoned him. Then when Gerard revealed Nate's fingerprints on the matchbook found at Randall's, he realized that Nate had been following him for a while. It really bothered him."

"I can imagine," Val said, spraying Willow's hair, so hurricane forced winds wouldn't touch it. "Did Gerard ever get the prints back on the card with the flowers someone sent you, or Nate's gun?"

Willow nodded before she remembered to use her words. "Yes, but neither of them were Nate's or anyone in the current system. I have no idea what to think."

"Today, you will not think about that. Let's get you finished and to your man."

Two hours later, they arrived at Big L' Ranch. Amelia and Quinton gifted them use of the barn where they'd held the Christmas party. Everyone at the ranch worked together to decorate the space with Val's help.

Yesterday, these same people helped move hers and Tate's belongings into Gerard's home. He offered to sell it and buy a new one that could be theirs together, but when Tate saw the game room and the bunk beds in the room, that would become his in about an hour, he was content and so was she.

Willow's parents were going to watch the boys for a week while Gerard took her to Aruba. She'd mentioned it was on her bucket list and Gerard said, "It's my honor to help you achieve all your dreams."

She loved her swoony sheriff. The man melted her heart. As Darlene and Emmanuel led the way down the aisle as junior bridesmaid and usher, respectively, Raddix escorted Val down the aisle as Best Man and Maid of Honor.

She heard the shifting of people moving from a seated position to standing. "Are you ready, my beautiful girl?"

"I am. Thank you, Daddy, for accepting Gerard despite his past."

"We all have one. Though we can't see inside someone else's heart, we can get a glimpse of their walk with Jesus based on how they live their life. I'm confident Gerard will keep Jesus at the center of your marriage." He wagged a finger at her like she was a kid again. "Make sure you do your part, too. Life is hard enough. Don't fight each other."

He wiped the single tear that slid down her cheek. "I know, Daddy. Thank you and Mom for being such great role models."

"And never keep anything as important as a grandchild from me again. No matter what you do, I'll always love you. Trust me."

She nodded, wiping more rogue tears. *Geez. I haven't even made it to the altar yet.*

The doors opened, releasing a wave of warmth and the cheerful chatter of the townsfolk gathered to witness Gerard and her begin their married life.

Her eyes instantly locked with Gerard's. The charcoal gray suit he chose pulled just right at his shoulders, mirroring the way the white button-up shirt underneath spread across his chest. The man's ability to look that good in a suit should be illegal.

All the decorations, thanks to her dedicated friends, were perfect. The sweet scent of Montana wild flowers captivated her senses as her dad led her down the aisle. The heady floral scent, accentuated with honey, grass, and spice, brought the lilies to life in the room. She felt like a princess with chiffon, white tulle arched over their heads, combined with eucalyptus garland; very elegant. More cultivated than her.

Zeke and Tate were standing with Gerard in matching suits. The boys wanted to be the Best Man, but Gerard wanted the boys with him as an extension of him, explaining that all four of them were marrying into this family and vowing to be the best self they could be for each other.

Swoon again!

Her dad kissed her hand when they stopped in front of her three boys. He placed her hand inside Gerard's palm and the boys placed theirs on top of hers and then they pig piled their hands on top of each other in fun. Willow knew married life was difficult. In the Bible, Paul tells people that lots of trouble comes to married couples, but she couldn't wait to marry this man.

Myles then took his place as pastor and began the ceremony. They kept the vows traditional, except her dad added in, "If he ever makes you feel less because you make a mistake, you best tell me." That got a chuckle from everyone in attendance. The best part was when he said the same thing to Gerard. Willow wiped a tear, knowing her dad thought of Gerard as the son he never had.

Finally, the best words, "By the State of Montana, I now pronounce you husband and wife. You may kiss the bride."

Gerard did not hesitate. Tipping Willow back, he pressed his lips to hers in a passionate kiss, fusing their lips and lives together as one.

Righting her in front of him, he whispered, "How does it feel to be Mrs. Gerard McDugal?"

A supernova of joy bursts in her chest, which she hoped was transparent in her expression since words clogged her throat.

Gerard cupped her face. "I feel the same way." He presses a long, lingering kiss on her lips. Lightheaded, she grabbed his lapel to steady herself.

"Let's go, McDugal's."

Hazel winked at them as they progressed down the aisle toward her. "Aren't you glad the ladies and I called your number now?"

"More than you now." He kissed a confused Willow on the head.

"Best auctioneers ever!" He kissed Hazel's hand and winked at Doris and Myrtle, who smiled in return.

Frank leaned over his wife and shook Gerard's hand. "I told you that you'd lose."

Gerard chuckled. "On the contrary, Frank. I won... big time!"

With linked hands, and a child under each arm, Gerard and Willow walked out of the event hall, ready to start their lives as husband and wife.

Thank you for reading Willow and Gerard's story. This will be the only book in the Big L' Ranch Series published this year, but don't worry, I have five more stories planned for this series that will be released in 2026. If you have a side character you want to read about, email me at karen@trueheartrom ance.com and let me know.

If you want to find out what happens between Rudy and Annika, you can read their story in the third book of the G & G Security Series, Keep My SEAL, coming out later this year.

For now, keep reading for a chapter from When the Dust Settles: A Sweet Romance with a Navy SEAL, where you can get to know Grady and Gunner, who become the owners of G & G security. Enjoy!

How About a Review?

Your feedback is valuable, so please consider sharing your thoughts. This will help other readers discover this book and my other works.

Thank you from the bottom of my heart for reading and reviewing my book(s).

Amazon

Goodreads

Bookbub

When the Dust Settles: A Sweet Romance with a Navy SEAL

Grady

G rady Gunderson stretched out on his couch after an extended mission. As the Officer in charge of his platoon, Grady spent most of his time gathering information and intel for the missions his men and he would carry out. However, the mission had worn him down emotionally for the past three weeks. They'd taken down Philippe Barnesto, a major player in the war on human trafficking. In all, the SEAL platoons assigned to this mission had released over three hundred and fifty women and children and had dismantled Barnesto's group using every necessary strategy.

It would be impossible for him to close his eyes any time soon. He'd need to bury the horror of the last three weeks like he always did after a mission before he'd sleep normally. It wasn't a great plan, but it seemed to work for him. Grady never took anything to help him sleep. He'd survived BUDs training in a sleep-deprived state. He refused to give in to outside help besides the good Lord's. Sleep would come when he needed it.

Grady had enlisted in the Navy at eighteen years old and had never regretted his decision. After three years with the Navy, he trained to be a SEAL and began his exclusive fight in the war on human trafficking. Six years ago, he'd been promoted to his current position. At thirty-three, he still fought the demons from his childhood. Carrying them on each mission, he used them to help eliminate the most vile offenders. He justified his actions every time he saw an innocent woman or child in captivity. Some of his missions over the years had involved releasing men and boys from debt bondage or forced labor, but an overwhelming percentage of the rescue missions had been to release women and children from sex trafficking. It made him sick to know that there was enough scum in the world for his and numerous other SEAL platoons to dedicate their lives to protecting others against human trafficking. He'd been fighting this fight nonstop for twelve years without an end.

His eyelids were heavy sandbags; he was losing the fight against a rushing flood. The doorbell jolted him, and he sprang up, whipping his feet to the floor. *Who could that be?* He thought he'd done a good job being incognito the last few weeks. No one other than a young boy he'd met in the woods behind his rented cabin knew he was here. He'd sent his men on leave. Maybe one of them couldn't get a flight and needed to stay with him for a day or two. Grady and his men had sixty days to recover from this past soul-sucking mission unless another mission popped up, cutting the time short.

Grady had his knife in his pocket and his 9 mm tucked behind his back. But neither of those weapons prepared him for what was on the other side of the door.

A beautiful blonde stood holding a dish that he couldn't will his eyes to look down at. This might not be someone wanting to hurt him, but it was definitely a dangerous situation. Grady and women didn't go well together. He didn't know how to act around them. *Them?* Like women were strange sea creatures. His men liked to set him up on dates, and sometimes he went, but they always ended up the same. They teased him endlessly about his lack of flirting skills, but he'd never felt the need to flirt.

Getting close to a woman had never fit into his life. He'd never be like his dad and leave, but a woman could leave him and take their child away or leave him to raise a kid alone. He or other boys from the group home had experienced all those scenarios. *No, thank you.* His SEAL buddies were his family, and that's all he needed. Now, the idea of leaving a wife behind as a widow left him feeling too guilty to try. Besides, he should have been married six years ago, but was too cowardly to go through with it. For one of his late SEAL brothers, he'd agreed to marry a woman he'd never even seen a picture of.

"Can I help you?" he asked, finally finding his voice. But before she could respond, he heard footsteps rushing towards them. He whipped out his Glock 19—the best 9 mm, in his opinion—and shielded her with his body. He wrapped an arm around him, resting it on her lower back to protect her from the approaching danger.

Scanning the area, his vision caught on two figures. Suddenly, he felt a hot breath on his neck. The woman behind him forcefully whispered, "Those are my children. Please put the gun away before you scare them to death!" Her voice's protectiveness and proximity filled his chest with an unfamiliar warmth.

The look of terror in the kids' eyes made his gun disappear. He released the tension from his shoulders and sidestepped, revealing their mother.

"See. I told you he was tough, Avery." The boy's words made Grady almost smile.

Avery shrugged.

Thomas took a step toward Grady. "You're like Rambo, but not as big. Taller, maybe that's why you seemed bigger."

Harboring a mischievous smile, Avery mumbled something under her breath that Grady couldn't hear. A sharp look passed from mother to daughter. Grady was probably better off not knowing.

"How tall are you, anyway?" The boy was now at his side, measuring himself against Grady. He almost reached Grady's shoulder. "Are you in the military?"

"I'm six-three, without shoes, and yes, I am."

The boy stared at him, worshiping Grady like he was a Greek god. Grady felt uncomfortable and shifted from one foot to another, rubbing his hand through his hair. The boy continued to stare. *He wasn't anything special. If he were, his dad wouldn't have left him to endure a fate Grady would never wish on any child.*

"How much do you weigh?"

"Thomas, you're asking some personal questions, and we don't even know his name," his mom gently admonished. Her angelic voice sent warm tingles through Grady's body. He'd been admonished plenty of times between his gruff foster families growing up and always having a higher-ranking officer to report to, but it had never sounded like this.

"I don't mind." Grady liked that one of the kids was a boy. He could relate to a boy. The beautiful woman, still holding the dish, was way out of his league; he didn't have a clue what to say to her. Even worse was her teenage daughter. Who in all the world knew what to say to a teenage girl? *Focus on the boy!* "I weighed in at two forty on my last check."

The boy's eyes widened. "Maybe you are Rambo. He was only five-ten; one ninety-seven. You must be way tougher than Rambo!" Looking at his mom, he asked, "Don't you think so?"

The blonde's flawless cheeks blushed. *What did that mean? What did he want it to mean?* He'd been in dangerous situations all his life, but none as alarming as the situation he found himself in now. He couldn't help but stare at her sea-green eyes. They shone brightly, like the sun, yet there was a haunting look that he'd seen on too many of his SEAL buddies' faces. Still, those beautiful eyes...

She ignored her son's questions and pushed the dish toward Grady. "My son told me we had a new neighbor in the cabin. Sorry, it took me so long to come and welcome you. We live right through the woods on the path if you ever need anything. Unfortunately, we made cookies. I can't imagine anyone that looks as good as you would eat cookies. I mean, SEALs train hard, so I imagine cookies aren't on your approved food list." Her face burned with embarrassment.

Grady bit back a grin. A light breeze hit him in the face. Her sweet, fruity scent with a hint of spice left him with a strong desire to move closer to the fit blonde occupying his little porch and soak in her scent.

"Thomas can be a bit overzealous with military men, something he aspires to be, so if he's ever...too much...please don't feel bad telling him to back off a bit."

"That's right. I've got six more years, then I'll be off to fight like my dad," Thomas interrupted.

Grady lifted the plate in acknowledgment. "Thank you."

"No. Thank you for your service." The blonde pointed toward the teenage girl. "That's Avery. She's always listening to music. She dreams day and night about becoming a singer, so she's always listening to her headphones. I think she uses them to shut out the world, but what do I know? I'm just Mom."

Grady let a small smile escape. He liked her carefree yet direct manner. *Was her rambling an indication of her nervousness? Did he do that?* She made his stomach flip-flop. He hadn't experienced that since he turned eighteen and signed his life over to the Navy. He hadn't thought much about his future when he'd enlisted. His dad had left him and his mom when Grady had turned two. Then, his mom had died of a brain aneurysm and left him alone at eight. He'd bounced from one foster home to another for the next ten years.

Thomas pulled Grady from his thoughts. "Our dad died on a mission, and she's mad at the world; that's why she's always listening to her music."

Grady understood completely. His heart ached for the young girl. It also made him wonder about the beauty who handed him the plate of cookies. How was she dealing with the death of her husband? His gut told him something about this situation seemed eerily familiar, and his gut was never wrong.

No matter how beautiful she was, it wouldn't matter. His past had made it nearly impossible for him to engage in a romantic relationship, so he'd never tried before, and he wouldn't start now. Besides, he was on temporary leave, further making the unfamiliar tightness in his chest a reason to avoid this woman. His life belonged to protect and serve—a SEAL for about two more years until he retired. Then, he'd probably work private security to save people from, or prevent, human trafficking.

He directed his attention to Thomas's mother and asked something he shouldn't have. "I'm so sorry. How long ago?" He never asked questions, keeping to himself to avoid connections with anyone outside of his inner circle of SEAL brothers, but the gnawing ache in his gut couldn't prevent him from wanting to get to know the woman in front of him.

"Thank you. Six years ago. He was a hero fighting the war on human trafficking."

Grady steeled himself. "So he was a SEAL?"

The woman shook her head proudly, but her face filled with anguish. Grady had learned to control his body language and his facial expressions. If her husband had died, as she said, then he may have known him. First, he had to know this woman's name. "I'm sorry you got left behind..." He waited for her to fill in her name.

"Olivia."

He wished she would have given him a last name, but he didn't blame her for being careful. In fact, he appreciated her precaution. He'd seen the effects of careless women too many times, and the thought of having to rescue the group standing in front of him from traffickers made him cringe.

"I'm Grady Gunderson." He reached out his hand. Olivia's face turned white, and her jaw dropped before she quickly snapped it shut as she placed her hand in his. "Is everything okay?"

She stuttered, finally spitting out, "G-Grady Gunderson?"

His smile faltered. She pulled her hand from his; instantly, he longed to feel the warmth of it inside his palm again. Then, as quickly as she had pulled her hand away, she bounded down the steps.

"Come on, kids. Leave this SEAL to his cookies and let him rest. He doesn't get much time off."

Grady wondered what caused the woman and her daughter to bolt. They were gone in a flash, but Thomas lingered. He asked Grady if he would share his military training with him so he could prepare himself to follow in his dad's footsteps.

Before he could answer, Avery appeared with her hand on her hip. "Thomas, Mom said you need to come right now."

"Go on, Buddy. When I return the plate, we can see what your mom says about that." Grady would have thought he gave the boy a million bucks by the way he smiled at him.

Stepping back into the house, Grady placed the cookies on the counter. Olivia was right; he didn't eat cookies very often, but he had an unexplained desire to do just that for her. He took a bite, and it melted in his mouth. Sensations exploded like he was eight years old again, eating Pop

Rocks. He hadn't had a cookie in that long, or the thought of returning the plate to the brilliant baker excited him more than he'd thought.

A pit formed in his stomach. How could this woman affect him so quickly? He wanted to know more about her. She'd started to break through the walls he'd developed long ago to protect himself. With how Olivia had just reacted, she clearly didn't like him, which definitely wouldn't work out in his favor.

About the Author

Karen Tucci, a public school teacher by profession, now tutors writing students online and homeschools her two children.

A native of Maine, she has trekked miles of the Pine Tree State and visited countless others. It is through her life experiences that the basis for her romance stories develop. One of her favorite things to say when out adventuring is, "...that is definitely going in my next book!"

Fun fact: Karen had only read and wrote non-fiction growing up. It wasn't until her late twenties that she embraced the joy brought forth by doing both — reading and writing — within the different romance tropes. Now she reads at least fifteen fiction novels a month and writes daily!

Connect with Karen:

Facebook Reader's Group

https://www.trueheartromance.com

Instagram

Goodreads

Bookbub

Amazon